Childhood friends and lost loves.

A former horse trainer turned stockbroker, Ryder Christensen planned to spend the rest of his life with Sal—the man he had grown up and fallen in love with. But nowadays, Ryder only has two things in that make him happy: his daughter, and his poker-playing. One night, he comes home to find his daughter dead. Then the loan sharks come knocking.

Back to square one...

Salvatore Lewis has spent the last six years running his late parents' ranch in Tryon, North Carolina. Between work on the ranch and helping his brother recover from an accident, Sal has almost gotten his old boyfriend out of his head. So, the last thing he needs is Ryder strolling back into his life. Sal tries to stay away, he really does. But the magnetism between the two men is undeniable.

Danger closes in...

Within a month, Ryder's taking care of Sal's horses, and the ranch-owner can't believe they're getting a second shot at happiness together. But there's more to Ryder's sudden return than he's letting on. As Ryder and Sal's relationship blossoms, Ryder's past in New York comes back to demand more than he has to give. Will Ryder be able to protect his new life from the threat that destroyed his old one?

LUCKY COWBOY

Ace Cowboy, Book One

Liz Borino

A NineStar Press Publication

Published by NineStar Press
P.O. Box 91792,
Albuquerque, New Mexico, 87199 USA.
www.ninestarpress.com

Lucky Cowboy

Printed in the USA
First Edition
July, 2018

Print ISBN: 978-1-949340-01-3

Also available in eBook, ISBN: 978-1-948608-90-9

Warning: This novel contains scenes of violence and references to the death of a child.

To Eugene, whose support and encouragement made the
last-minute rush more bearable

Prologue

RYDER CHRISTENSEN'S MIND raced as he stared at the photo collage above the opulent coffin holding his daughter, Gabriella. The air grew thick and hot with every exhale in the cathedral. Between the priest's homily and the eulogy, Ryder struggled to breathe. He couldn't name even half of the people here. *But that's what happens when death is sensationalized. People read a tragic story and think they have the right to share in the grief.* Ryder just wanted to disappear.

Finally, the service ended. *One more event to get through and then...* Ryder glanced over at his mom and dad and sighed.

"Looking for me?" a gritty voice behind him asked.

"No." Never. Ryder never sought the man with dark glasses who towered over him.

"You should have been."

Ryder growled low in his throat as he nudged the man out of the throngs of people leaving the cathedral. "You come today, of all days? Don't you have any respect? This is my daughter's funeral."

The man—who had never given Ryder his name, maybe for fear it might humanize him—crossed his arms over his chest. "And whose fault is that?"

Asshole. Ryder clenched his hands into fists. He shot his gaze around to see if anyone noticed he was missing yet. As the bereaved father, Ryder had to be on hand for the condolences of friends, family, and strangers. *If I relax my posture, I can convince them that's what me and tough guy here are doing.* With that, he released his fists and shrugged the tension from his shoulders.

"Word on the street is that you're leaving town soon. You weren't thinking about doing that without saying goodbye, were you?"

"I planned to stop to see your boss tomorrow." Ryder caught his dad's eye and raised his finger, signaling that he'd be right there, hoping with everything in him that his dad wouldn't come over or draw attention to his whereabouts.

"Well, if you have the money now, I could save you a trip."

Right, because handing over an envelope of cash at a funeral won't raise anyone's suspicions. "It's in my car. Listen, I'll—"

"You'll walk me over there, hand me the money, and *I* won't cause a scene." The man moved so that the handle on his revolver glistened in the sun. A pointed reminder of just what kind of scene he could cause, if given the chance.

Ryder raised his hands in surrender. "Follow me." He realized the futility of his words as soon as they left his lips. Keeping his focus on the uneven pavement under his unsteady feet, Ryder led the goon to his father's pickup and opened the driver's side door.

"Nice car."

"I sold my nice car." *And my nice house. And my nice retirement fund...* Ryder swallowed the bile of emotions the thoughts brought up as he extracted the thick envelope from the glove compartment.

"This is everything?"

Everything I have. "That's what Boss and I agreed on."

"Hmm. I hope for your sake he remembers that agreement. Later, Cowboy."

Me too, Ryder thought as the goon tucked the envelope into his jacket pocket and strode toward his black, tinted-window SUV.

"Son?" Ryder's father asked from behind. "Are you in trouble? Something your mom and I should know?"

Ryder scanned his face for any indication of how much his old man had heard, but Victor Christensen was never one to give too much away. "No, Dad, don't worry about it. I took care of it."

Victor nodded, though Ryder could tell he didn't entirely believe him. "Why don't we drive over to that luncheon together? Your mom took our car when the service let out. Too many people for her."

Ryder passed his dad the keys and sat in the passenger seat. Manhattan always had too many people for his parents. "I imagine so. I appreciate you two coming though."

Victor made a noise from the driver's side. "I'm going to pretend you didn't imply that we'd miss our only granddaughter's funeral. We'll always be there for you, son."

"I know, Dad. It's just—"

"Nothing. We'll go to this luncheon, sleep for a couple of hours, then head home."

Home. It had been a long time since he called the small North Carolina town of Tryon home. Something painfully ironic about starting over in the place he grew up itching to leave.

Chapter One

SALVATORE LEWIS SWEPT his palm over the cropped chestnut mane of the warmblood stallion being offered to him. "Strong muscles."

"Of course," Jack, the farmer from Vermont, said. "Patches here comes from the finest lineage. Both his parents are world-class dressage champions."

Patches. That's a name for a damn guinea pig or maybe a house cat, but it's an insult for a nearly six-foot horse. Sal stopped himself from rolling his eyes. *It's not the horse's fault his breeder gave him a stupid name.* "But he hasn't been in any competitions?"

"Too young. He has been training along with his parents since he was one."

A year. Great. Stallion-in-need-of-a-new-name would require extensive work and breaking in before Sal could do much with him. Sal reached into the food bucket and extracted a carrot, which the horse took gently. "Good boy." Sal stroked the stallion's snout as he munched the vegetable. In the horse's gaze, Sal found more humanity than resided in most people he knew. He sensed a willingness to improve, adapt, despite the stallion's relative youth. "I'll give you $10,000 for him."

"Are you out of your mind? His parents are champions! He's gorgeous! Anything below $15,000 is absurd."

Sal schooled his features to appear bored. "He has little training. He's young enough to be unpredictable. So, the time, money, and resources required to make him useful is worth at least $5,000." He adjusted his glasses in the hot North Carolina sun. The transition lenses were struggling to keep up with the changing cloud cover. He leaned forward. "But let's be honest, you know all of that or you wouldn't be selling this champion-bred warmblood stallion as he's approaching the prime of his trainability. Since I see nothing in his medical file to signal health issues, I suspect you'd rather not spend those resources. So, would you rather take my $10,000 offer or bring him round to three more farms, where you'll get less?" Sal was grateful for the clarity in vision the shade brought. It allowed him to watch every emotion play out over the farmer's face.

An hour later, Sal had signed the papers and was settling Bishop into his new stall. "Okay, Bishop, after the vet checks you out, we'll introduce you to King."

"Bishop?" Jason asked. "You are such a fucking chess nerd."

Sal turned to find his younger brother sitting in his wheelchair and his face fell. "Bad pain day?"

"Only when I'm walking. Or talking about it." Jason tucked his hair behind his ear. His pit bull, Petey, a trained seizure dog, followed dutifully at his side.

"You can—"

"Rag on you for the chess obsession you never let go of? I was trying to." Jason rolled in closer, but stopped a few feet short of the stallion. "He seems really calm for his age." Jason grabbed the binder with all Bishop's information and flipped through it. "When's the vet coming?"

"Tomorrow morning." Sal studied his brother's movements, but decided asking him for health details would be an exercise in futility.

Jason bobbed his head and returned Bishop's binder to the table. "Speaking of high school…"

"Wait. What? When were we talking about high school?" Sal gave the stallion a pat and motioned for Jason to follow him out of the stall to give Bishop time to warm up to his surroundings.

"I was sort of referencing high school when I was mocking you for your chess obsession."

"It's not—"

"Important! God, can't you recognize a leading phrase when you hear one?" Jason huffed as he rolled along the sidewalk they had built around the property after his accident. "Have you seen the paper?"

Sal stopped walking and narrowed his eyes. "Do we still get a newspaper? On second thought, never mind. No, I haven't. What's in the paper?" If he didn't move the conversation along, Jason could spend all day finding his point, and neither of them had time for that.

"Did you hear about Ryder Christensen coming to town?"

He sucked in a breath. "Well, I hope he, his wife, and kid enjoy their visit with his parents." Sal picked up his pace, but even his longest strides were no match for the motor on Jason's chair.

"Sal, do you really think I'd tell you that if Felicia and Gabriella were here?" Jason barely paused before he answered his own question. "I know better than to torture you with him."

"He doesn't torture me."

"Bullshit. Tell that to the last five guys who didn't measure up."

"You don't know what you're talking about."

"Yeah, right. Look who you're talking to. I'm the guy who shared a bunk bed with you, remember? I do. The fall fucked up my legs, not my memory."

Sal cursed his shaking hands as much as he cursed his curiosity. He glanced around the vegetable farm where workers were tending to plants. Around dusk, he would check their progress, but he saw no reason to micromanage them. "What about Ryder? And why is whatever it is in the damn paper?"

"Local papers usually report on murders of former residents."

Sal's jaw dropped along with his stomach. *Ryder's...dead? How? Why? What?* Try as he might, he couldn't make his mouth work to expel his racing, heart-stopping thoughts.

Jason's eyes widened at Sal's reaction. "No, no, I'm sorry. Not Ryder. Gabriella, his daughter, died when she was alone with a babysitter."

"Oh, Jesus Christ, Jay!" Sal pressed his hand to his chest and lowered himself to a squat, willing his heart to slow. "The fuck is wrong with you?" Somewhere in the back of his mind he knew he should be sad for Ryder, but all Sal could conjure right then was relief. He didn't bother analyzing why he cared as much as he did, considering Sal had cut contact with Ryder when Ryder had chosen the baby's mother, but... Sal didn't finish the thought, instead petting Pete, who came to check on him. "I'm okay, buddy."

"Sorry." Jason placed his hand on Sal's arm. "I didn't mean for it to come out like that."

Sal sighed and climbed to his feet. "Bang-up job of showing I didn't care, huh?"

Jason shrugged. "Wasn't gonna comment."

"Appreciate that." He inhaled deeply. "I'm going for a ride." Perhaps not the most responsible thing with the constant flow of work to be done on the ranch, but Sal and Jason both knew Sal wouldn't be able to focus until he cleared his head.

Jason gazed at the stalls. "Take Nelly. She can use the exercise." He flipped his chair around and headed toward the house.

Sal crossed the path between the stalls until he reached the farthest and largest, where the coat of a sleek black mare shone in the sun. "Hey, girl," he said with a pat. "Sorry Jason couldn't visit with you today. He's not feeling great." He attached the mare's saddle as he spoke. "I know you miss him when he can't see you, but we all love you. How's about you and I go for a jaunt?"

He paused to gauge her reaction to wearing her saddle. She seemed restless, but not distressed. Had she shown signs of being unhappy, he would have taken more time before mounting her. Once on the saddle with his boots securely in the stirrups, Sal clicked his tongue and let her lead him out of the stall.

Chapter Two

AFTER TWO WEEKS of staring at the wall and playing with the puppies on his parents' farm and dog-breeding facility, Ryder had to get off the property. Since the story of Gabriella's death had been reported in the local paper, he feared the town gossip mill would be in full swing. Though all the stories that he read were short and only mentioned him in passing. Despite his hesitancy, one more puppy yip would push him over the edge—into what, Ryder wasn't sure, but the fall would be long. In exchange for picking up groceries, his mom gave him permission to take the truck into town.

The familiar roads were nearly deserted in the middle of the day. *Because most adults have jobs.* The thought brought out a sigh. It wasn't that Ryder didn't want to work. He did, but his experience as an insurance actuary didn't position him for many opportunities here. And given that he couldn't currently afford to pay rent, here was the place to be. Ryder hated asking his parents for money even more than he had in high school, since that was the last time he'd had to. *I'm lucky,* he reminded himself. *Other people in my situation would be homeless or dead, if the sharks had their way.*

Ryder shook his head as he parked the truck. Pity parties didn't suit him. He vowed to ask around town to see if anyone was hiring. Any job would be better than the nothing he had now.

"Ryder?" a familiar, tentative voice asked.

"Cat?" He lifted his gaze, and the sight of his old friend tugged the corners of his mouth upward.

"You just gonna stand there?" Cat extended her arms and pulled him into a hug that took his breath away. Though petite, she was far stronger than she appeared. "How are you? Never mind. That's a stupid question. Do you have anywhere to be?" she asked when she released him.

"No...not really."

"Good! You must try the new donut place then." Cat grabbed his hand and pulled him down the cobblestone-lined street. She stopped so suddenly he almost ran into her. "You're skinny. You aren't on a ridiculous low-carb diet, are you?"

"No, I—"

"Thank God! I worried New York may have killed your spirit. I know how those Yankee types can be."

Considering Cat's only exposure to people outside of their small North Carolina town was through dog shows, where she competed with her German shepherds and Afghan hounds, she did not have as firm a grasp on Northern personality types as she'd like to believe. But Ryder saw no reason to point that out.

Cat led him inside a bubblegum-pink bakery that had fake lollipops hanging from the ceilings, giant rainbow-sprinkled cookies on the walls, and a dizzying array of baked goods displayed behind glass. *Holy shit! Ow! It's like...a child's princess party threw up in here.* Ryder blinked hard in attempt to adjust his vision.

"Did you say something?" Cat asked.

Did I? God, I hope not.

Before Ryder could reply, a woman wearing a uniform that matched the decor stepped out through the curtain separating the back from the front. "Good morning, darlings! Welcome to Sweets on Main! What can I do for you?" Her deeply cheerful Southern accent echoed off the walls.

Ryder opened his mouth to answer around his plastered smile, but Cat cut him off.

"Ryder is back in town after spending too much time up North. I thought I'd bring him here to remind him of why he should never leave again."

"Well, you've come to the right place. What's your pleasure, sugars?"

"We'll have two Heavenly Berry donuts."

"You're in luck! They just came out of the oven. Take a seat anywhere, and I'll bring them right over."

"Thanks, Belinda."

Ryder followed Cat to the corner booth. "This place is...nice."

Cat rolled her eyes. "The decorations threw me at first, too, but the donuts are to die for. Trust me."

Long as the pink doesn't kill me first. The decor reminded him of Gabriella—but not because she enjoyed the typical girl colors. She hated them, much to her father's relief. The memory caused a wave of sadness to wash over Ryder.

"What did I say? Die for...oh, my goodness, Ryder, I'm so sorry. How could I be so insensitive?" Cat's features flooded with such profound remorse that Ryder couldn't help reaching out and squeezing her hand.

"It wasn't that. I just get sad sometimes...a lot of the time."

"Well, of course you do." Cat clamped her mouth shut when Belinda brought their food. They both thanked her, and once she was out of earshot, Cat asked, "How are you handling everything?"

Ryder picked up the pink, flaky donut and took a bite—partly to buy himself time and partly because the aroma was making his stomach growl. Since Cat still looked at him, waiting for an answer, he offered a one-shoulder shrug. "I don't know, honestly. Some days are better than others. It's especially difficult because I don't have much to occupy my time."

Cat quieted for a moment as they ate their pastries. "You used to work with money, right? Is that the kind of thing you could do online?"

"Not easily. One of these days, I'll take a trip to Asheville to see if they have openings available."

"Well, I'm sure in a city that size, you'll find something, but perhaps Sal would need help at the farm."

Ryder jerked his head up. "Sal Lewis?"

"Is there another in our friend group?"

"I thought he was in Raleigh. Did he come back after college?"

Cat scrunched up her face. "He only got to work in the city a few years before Jason's accident..." She shook her head. "It's not my story to tell. You'll have to ask him."

Ryder scoffed. "I highly doubt Sal wants the first thing to do with me."

This time, it was Cat's turn to reach across the table to touch him. "Then you don't know the first thing about him, or the rest of us, for that matter." She patted his arm, then ran her fingers through her dark brown hair. "Listen, I have to get going. A group of us gets together at the pub on Friday nights. You should join us. Might take your mind off your grief for a while. Let you make some connections?"

He rose and hugged her. "Thanks, Cat. I'll try."

"Do better than try. If I don't see you this week, I'll be dragging you out next week."

Ryder laughed. "With incentive like that, how could I resist?"

"You can't." She beamed her radiant smile. "I'll see you at eight sharp tomorrow night."

RYDER'S MIND CHURNED over the new information all the way home. It hadn't even occurred to him that Sal would be in town, much less that he would want to see him... *No. He doesn't, regardless of what Cat believes. She doesn't know the whole story. At least, I hope not. Of course, she doesn't know what happened. If she did, she wouldn't have invited me out tomorrow. I shouldn't go.* As sure as Ryder was that it would be wrong, and maybe even selfish, to join them at the pub, he couldn't help wanting to see his old friends again. Even if Sal told him to fuck off, Ryder would know he was okay. Healthy. Happy... Taken?

That possibility should not have roiled Ryder's gut the way it did. His breakup with Sal had been...messy, if he wanted to use a vast understatement. The phone ringing in his headset interrupted his thoughts. "Hello?"

"You're driving," his mother said, disappointment coloring her voice. "Are you almost home?"

"'Bout ten minutes away. What do you need?"

"I forgot to include yeast on my grocery list, and I can't make the bread without it."

Ryder chuckled. "I am certainly not going to stand in the way of fresh bread. Is the mart down the road still open?"

"That mart has been here almost since the town's founding. I'm convinced it'll be there until the second coming."

"All right, Ma. I'll stop by there and be home soon."

"Thank you, dear."

Ryder ended the call after saying goodbye and turned off at the next exit. Charlie's Mart was a convenience store passed down through four generations of Charlies. The patriarch of the family had damn near had a heart attack when his son had only had a girl. But they kept with tradition and named her Charlotte—just so they could call her Charlie.

Ryder parked the truck, climbed out, and locked the door.

"You aren't in New York anymore, Cowboy," Phineas Killman, a friend of his dad's, drawled on his way to his car.

"Old habits." Ryder forced a smile. No matter where you went in this town, you were bound to run into someone you knew. Tired, sick, happy, or sad, you had to make small talk everywhere. "How ya been?"

"Hanging in there." A shadow crossed over Phineas's features. "I'm real sorry to hear about your little girl."

"Thanks. It's tough, but—"

Phineas clamped his hand on Ryder's shoulder. "But she's with God now, and that's a heck of a lot better than the hell this country is turning into." Ryder bit the inside of his cheek to keep from disrespecting the older man, but thankfully, he didn't seem to notice the sudden tension. "I have to head back. Those eggs aren't collecting themselves. You come on down if you need anything, hear?"

"Yes, sir. Thank you," Ryder managed around the metallic taste of blood. He willed his legs to move toward the door.

Someone up there was looking out for him because he was able to collect and pay for the yeast while only exchanging a few words with the cashier. After filling up the truck's tank, he completed the journey home.

"Ryder, is that you?" Ma called from the kitchen.

"Yes. Sorry it took so long. I ran into Phineas Killman and—"

"You were lucky to get out of there alive?" She smiled when he handed her the yeast.

"I wouldn't go that far," Ryder said as he put the remaining groceries away.

Ma rolled her eyes and motioned for him to sit at the kitchen table. "That man would drive the saints to alcoholism."

"Can I help?"

She opened her mouth, a reflex action to refuse, but then closed it and handed him a pot of potatoes and a bowl. "Skin those for me?"

"Absolutely." Ryder was grateful that she didn't brush him off. He appreciated the chance to contribute something, even if it was only dinner prep. He glanced at the clock. "How come you're home in the middle of the day?" As a vet with a constant stream of patients, Ma didn't often have the luxury of random weekday afternoons at home. Nor had she ever seemed to want it.

"I had a cancelation. Thought I would make dinner before going back," she replied, then returned her focus to her task. "Did you have a nice time with Catherine?"

Ryder scrunched his forehead. "How did you...?"

"Millie called me when she saw you two at the bakery. We had a nice chat. I didn't know you and she were in touch."

Now, I remember why I left this town as soon as I could. Ryder suppressed a groan. "We weren't until a couple of hours ago when I ran into her."

"Oh." Fresh disappointment crept into her words. "I thought perhaps you had planned the outing."

"No, though she did invite me to hang out with her and her friends tomorrow evening. She said most of our high school friend group is still in town."

Ma hummed her confirmation. "People tend to return to their roots eventually. You *are* going, aren't you?"

"Probably."

"I think you should. Your dad and I can't be the most interesting companions." Ma prepared the bread dough while they talked. She was too short to comfortably work on the counter without her step stool, the same one she'd been using as long as Ryder could remember. Why she didn't sit to prep, he had never understood.

Ryder dropped the third peeled potato into the pot. "So, Cat mentioned that Sal is back in town."

"Yes, tragedy that. Now Salvatore is working on the farm, of course. He's a wonderful asset to the community," she added. "But poor Jason." Ma sighed.

Ryder let a few beats pass before asking, "What happened to him?"

"He was riding his black mare in a competition. What's her name?"

"Nelly?"

"Yes, that's it. Beautiful horse."

"She is." Ryder had been with Jason and Sal when Jason had chosen her not more than a few months after their parents died. Her sleek coat caught everyone's attention, but she only had eyes for Jason. Sal and Ryder gave Jason shit for allowing such a powerful, gorgeous creature to keep the name Nelly. But saying "Whoa, Nelly" amused him, so his grandparents gave in. She took to him right away. It was months before anyone else could ride her. Not that it mattered. Nelly and Jason were in almost year-round competitions throughout middle and high school. After that, Ryder and Sal were in college and Ryder lost track of the equestrian world, and his hometown. "What happened at the competition?" he pressed his mom.

"Something spooked the horse, and she bucked him clear to the other side of the arena circle." Ma shook her head. "The medics on-site said he got lucky. If he hadn't flown so far, she very well may have trampled him."

"I can't believe she'd hurt him intentionally."

Ma turned around and pointed the wooden rolling pin at him. "You damn well know better than that. Intention has nothing to do with it. When animals are scared, they don't think about not hurting the ones they love. They don't worry about consequences. They react. Same as humans."

Ryder lowered his gaze to the potatoes again, focusing all his effort into the task of paring the skin. "Is Jason okay?"

"From what I understand, after many surgeries, he's left with pain, limited function in his lower body, and seizures. Salvatore had to come to help him with the farm because their grandparents couldn't manage it anymore."

"Limited function? What does that mean? Can he walk?" He glanced up from peeling. "Does he still ride?"

She let out a long sigh. "Not professionally, and I believe the answer to your other questions is usually he can walk, but sometimes he uses a wheelchair. The family keeps the details quiet." Ma knitted her eyebrows together as she appraised the pot of potatoes. "No more chitchat until you finish the spuds. At the rate you're going, they won't be ready to mash until Christmas."

Ryder zeroed in on removing the skins as quickly as he could. A mindless task that let his brain meander back to his conversations with Cat and his mother. Had Cat suggested he apply for a job at the Lewis farm because Sal was struggling, or was it a matchmaking attempt? He laughed at the thought of pursuing a job because you wanted a relationship with the boss. *What do I think this is, a goddamn romantic film?*

Chapter Three

SAL REMOVED HIS Stetson and mopped the sweat from his forehead with a rag he kept on his belt. Bishop wandered over to his water bucket. "Okay, boy. Can't deprive you of water. But we still have at least another thirty minutes." He rarely trained the horses after lunch in the summer months. Both he and they worked better in the morning and late afternoon when the sun wasn't trying to recreate hell, but the forecast called for thunderstorms later, so he had to get it in while he could. Then again, he didn't need to consult the weather channel to know when storms were on the way. The fact that Jason was in his chair for the second day in a row told him all he needed to know about the weather.

Bishop stomped on the ground. "You ready?" Sal grabbed the reins and led him around the running circle. The colt had proven to be receptive to guidance in the short amount of time they'd worked together. Tomorrow, Sal would add the obstacle course to Bishop's agility training.

"Is this the new kid?" Cat asked from outside the fenced-in area.

Sal clicked his tongue and slowed Bishop to a walk. "This is Bishop."

"He's a beauty. Friendly?"

"Long as you aren't putting a saddle on his back." He got the horse to stop in front of her, and Cat stroked Bishop's snout.

"That's a problem, isn't it?"

"Eh, not yet. He just came yesterday. We still need to get to know him and his preferences. Maybe he's picky about the kind of material he'll wear. Some horses don't like leather; others won't use anything but." Sal waited for Bishop to give the signal that he was becoming restless, then led him to his stall. He had moved Bishop to the stall next to King earlier in the day, and they both seemed to appreciate the company. "My hope is that King is a positive influence on him." After settling Bishop in his stall, he turned to Cat. "But you're not here to discuss horse care."

She offered her thousand-watt smile. "You know I love them, especially when they're so young and adorable." Sal couldn't hold in his snicker. "What?"

"Would you keep your dogs' puppies forever?"

"Forever, no, but that doesn't mean I don't want to kiss their faces when they tumble around and chase their tails."

Sal shook his head. "I'd stick to pictures of puppies and colts, if I had my way. Bishop is as young as I would go."

"With the exception of those born here?"

"Obviously." He slung his bag over his shoulder. "Seriously, though, what's up?"

Cat gave a look of mock offense. "Saying I can't stop by to check on my oldest friend's new colt?"

"In the middle of the afternoon when we're meeting later today, and with a storm coming, to boot? No. Probably not the most advisable timing." Sal softened it with a smile of his own. "Do you have time for tea?"

"Always."

The two of them cut diagonally through the grass toward the house. "Fair warning, Jason isn't in the best of spirits today."

Cat's features crumpled in sympathy. "The storms must make it hard for him."

That was an understatement. Jason rarely discussed his pain in explicit detail, though he had gotten to the point of accepting unprompted assistance from Sal. Which meant Sal always had to be on guard for nonverbal signs. Sal and Cat made it to the kitchen door, where Pete greeted them with a wagging tail.

"Hello, Petey boy!" Cat stepped off to the side with him while Sal unlaced his boots to leave them in the entryway. Habit ingrained in them since childhood, but it probably saved them hours of cleaning each week, so Sal had no intention of breaking it.

"This is a surprise, Cat," Jason said as he wheeled in from the living room. His voice was lighter, and the stress lines around his eyes had faded a touch. This signaled to Sal that his new medicine must be working.

Sal let out a breath. Apparently, he was more concerned about Jason being receptive to a guest than he realized. "Says she wanted to see Bishop."

"Beauty, isn't he?" Jason wheeled over to the stove. "Tea, right?"

"Yes, thank you." Cat lowered herself into the seat at the table Sal motioned her to.

He then took three mugs from the cupboard and arranged them along with a tin of cookies on a tray for Jason to carry over. Yes, it would have been easier for Sal to put everything directly on the table, but that wouldn't give Jason satisfaction. Once all three were seated, Sal focused his attention on Cat. "Now, will you tell us what prompted the visit?"

"Why does anything have to prompt it? I was in the neighborhood. You have a new pony."

"Horse," Sal and Jason said together.

"I know." Cat giggled. "I just like the color your ears turn when I say it."

"Jerk," Sal scoffed without malice.

"Have you gotten around to mocking him for naming another future stallion after a chess piece?" Jason asked.

"You already did that," Sal reminded him.

"Everyone should take a turn. Might be the only way to get it through your thick skull." Jason swirled milk into his tea.

"Bishop is more than just a chess piece."

"Yes, it's also a position in the Catholic church. Gonna tell me he was named in honor of a clergyman you admire?" Jason added a cookie to his plate.

Sal glared at his brother but couldn't muster enough emotion to look intimidating. Truth be told, he was too happy Jason could joke around. This morning that hadn't been an option. Cat's laugh brought him back to the present. "Sorry."

"For what? You two are hysterical." Her eyes widened as she bit into a cookie. "These are fantastic. Who made them?"

"Grams, who else?"

"She's still up to baking?" Cat held the cookie between her plate and her mouth.

"I swear she's going to die while in the middle of cooking dinner." Sal paused. "Now that I think about it, that's probably exactly what she and Pops would want."

"Then he wouldn't have to live without her, assuming the house burned with dinner."

Cat furrowed her brow. "But it wouldn't with you two living on the other side of the property."

Sal gazed out toward his grandparents' smaller home past the stables. They'd moved there after Jason's accident, since this house had to be remodeled to accommodate his wheelchair, which the doctors were sure he'd need to use full time. Grams and Pops couldn't have taken the upheaval of the remodel, and by the time it was completed, they had settled in the other house. "No, we'd never let it happen if we saw it. Obviously. We're just saying they couldn't imagine living without each other, and neither one of them do well with being inactive."

"Speaking of spouses," Jason cut in, "is Owen still due to get back from deployment at the end of the month?"

"As of when we talked last week. But you know the goddamn navy. It feels like they change their minds with the wind."

Sal only "knew the navy" through listening to Cat's struggles, and that was just fine with him. "Isn't his four years almost up?"

"December, thank God."

"No chance of him reupping?"

Cat's laugh was tinged with incredulousness this time. "Not if he wants to keep a wife at home." She tipped her teacup back like a shot, and Sal winced, imagining the inevitable burning in her throat. "I ran into Ryder Christensen downtown."

Sal half choked on his tea. "Yeah? How's he doing?"

"About as well as you'd expect a man who lost his baby to be doing, I suppose."

"I'm sure he's getting plenty of comfort from the mother."

"His mom's doing her best, but—"

"No. The baby's mother." Sal knew he sounded immature, but he couldn't seem to let go of his anger. Sal and Ryder had been happy together—no more doubting or trying to hide their sexuality from the world. Then this bitch came in and swore the kid's doctor ran a blood test that found Ryder to be the father.

That was it. Ryder chose the girl and her daughter over Sal. "It was the right thing to do," he had said. "Have to take care of the child."

Sal never—would never have—disputed that, but that did not have to involve being with the gold digger of a mother. He buried the emotion at the sound of Cat's voice. "Sorry, what did you say?"

"He hasn't been with the kid's mother for years." Sal blinked, and Cat's eyes widened again. "Oh, my God. You really don't know?"

"He broke up with me to be with her."

"I'm not sure about that, but he's been raising that little girl on his own."

"Why? What…?"

"I don't see why that matters," Jason said. "Ryder still left Sal for the mother of his baby."

Sal's head spun. *Ryder did say he was leaving me for her, didn't he? Or was it that he felt like he had to take care of her? Is there a difference?* "Fuck," he muttered. "What if I got it all wrong?"

"Wouldn't he have told you at some point in the last six years?" Jason wheeled to the door to let his whining dog outside.

"I didn't really leave the door open for communication."

Cat shrugged. "Might be worth talking to him. You can start tonight." She climbed to her feet.

"Tonight?" Sal's brain was still jumbled.

"Yes, I invited him to our weekly pub meeting." She swung her purse over her shoulder. "Don't make me come looking for you." On her way to the door, she called back, "Thanks for the tea and cookies! Stay safe with the storm."

"I can almost understand why her husband is in the navy. She'd be a head trip twenty-four seven." Jason wheeled up behind Sal as they both stared after her. In response to Sal's noncommittal grunt, he asked, "Are you going?"

Sal exhaled. "If I get all my work done, probably."

"Okay, Cinderella." The eye roll was clear in Jason's voice as he turned around to open the door for Pete.

"What if I said, 'I'll go, if you do'?" Sal kept his hands busy loading the dishwasher with their snack plates and mugs.

Jason quieted. "Then you will be a very lonely man, because I am not leaving."

"So, you finally admit you're lonely?"

"No, but you would be." Before either of them could continue their oft-repeated argument, their cell phones dinged at the same time. Jason grabbed his from the table first. "Shit. Tornado."

"Watch or warning?" Sal was already lacing his boots as he asked the question. The answer would only tell him how fast he moved.

"Warning. Touchdown five miles out." Jason fitted his shoes on.

"You don't—"

"Yes, I do. I'm fine. One of us needs to bring Grams and Pops over here."

Sal bit his lip. Their grandparents' house was fine most of the time, but they didn't have the secure shelter Sal and Jason had over here. "Okay, but you don't have to walk."

"Salvatore." The low growl leaving Jason's lips as he leveraged the back of the chair to climb to his feet would intimidate people who hadn't lived with him all his life—or those who didn't see the flash of anguish twisting the glare that accompanied it. "Go lock down the stalls, and I'll fetch Grams and Pops."

Jason left the house and sprinted—in what Sal could only imagine was very painful fashion—toward their grandparents' home.

Chapter Four

AT 7:50 ON Friday, Ryder approached the local pub. The corners of his mouth lifted when he saw the rainbow inverted-triangle sticker in the window. "Times they are a-changin'," he muttered.

"That'll happen in seven years," Neal Marcus, a man who had not changed much from his high school glory days as a quarterback, told him.

Ryder almost countered that he had only been gone six years, but that wasn't true. Gabriella had been born six years ago. He hadn't been back to his hometown since the year before. The thought of his daughter once again brought sadness rushing back to him. *What kind of monster am I for going out partying so soon after she passed?*

Just as Ryder was about to tell Neal he had made a terrible mistake and had to head home to self-flagellate, Cat bounded up. "Good lord, are you two just going to stand outside? Come on. I need a cold one."

Ryder murmured his thanks to Neal for holding the door for him and Cat. The live band sat on the stage tuning their acoustic guitars and sound checking their microphones. Ryder's heart raced as the energy of the people pulsated around him. The place was packed, but Cat led them to a somehow empty booth in the back. "How many people are coming?"

"Between five and seven. We'll add a table if we have to." Cat waved to the server. "Pitcher, please!"

"Pitcher of what?" Ryder asked.

"The house microbrew," Neal answered. "Same thing every week. Only now that we've gotten older, we've started coming earlier."

"Oh, hush, you don't have puppies who wake you up at 4:00 a.m."

"No, I have a goddamn hen house. Those roosters are well-known for not letting people sleep in."

"Only get worse when the baby comes." A very pregnant Lilly sat next to Cat. "Phil is parking," she said of her probable husband. "Ryder! I didn't know you were coming."

"Cat invited me when I ran into her the other day. I hope y'all don't mind."

Lilly opened her mouth, but Cat waved her off. "Ignore him when he says shit like that, and hopefully he'll stop." Cat gave him a pointed look. "How about that wind this afternoon?"

"Oh, my God, it shook the damn house. We didn't see the funnel, though, did you?" Lilly answered. Phil shook Ryder's hand silently before easing in beside his wife.

Cat focused on Phil. "Now, why would you box the pregnant woman in? You're only gonna have to move again. Sit by Ryder."

Ryder stood up because he did not want to be trapped on the inside of the booth either. His nerves frazzled with the growing crowd. "I don't remember you being this bossy, Cat."

"Someone has to keep Owen in line when he's home from the service. Would hate to see him get undisciplined."

Phil almost choked on his drink. "Don't believe he'd appreciate this conversation."

The server set down a pitcher of beer, five glasses, and a pop for Lilly. She came back a moment later with a rum and Coke and set it in front of Ryder. "From the gentleman at the bar." The server winked and pointed to a young man in the middle.

Ryder blinked around the table at his friends. "What the hell?"

"I'd say he's interested." Neal poured the beer and passed around the glasses.

"How does he know that won't earn him a fist to the face? You can't make assumptions like that." Ryder ran his fingers through his shaggy hair. The table fell into silence—as much as could be afforded in a crowded bar, anyway. "What?"

Cat shrugged. "Guess he felt comfortable 'cause he knows you bat for both teams. Your relationship with Sal wasn't a secret."

Ryder licked his lips and tried not to allow his nerves to make him fidget, but he couldn't stop them from affecting his digestion. The guy at the bar caught his eye. Handsome though he was, the attention did nothing to ease the knot in Ryder's stomach. "I have to go to the bathroom." He didn't wait for a response. Crowded bar on a Friday not was not his best idea. If he wanted to see his old friends, which he thought he did, he would have been better off setting up something in the daylight, without alcohol. Or rather, asking Cat to set it up, since she seemed to be the leader. Ryder pushed the bathroom door open, eyed the row of urinals, and chose the second stall. Another advantage to being here early—the bathroom was relatively clean. When he was halfway through peeing, the outer door opened and closed. *Shit. Doesn't matter. Men don't congregate in the bathroom to chitchat. Not even gay men.*

After tucking himself back into his jeans, Ryder slid the lock on the stall door. He kept his eyes fixed on his shoes as he walked to the sinks.

"Not a rum and Coke guy?" a voice behind him asked.

"Not really. I appreciate the thought though." Ryder washed his hands quickly but thoroughly. He used one paper towel to dry and plucked another down to open the germ-ridden door handle. As he reached for it, the rum and Coke guy grabbed his arm. "Hey, I don't want any trouble."

"Neither do I. No reason to rush off, is there?"

"I'm here with my friends—"

"Something wrong with making a new friend?"

Ryder pressed his lips together but released them to breathe from his mouth. The stench of booze on this wanker assaulted his nose. "Let me go."

Wanker—as Ryder would now be referring to him—pushed Ryder's shoulders against the wall next to the urinals. "You a cocktease? Gonna lead me on and then not follow through?"

"What the fuck did I do to lead you on?" *More importantly, what the fuck is wrong with me? Why am I engaging him at all?* Wanker had about fifty pounds on Ryder's lean but fit frame.

"I bought you a drink; then you gave me the signal to meet you in the bathroom. That's a clear choice. Am I supposed to deal with blue balls because you changed your damn mind?"

A mix of adrenaline and anger heated Ryder's upper body. He shoved Wanker back suddenly enough to knock the asshole off balance. "You need to work on your definition of consent. Avoiding the person hitting on you does not indicate a come-on in any sane human." Ryder clenched his hands into fists as he narrowed his gaze at the other man, who found the sense to stay back. "Don't come near me again."

When Ryder stalked out of the bathroom, the now pounding music pinged off every electrified nerve ending in his body. With a fortifying breath, he made his way past the throngs of customers to his table. "I have to head out." He plunked down five dollars for the beer he didn't drink.

"But what about—" Cat stopped talking when Ryder shook his head.

"I'll talk to you all later, but I gotta get out of here now." *Before the asshole rounds up his friends to come find me.* Ryder received hesitant nods from the rest of his group, and he zigzagged through the crowd toward the parking lot. Maybe he was being paranoid, and the asshole would slink back to whatever hole he came from. Ryder may not have dated much—or at all—since his split from Sal, but he knew enough about romance to know that many men did not take kindly to rejection. He rejoiced in the late summer sunset. He hadn't relished the idea of navigating the parking lot in the dark. *Now, I'm definitely being paranoid.*

The drive home was faster than normal, due to the absence of traffic, and the last rays of light fell behind the horizon when he reached the driveway. After spending a moment in the truck just breathing, Ryder stepped out and approached the kitchen door, where his parents waited on the other side. They stared as he walked in.

"You drove home? I thought for sure you'd take a cab," his father said. "Any amount of alcohol can—"

Ryder raised his hand. "I didn't drink."

"Then why are you home so early?"

"I have a headache." He opened his mouth to say more but stopped when he spied one of the puppies in the laundry room pen. "What's wrong with Elle?"

"Her mother rejected her, and her siblings followed suit." Ma sighed. "We're going to try to bottle-feed, but usually rejection means there's something wrong with them. Though I couldn't find anything. She's four weeks old. So, the feeding schedule is not as intense as it would have been two weeks ago."

"Also worth noting that Carrie had a large litter this time, so she may have been overwhelmed," Dad added.

Ryder approached the pen and crouched to Elle's level. "You and your family not getting along?" He scratched behind her ears and down her neck, for which he was rewarded with a lick to his wrist. "Let me care for her."

His parents exchanged a glance. "Do you want to keep her or get her ready to be adopted with her littermates?" Ma asked.

Ryder lifted her out of the pen, and she snuggled close to his chest.

"Well, that answers that, then." Dad tried to look dismayed, but he had been wanting a second pet dog in the house since he lost his Lab last year. At least he'd get his wish for as long as Ryder lived there.

"Thanks. I'll set up her crate in my room." Ryder's heart lifted when she wouldn't move away after being set on the ground.

"Her feeding schedule is posted on the fridge. You have to stick close to it."

"I know, Ma; we've been raising puppies since I was a baby." Which meant he also knew how difficult it was to adopt out the "different" dogs. Potential owners were nervous about puppies who weren't accepted by their mothers because if not handled well, those dogs could develop severe behavior problems. He pecked her cheek and led Elle to his room, where he set up her crate with soft blankets. Ryder could have pretended that he would nurture her until the rest of the litter was at an adoptable age, but he didn't see wanting to give her up anytime soon.

Once he'd fed her and taken her outside, they settled in for the night. It wasn't until the lights were off that Ryder thought back to the asshole at the bar. *Will he talk to Cat and the rest of the group? What if he says something to Sal? Does it matter?* The last answer was, of course, yes, it did matter. Ryder may have fucked things up with Sal beyond repair before Gabriella was born, but that did not mean he wanted Wanker to control the narrative of the story.

God only knew what he'd say, or what Ryder's old friends would believe. They hadn't known him for a long time. None of them had seen him juggling caring for his daughter on his own while he tried to make it in the cutthroat financial industry. He'd had to give up on being a stockbroker so he could keep humane hours. Not that anyone would complain about the salary he had made as an actuary. But he had blown it on—

Elle yipped and whined from the floor. Ryder climbed out of bed and lay next to her crate. "Thank you, girl. My head was going nowhere good fast." He reached in and scratched her. "I understand that no amount of blankets can replace your mom and siblings. But the crate is only temporary. Hopefully we can ditch it after a few weeks." She whined again after he stopped touching her, so he stuck his hand in a second time. "Okay, you're right. It will probably be months, but it'll make things easier going forward." He kissed her head between the bars. "We'll get through it together. I promise."

AT 10:30 THE next morning, Ryder was throwing a ball for Carrie and her pups, all except Elle, anyway. He and his parents decided they would reintegrate Elle and Carrie after the other puppies found homes. In various areas of the farm, people worked to sheer the sheep, mow the grass, and check on the chickens. Ryder had gotten up early to feed the chicken and collect the eggs. Ryder's parents' farm was unique in that none of the animals were killed for food. They bought all their meat from other local humane farmers. Ma said that was a stipulation of marrying Dad—no eating the animals they raised. The family still sold the milk, eggs, and refined wool, in addition to the hay to support dog breeding.

The churning of the lawn mower puttered to a stop in the middle of the field. Ryder raised his hand to shield his eyes from the sun's glare to see if the farmer jumped down to inspect the engine. But, no, the worker waved to someone riding a black-and-white spotted horse with a luscious, thick tail. Ryder's pulse picked up speed as the figure drew closer and Sal's broad shoulders, toned torso, and defined jaw became clear. Another couple of strides would reveal the soft, pink lips perfectly contrasted by Sal's summer tan. The sight of Sal riding through the field on a horse transported Ryder back a decade. Their properties were close enough that while they were growing up, Sal would often visit on horseback instead of wasting time with the car. Depending on the horse, it could even be faster. A glance down at his own dirty clothes brought heat to Ryder's face. He would have much preferred to have been more put together when he saw Sal after all this time. *Then again, he might not even be here for me. He could be coming around to place his hay order. Without his truck? I said place it, not pick it up.* As the voices in Ryder's head warred, he wondered if other people experienced the same internal arguments.

One of the puppies growled around the tennis ball in his mouth. "Hey! None of that, little guy." Ryder waited for him to sit before taking the ball and tossing it in the other direction. A stampede of puppies chased it down, tumbling over each other in the process.

Sal stopped his horse a few feet from Carrie, who was lying in the sun. She lifted her head and wagged her tail. "Pretty Mama," Sal soothed. "Are your babies wearing you out?"

Ryder's mouth suddenly lost all its moisture as he watched Sal bending over to fuss on the dog. The man's body hadn't lost a centimeter of muscle mass in the six-and-a-half years since Ryder had seen him. *Why is he here? I could...should, no, will ask, but I'm not sure if I want to know. Holding on to the thought that he may have forgiven me is more attractive than knowing for sure that he hasn't.* "Hi," he said, while congratulating himself on his originality.

"Hi." Sal straightened to his full height and walked over. The darkened lenses Sal wore prevented Ryder from reading his eyes. The silence stretched out between them so long that Ryder considered running into the house—or the lake on the other side of the property. *Certainly the more dramatic choice.* "Cat said you left suddenly last night. Everything okay?"

Ryder swallowed to lubricate his throat enough to speak. *Should I brush it off? Tell him a version of the truth?* While the latter seemed to be the better choice, he couldn't think of a way to phrase it that didn't make him sound weak. "I'm fine now. There was an asshole at the bar who hit on me and didn't appreciate the rejection." He offered what he hoped was a convincing smile. "I'm sorry I missed you."

Sal lifted a shoulder and let it fall nonchalantly "No big. She was worried though. Thought maybe you got hurt."

"I didn't let him get that far." Ryder pretended he was checking on the playful puppies as an excuse to avoid Sal's raised eyebrow. "Do you have time for some fresh lemonade and apple fritters or do you need... What?" he demanded in response to the grin cracking Sal's face.

"Nothing. Just…fresh lemonade and apple fritters has to be the most Southern offer I've ever received." The amusement in Sal's voice was music to Ryder's ears, even if the joke was on him.

"You hungry or not?"

"Yeah, I could eat. Let me tie King to the tree."

"Might want to take him to that one." Ryder pointed to a tree with higher branches and lusher leaves. "Shade's better. The water bowl was just changed, so it should be fresh and full, but let me know if you want more." The sweat coating Ryder's palms had nothing to do with rising heat. He whistled for the puppies, then glanced at Carrie. "Sorry, girl. I'll bring you out here in a while." Like the tired mother she was, Carrie rolled on her back a few times before getting to her feet and barking for the pups to follow her in. Once all the animals were settled in their respective places, Ryder let Elle out of her crate. "Go right outside." She sped out the door as Sal was coming in.

"Where are your parents?" Sal asked as he removed his Stetson and boots, as Ryder had done. They all knew better than to track mud into the house.

"They went to see my aunt overnight." *Shit. Does that sound like a come-on?* "One cube of ice with your lemonade?"

"You remembered."

"Hard to forget something I did for two-and-a-half decades." Sal liked his drinks cold, but not watery. He had perfected the one-ice-cube method around middle school. Ryder washed his hands, then plated the warm apple fritters. When he turned around to see Sal still on his feet, he waved to the table. "Sit. Sit."

Sal lowered himself into a chair and waited for Ryder to take the one across from him. For his part, Ryder was grateful when the indoor lighting changed and it was apparent Sal was wearing transition lenses to allow Ryder to read emotion in his chocolate-brown eyes. "So...what made you decide to come back here?"

"Honestly? I didn't have many options." He fidgeted with the ring on his middle finger—the one he had worn for years. It had the word "Peace" in a Native American language inscribed around the silver band.

"I'm confused. Tell me to mind my own business if you want, but didn't you have a job in New York? Friends?"

As Ryder licked his lips, he contemplated how honest he should be. He had little doubt that the truth, at least most of it, would come out eventually, but he wasn't sure if he could stomach laying it out on the table right that moment. "I...fell off the proverbial deep end after I lost Gabby and—"

"Gabby was the baby?" *Who tore us apart,* was left unsaid, but very much felt by both men.

"Gabriella was my daughter, yes." He fumbled for his phone and showed Sal his lock screen—a selfie of himself and Gabby in Central Park, Gabby's expression alight with mischief.

Sal managed a ghost of a smile. "She looks..."

"Like trouble?"

He laughed, a short, yet sweet sound. "I was gonna say 'like you,' but same thing I suppose."

For the first time in what felt like forever, Ryder let a chuckle escape his lips. "Thank you. Though she was much prettier than I will ever be."

"Oh, I don't know about that," Sal crooned. "Seem to remember you placing in the college drag competition."

Ryder let out a put-upon sigh. "If only they hadn't let a professional enter, I would have won."

"Yes, and you would have gotten so much use out of the Sephora gift certificate." Sal rolled his eyes, but his features softened as he handed back Ryder's phone. "I'm real sorry for your loss. I can't even imagine what you must be going through."

He paused to study him. Sal did know loss. His parents had passed on way too young. Ryder thanked his lucky stars every day that he still had his ma and dad. He had no idea what would've become of him without them. But losing a parent and losing a child had to be different because if Ryder had to go through this pain three separate times, he was sure his psyche would never recover. "Thanks. I can tell you mean that."

"Course I do, Ry. No one should have to go through that." Sal looked hurt by the implication that he wouldn't, and Ryder immediately regretted his words. He opened his mouth to backtrack, but Sal continued, "Do you...want to talk about it? I don't know what happened, but..."

Ryder shook his head violently. "No. Not yet." *Maybe I can tell you all about the biggest mistake of my life, if you stick around. Don't,* the counter voice in his head warned. *That's far more than you have a right to hope for. Besides, if you ever did tell him, you can bet it'll be the last thing you get the chance to share.* True though Ryder knew the argument was, it caused an unexpected pain in his chest. "What about you? I heard Jason had an accident. Is he doing better?"

Sal offered a half shrug as he reached over and scratched Elle's ears. "Most days. He's on a strict pain-management regime. Trying hard to stay away from opioids, but there aren't too many options for when the pain is unbearable."

"Can he ride still?" To most people, that would be an insensitive question, but for Jason, the ability to ride a horse was as fundamental to living his best life as walking would be for the rest of the population.

"On good days, he can go for a trot." Ryder winced and Sal nodded. "That's how we feel."

"So, what does he do? Can he help out on the farm? Train the horses at all?"

Sal pushed his glasses up his nose, but studied his food instead of looking at Ryder. "He does what he can, but mostly he sticks with the business end of things."

Again, Ryder could barely contain his grimace. Jason hated school and anything that forced him to be inside and still for a significant period of time. Taking care of the farm's business needs had to be a special sort of hell for him. "I'm sorry. I'd ask if I could help, but I wouldn't want to take over what he's able to do."

That brought Sal's gaze to him, and Ryder exerted a great effort not to squirm under the intensity. "No, I couldn't hand you the books, but I'd appreciate another set of hands with the horses, if you'd be up for that. I mean, I know it's probably nothing like what you were doing in New York…"

Ryder's lips twitched upward. "If I belonged doing what I was in the city, I'd still be there." He paused to wipe his mouth of crumbs that may or may not have been on his face. "I'd love to help, if you'll have me." *God, could I sound more pathetically eager? He's offering me work, not a fucking relationship.*

Much to Ryder's chagrin, Sal downed the last of his lemonade. He leveled their gazes, his chocolate eyes a mask of neutrality. That was a new skill, one Ryder was not particularly fond of. Ever since Sal and Ryder were little kids, Ryder could read him regardless of the emotions playing out in his head. *I haven't earned the right to openness. Hell, I don't even deserve the civility he's giving me.*

Sal must have found what he was searching for because he said, "Let's try it. We'll see how we work together."

"Thank you. I appreciate you being willing to take a chance."

Sal's tongue darted out to wet his lips as he fidgeted with the napkin on his lap. "You've always been a good worker. I've no reason to believe that would have changed. But if we're going to be together day in and day out, there's something I need to ask you."

"Long as it's not about what happened to Gabby, I'll tell you whatever you want to know."

"No. I wouldn't insist on that. Not that much of an asshole."

"Not an asshole at all if I remember correctly." *That would be me. I'm the asshole. Always have been.* A tiny voice buried in the depths of his subconscious tried to argue the truth of the thought, but Ryder wouldn't engage it.

A half snort, half laugh emerged from Sal's lips. "Your memory is in trouble. Might want to get that tested." Sal shook his head as though to find his train of thought. He opened and closed his mouth several times before blurting, "Where's her mother?"

"Gabby's?" With Sal's affirmation, it was Ryder's turn to shrug. "Fuck if I know."

"I...what? How?" Sal's apparent confusion deepened the creases of his brow.

"Haven't heard from Felicia since she started using again the day after I brought Gabby home from the hospital."

"Using?"

"Meth, coke, probably things I didn't even know existed." It had taken a long time for Ryder to get over the bitterness of that period in his life, but he mostly kept it in check now.

Sal leaned back in his chair and stared at nothing to the left of Ryder, but finally Ryder witnessed emotions playing across his face. Confusion, sadness, and, maybe, a touch of relief? "I don't know what to ask first." Sal cleared his throat. "Was she using while she was pregnant?"

"No. I helped her get clean so that Gabriella would have a chance at a decent start to her life. Would have hated for her to be born with the same addictions her mother battled." If "battled" could even be considered the right word. More often than not, Felicia embraced the addictions and took them out for drinks. "The deal was Felicia would have a place to live during the pregnancy if she never used. Best as I could tell she stuck to it." Ryder tilted his head to the side. The physical markers of Sal's confusion only seemed to grow the more he spoke. "I told you this at the time."

"I heard 'the woman I slept with while you and I were on a break is pregnant. I have to take care of her.'"

"Doesn't mean I had an interest in fucking with her."

Sal narrowed his gaze. "You did once. Can't argue it was too much of a stretch to assume you'd want to again."

Ryder shrugged again. "Not a stretch, no. But I tried to tell you as much, and—"

"And I wasn't keen to do a lot of listening." He blew out a breath. "I'm sorry. I guess I should have—" A wave of Ryder's hand cut him off.

"We both should have done a great many things the last few years, I'm sure. Know I should have, at least."

Indecision colored Sal's features again. "So, you raised the baby on your own?"

Ryder bristled. "Do me a favor? I don't mind getting most of this out in the open, but please use my daughter's name when you talk about her. Gabby was a bright, beautiful person in an otherwise gray life. She loved science fiction and aliens and wanted to be an astronaut/hairdresser/vet. For her seventh birthday next month, I promised to get her a puppy because she had been asking for one for the past three years. She was funny and smart, and the best part of me." Ryder cursed his cracking voice and the moisture forming around his eyes. He blinked it away and lifted his gaze with a deep breath to find remorse on Sal's face. A sign his words were getting through, which gave him the strength to continue. "Yes, I raised her alone. But when the alternative was having a mother who cared more about her next hit than making sure you had all your vaccines, I figured she'd be better off without her." Ryder focused his vision on his empty plate. "Maybe I was wrong. Maybe if she had been there, Gabby would still be alive, debating the best breed of puppy for city living." Ryder sucked in a breath when Sal's warm hand engulfed his, which had borrowed the chill from the glass.

With the hand not covering Ryder's, Sal tucked his thumb under Ryder's chin and nudged it up until their gazes met. There was no mistaking the sadness in his eyes. "I am so sorry, Ry. I was being insensitive. Gabriella sounds like a wonderful little girl. I'm sorry I never got the chance to meet her." Sal let the hand supporting Ryder's chin fall to the table, but kept his other one in place. "What I don't understand is why you chose to go it alone."

Ryder drew his eyebrows together. "I told you, her mother—"

"Forget her mother. Why didn't you bring Gabby down here where you have family and...friends?"

"And you?" Ryder didn't wait for an answer. "I thought about it many times, especially when she was a baby and I was spending half my wages on decent childcare. But—" He paused in an effort to get his thoughts in an order that they'd make some semblance of sense. "I didn't know if I could see your family—since you weren't here at the time—day in and day out without falling into self-pity for fucking things up the way I did. Didn't want to be surrounded by memories, reminders of dreams of what could have been." He warred internally between reaching for his drink and prolonging the warmth of Sal's hand on his. The latter was winning out. Who knew how long it would be until Ryder was touched this way again? He almost purred when Sal stroked their thumbs together.

After a moment of searching each other's eyes for answers clearly neither of them had, Sal shook his head again. "We fucked this up nicely, didn't we?"

"I fucked a lot up, far more than I could ever atone for, but I'm gonna try to..." Ryder couldn't find the words he needed, wasn't even sure they existed. "I don't know. Start over, maybe?" *No, that's not right. That would mean I'd forget her, and I couldn't do that, even if I wanted to, which I don't. But it's the easiest description.*

"Your head seems like a busy place."

Understatement, if I ever heard one. Ryder didn't say that, or anything else, for that matter.

Sal's features had softened from their earlier mask as he eased his hand away from Ryder's. "Sounds like we could both use a friend."

Ryder opened his mouth to agree, but the ding of his cell phone jolted his back straight. The noise jarred a bark from Elle. "Shh, girl, it's fine." He tapped the screen to reveal *Text message from unknown number.* Ryder flipped it over so he couldn't see the flashing light. "Friend? Thought you wanted to be my boss."

The grin cracking Sal's face shattered any remaining tension. "Here I thought you liked those qualities together."

"Only for you." Their banter was the easiest conversation Ryder had had in a long time.

"I can live with that." Sal stood, and Ryder followed suit. They had more to say, much more, but it would have to wait. "See you at six?"

"A.M.?"

"What do you think this is, Wall Street? You're going to work on a farm. Yes, 6:00 a.m." He laced up his boots and fitted his hat on his head. "This was good."

"I agree. I'm glad you came."

"Me too." Sal tipped his Stetson at Ryder, then patted Elle's head. "Feel free to bring her when you come. I bet she'd like to play with Petey."

He was out the door before Ryder could ask who exactly Petey was. Another dog, probably. Ryder stared at Sal as he mounted his horse and rode away until he could see no more than a speck on the horizon. His phone gave a reminder ding, and Ryder snatched it up. After unlocking the screen, he read the text message with a sinking heart.

Hope you're getting the rest of the money together, boy. Boss always gets his dues.

The rest of the money? What? The only person who would be talking about money is the shark. No, we had a deal. This is just one of his goons fucking with me.

Ryder deleted the message and started cleaning the kitchen. But his good mood was destroyed.

Chapter Five

BY FIVE O'CLOCK the next morning, Sal had given up sleeping and thrown on his shorts. *May as well get a run in before the day starts. Before Ryder gets here, you mean. Right.* Sal exhaled. He had spent all night trying to deny how heavily Ryder had ingrained himself in his brain since their conversation yesterday. He double knotted his shoelaces and jogged down the steps two at a time. With a glance at Jason's closed bedroom door, he cranked the music up through his headphones, grabbed a water bottle, and eased the back door shut behind him. Not even the loud beat of Run-DMC could drown out the questions that plagued his brain all night.

Did I really remember the most significant moment of my life—when things ended with Ryder—incorrectly?

How could I have managed to misinterpret his words that badly?

Maybe I didn't. What if I heard correctly, but he changed the story later to save face? Sal pounded his feet on the uneven ground, as though trying to beat the idea out of his brain. The only thing he had a harder time believing than misunderstanding the situation was Ryder intentionally misrepresenting what happened. Ryder was a lot of things—stubborn, passionate, tenacious, driven, kind, difficult—but liar was nowhere on the list. Hell, he couldn't even lie to get out of trouble when they were in school. Sal would be shocked if he'd developed the skill over the last six-and-a-half years.

The thoughts looped through his brain, as they had for the past ten hours. Nothing had stopped them yet, not a desperate need for sleep nor the run that should be flooding his brain with endorphins. A glint of metal underneath a pile of dead leaves off the side of the path caught Sal's eye. He halted his run too fast, which left him panting for breath. After downing a third of his water, Sal removed an earbud as he approached the shiny metal. He used a long stick to clear the brush. The second he uncovered enough to identify it, the bear trap snapped the stick in half. "Fuck!"

A glare around the wooded trail gave him no more information about who had set the trap. But whoever it was had surely put out more than one. Sal snapped pictures on his phone, then went down the way he came, his anger now fueling his speed. No one who lived around here would set anything like that. Not with the way the animals were allowed to run through the woods.

When he reached his property again, Sal spied his grandfather coming out of his house.

Pops raised his hand. "Little early to be in the woods, isn't it, son?"

Sal shut the music off and pocketed his headphones. "And when would you like me to run? At high noon?" He made sure to keep his tone light and accentuate his words with a small smile so his grandfather knew he was joking.

"I used to wait until at least dawn."

"Good thing I went before our day started. Found a bear trap about a mile yonder." Sal gestured northeast.

Pops' eyebrows, which had nearly grown into one, shot up as he glanced through the photos Sal showed him on his phone. "Better call county."

"Think they'd come out on a Sunday?"

"Proa'ly not, but if you leave a message now, they can make it a priority tomorrow." Pops handed Sal's phone back to him. "Come have breakfast with your Grams and me."

"Much as I appreciate the offer, I can't eat so soon after running." His breathing was just now settling. "Besides, we have a new employee starting at six, and I should probably rinse the sweat off me before shaking his hand, dontcha think?"

Pops gave a shrug. "Not sure how important that is when you and the new employee used to get sweaty together."

Sal choked on the water he had just drunk. "Can you please do me a favor and never reference my previous or current romantic relationships like that again?"

"Like what, son? I was referring to the times the two of you spent playing as children."

"Sure you were." Sal couldn't keep the chuckle out of his voice. Despite how religious his grandparents were, they had never treated him differently because of his sexuality. They loved him just as much as before he had come out, though they did lament the loss of grandchildren when Jason had followed suit. Technically, Jason was bi, but Sal hadn't heard about him dating a woman in years before the accident. After...well...he didn't see much of anyone who wasn't family.

"What will you have him do?"

Sal blinked to refocus on the conversation. "Ryder? He's always been good with the horses."

"He hasn't worked with them in years."

"He spent the majority of his life on a farm. And if, for some reason, he can't train the horses anymore, he's experienced enough to replace the riding teacher we lost last week." To bring in extra money, Sal and Jason had added riding lessons to the breeding. After scrutinizing the books prior to the addition, Sal had questioned how the business stayed afloat without it.

A smug smile twitched the corner of his grandfather's lips upward. "So, you hired him without a specific job? Sounds like you're definitely acting with the interests of the business in the forefront of your mind."

Sal opened and closed his mouth. "I...have to go. Talk to you later, Pops." He jogged toward the house with his grandfather's laugh trailing behind him. Sal's pulse raced again as he came around the stables to find Elle and Petey sniffing each other out. "You two be nice, you hear?"

"Good morning," Ryder called. Today, he wore a tight black T-shirt, denim shorts, and sneakers. His calves were lighter than Sal had ever seen them this time of year, but that would probably change after a few days in the sun. Already the rising light was accentuating the freckles on the bridge of Ryder's nose, only a few, but he used to call them "proof the ginger is real."

"Morning. Are you early, or am I late?" Sal had slowed to a walk. He would have sworn he saw Ryder check him out the same way he had done to him, but Ryder's gaze returned to the dogs so fast it could have been Sal's wishful thinking at play. *Employee,* he reminded himself. *Try professionalism. Yeah, that's gonna last.*

"Maybe a little bit of both?" Sal opened his mouth to apologize, but Ryder waved him off. "No worries. I was talking to Jason for a few. He went in to cook a couple of the eggs I brought."

Hopefully, that meant Jason felt well enough to work today. Not because Sal desperately needed his help, especially on a Sunday, but Jason always felt better about himself when he could work with his hands. "Great. Let me clean up fast; then we can figure out where to start." Sal cast a glance at the dogs. "You can come inside and wait if you like. They seem okay."

Ryder hesitated. "First, is what I'm wearing okay? I was caught between dressing for the weather and dressing for the work. I didn't know what we'd be doing."

"Uh, it should be."

Ryder studied Sal for a second. "You don't know what you want me to do, either, do you?"

There's a lot I want you to do. Wow. My professionalism is overwhelming. The inappropriateness didn't even touch on the fact that before yesterday, he would have said he didn't wish to be in the same space with Ryder, forget attraction. "Let's see what you remember about the horses and go from there. If you need long pants for anything, you can borrow a pair of mine. Be right back." Sal went in the house before Ryder had a chance to answer.

"There you are," Jason said when Sal entered the kitchen. "Want an egg sandwich?"

"Please." Sal eyed Jason as he scrambled eggs. "You're looking well."

"Yeah, I feel great." Jason glanced his way. "Reason you're standing around stinking up the kitchen?"

"Thought I'd give you a taste of what the rest of us deal with whenever you walk in a room." Sal toed off his sneakers and headed for the stairs. "Oh, hey, careful in the woods. Found a trap."

Jason whipped around. "Are you serious? Who the hell would set traps around here?"

"Same people who set them elsewhere—assholes." Sal pointed back to the stove. "Watch what you're doing. I gotta go get clean." With that, Sal hurried up the stairs, shedding his shorts and dropping them in the laundry basket on the way to the upstairs bathroom next door to his bedroom. No one but him ever used it, and Jason rarely even came up here since they'd relocated his room to the first floor.

By the time he finished his utilitarian shower and came down the steps five minutes later, he found Ryder and Jason in the kitchen with the dogs sharing a water bowl. "That didn't take long."

"No. I was a little concerned because she was ostracized by her mom and littermates. But the two of them seem to be doing okay." Ryder took a drink of his orange juice while Sal poured coffee from the pot and took his seat next to Jason.

The three men ate silently, none wanting to pause for conversation. Sal realized he was hungrier than he thought. When Ryder had polished off his sandwich and most of his juice, Sal eyed his plate. "Did you really come to work without eating breakfast?"

"I woke up later than I intended. So, I had to rush through the morning chores."

"When do your parents come back?"

"This afternoon, if they don't run into too much traffic." Ryder waited for everyone to finish, then cleared the table.

"You don't have to do that, Ry," Jason told him.

"I know, but you cooked."

"And you brought the food, so Sal should clean up."

Sal parted his lips to say something but stood and took over for Ryder. Not worth the argument that would likely end with him doing it regardless. "I got it."

"All right, but I don't mind helping." He put the food and drinks away while Sal rinsed the dishes.

Jason stretched his arms and climbed to his feet. "Isn't that cute? The two of you working in the kitchen like—"

"Jay—" Ryder barely stifled a snort that turned into a full-on laugh when Sal hit him with the end of a dish towel. "Don't encourage him!"

"Like I need encouragement." Jason leaned his hip on the table. "Ryder and I were talking while you were upstairs compensating for lack of beauty sleep—"

Sal faced him. "Do you think the next time you get hurt you could damage your vocal chords instead of your lower body?"

Jason dismissed the suggestion with a wave. "Then you'd have to listen to me bitch through a machine, and that would be even more grating. *Anyway*, since you don't have a particular set of tasks in mind for Ryder, maybe we should take the trucks and go looking for the traps."

"Pops said the county will handle it."

"At some point, I'm sure they will. But everyone in a five-mile radius uses those woods, for training, riding, or hiking. We can't wait around for them to decide it's worth doing."

Sal made eye contact with Ryder, silently begging him to go along with what he was about to say. "I think we oughta wait for them. Today, I need to see where Ryder's at. Make sure he hasn't lost his touch with the horses."

"You can do that in an hour."

"You might be underestimating how much work I need. It's been a long time since I worked with horses," Ryder cut in. "Besides, my dad has some pull with the county. He can convince them to haul ass."

"But nothing he says is going to make them work on a Sunday." Jason's frustration came through in his barely controlled breathing and the way he wrung his hands. "We can't do tomorrow's work unless the woods are safe. Hell, we should be rounding up the neighbors to help."

"I'm not saying no, Jay, but we need to get things done here first." The tension in the small room had risen to an uncomfortable level.

"Fine! I'll be in the barn with Nelly. Come on, Petey." Jason stormed out of the house and let the door slam behind him.

Several beats of silence passed before Ryder said, "Accident didn't improve his temper, huh?"

Sal gave a half laugh. "No, no, it did not. His emotions are as volatile as ever. Maybe worse, since he doesn't consistently have his preferred method of release."

"So, should I play dumb to avoid going out there?" At the twitch of Sal's lips, Ryder shook his head. "I know, I know. I wouldn't have to play."

"I didn't say a word." Sal laced on his boots. "Grab the water bowl for Elle, and we'll get her set up in one of the empty stalls. Let's go see the horses."

Chapter Six

RYDER SHOULD HAVE known better than to wear shorts today. *Why am I acting like a goddamn novice? Because Sal is turning my brain into mush.* All night, he had been thinking about their conversation yesterday, tormenting himself with questions about whether he said too much, not enough, or... He gave himself a shake in the hopes of scattering the musings. Sal didn't seem to be worried about it. *And why should he? He barely stopped hating me.*

As the two of them crossed the property to the stables, Elle ran alongside, pausing to sniff every couple of feet. But she was already receptive to Ryder's command and would follow again at his whistle. Sal unlocked the barn area.

"Wow. You've been expanding."

"We have around twenty horses now. I'm assuming we can skip the basic care instructions."

"You mean like how to approach them, brush them, and feed them?"

"And how to keep the stalls clean."

"I'm pretty adept at shoveling shit." Ryder snapped his fingers at Elle when she got too close to a brown horse's stall.

"Brandy won't bother her," Sal told him.

"I was more worried about her bothering Brandy."

Sal stroked the mare's snout. "Nah, they'll both be fine. I just think Elle would do better if she had a chance to get used to the smells of the stables before introducing her to the horses." After Ryder gave him his silent agreement, Sal opened a stall that was empty except for fresh hay. "She should be okay in here for a bit."

Ryder walked her in, set up her bowl, and promised to check on her in a little while. Her whimpers were like daggers into Ryder's heart. "Shut up," he mumbled at the sight of Sal's barely contained smirk.

"I said nothing. I think it's sweet." Sal opened Brandy's stall. "Brandy, meet Ryder."

"Hey, girl. Your mane is so stylish." He offered her the carrot Sal passed him, which she took very gently. "She's a sweetheart. How old?"

"Five. She's a cancer survivor, so we can't breed her, but she's great with the kids." The confusion must have been clear on Ryder's face because Sal laughed again. "We give horseback riding lessons now to bring in extra money, though to be honest, it makes up a good deal of the profits." Sal paused. "Will you be okay to help with lessons?"

Ryder hadn't planned on working with children. He assumed Sal needed help with training and caring for the horses. But Ryder also knew enough about farm life that he didn't have illusions that anyone could stick with one job. Everyone had to be capable and willing to do everything from shoveling manure to assisting with births. Children were usually more pleasant than either of those tasks—even spoiled rich ones. "I may have to shadow you for a bit since I've never given lessons before, but it shouldn't be a problem."

Sal studied him for a moment. "We'll figure it out. I'll show you where to find the feed and tools." He gave Ryder the full tour of the stables. Sounds of a leather saddle going into place echoed from the end of one of the rows. "He's gonna try to ride her."

"Is that bad?"

"Guess that depends on her mood. Usually I like to run her down first, but I'm not going to say anything if he stays on the property."

Ryder couldn't imagine this controlling dynamic working well with Jason, but he kept his opinions to himself. Wouldn't do to argue with the boss on the first day. He reached for the clipboard hanging by the tools. "This is very well-organized." The horses' stalls were mucked out every other day on alternating days. With so many horses, it made sense. "How many workers are here on a daily basis?"

"Around five. Depending on what you remember from before college, we can decide where it makes most sense to have you start."

What I remember... Ryder released a slow, careful breath. On his inhale, memories of traveling with Sal and Jason to shows flooded back to him. Occasionally, he and Sal would compete, but more often, they worked behind the scenes. Ryder thrilled at rehabilitating struggling horses, and Sal excelled at training their riders. *Together, the two of us made a dynamite team. But we both chose to leave. Yet, here we are.*

Sal had been quiet so long Ryder realized he was waiting for him to say something. "No use standing here. Let's start on the Sunday schedule."

"I'm gonna have you follow me for today to make sure we're all on the same page."

Not because you want to spend time with me. Ryder shut the thought down. Whether or not the postulation was true, it wouldn't do any good to get cocky. While the methods of caring for horses may not have changed in less than a decade, the time away had likely rusted Ryder's skills, and with animals as powerful as horses, human arrogance could prove deadly. "Works for me. I'm going to change into the long pants I packed in my bag." Shorts around all that hay would make for sunburned, cut-up legs. *Another thing I should have thought about before heading over. Could be worse. At least I brought an extra.*

Sal nodded once. "I'll start letting the horses out to pasture. Meet you at the third stall."

He went into the stall where Elle and his duffel waited. "Hey, girl." He scratched her head as he switched his bottoms. "I have a timer set for when you need to eat next. Promise you won't get off track." After another vigorous scratch behind Elle's ears, Ryder jogged toward the stalls where Sal lured the horses out. "Any interpersonal problems?"

"Huh?"

"Between the horses. Do they all get along?"

"Oh." Sal clicked his tongue at a smaller gray spotted one, who was not as eager to turn out as most. "They're mostly fine. The only ones we've had problems with are Ace and Kesha, but we don't let them out at the same time."

Once all the horses were free from their housing, Sal and Ryder got to work cleaning the hay and scrubbing out the food and water containers.

"Sal," Ryder called as he stood in front of a dirty stall. The manure spread away from its main pile and "decorated" the walls with what appeared streaks of rancid, brown paint. "I think we have a sick one."

"Shit," Sal muttered.

"Accurate assessment." Ryder studied her information. "Has Brie had digestive issues before?"

"When she gets nervous, but not normally so bad." Sal gazed out into the meadow at the aforementioned horse.

"Why don't you check her out? I'll get this cleaned up."

Surprise flashed across Sal's face, but disappeared quickly. "Thanks."

Did he think I'd argue? Clearly, it makes more sense for him to check on the mare. He knows her best. Ryder shook the thought, found a scrubbing brush, and went to work on returning the stall to a sanitary condition.

He was putting fresh hay in when Sal came back. "Looks good. You work fast."

"Years of practice comes back quicker than you'd guess." Ryder removed his gloves and dropped them in the bucket to be hosed down and sanitized. "How is Brie?"

"I called for the vet to come tomorrow morning. He told me to keep an eye on her temperature throughout the day, though, and if it gets above a hundred and two, I should let him know and he'll head out today." Sal took off his own gloves. "It's at an even hundred now."

Ryder licked his lips. "Should we keep her away from the others until it stabilizes?"

"Not a bad plan, probably." He went out to the field to catch her and lead her to the isolation stables. "That's done," he said once she had been quarantined. "Let's wash our hands. There's someone I want you to meet."

Intrigued, Ryder took his turn at the outdoor faucet. He then trailed Sal to the second set of stables. "Hi, King." He offered the horse who Sal had ridden over to his house yesterday a carrot. But Sal stopped at the next stall, where Ryder found a smaller horse with bright eyes and a chestnut mane. "Wow, he's gonna be a big boy."

"Yep, that's Bishop. We just got him last week. He's young, so we can train him how we like, but..."

"He's young, so you have to train him *more* than you'd like."

"Exactly." Sal offered the stallion an apple, which he took hesitantly. "He comes from excellent breeding stock, so it shouldn't be too hard."

Finally, Ryder understood. "You want me to focus on him."

"I'd like to see what you can do."

Ryder's controlled breathing was meant to calm his nerves. It would do none of them any good to let the horse in on his apprehension. "Hey, buddy boy. You have such a beautiful mane." As he spoke soothingly to the majestic creature in front of him, Bishop dipped his head for a stroke. "Have you had him out yet?" Ryder asked Sal without looking at him.

"He's been in the smaller run. Once by himself and once with King."

"How'd he react?"

"Like you'd expect. He's not too keen on following commands but doesn't object to the harness."

Ryder faced Sal and noted the strangely captivating expression in his eyes. *Focus. He's admiring the horse, not you.* "What are your goals for him?"

Sal shrugged. "Depends on how he develops. If he turns out to be gentle, we might use him for riding lessons, but if I had to guess, I would say he'll be athletic."

The comment jarred Ryder. "You'd ride him in competitions?"

The smirk that played on Sal's lips warmed a part of Ryder that had lain dormant for so long Ryder almost forgot it existed. "I can ride, ya know."

"Well, sure, but..." *You never have. At least not professionally.* Ryder opened his mouth to find a diplomatic version of that but closed it when he noticed the smirk had widened.

"By the time we're ready to make that decision, we can hire a jockey if need be." Sal passed him the harness. "Do the honors?"

The hesitancy Ryder felt earlier melted away when his hand touched the cool leather. He slipped it over Bishop's snout with ease, then attached the lead. "What a good boy."

Sal stepped back, keeping an evaluative eye on Ryder as Ryder opened the stable gate, followed by the one leading to the run. After coaxing Bishop into the run and closing the gate behind him, Ryder unclipped the lead and stood on the opposite side of the run's fence. "Nice job, Ry. Very smooth."

Heat rose in Ryder's cheeks at the praise. Of course, had he been asked, he would have blamed the sun. "Thanks. I thought I'd let him run on his own, then catch him for a tandem trot."

"Good plan. I'm going to check on Brie. Shout if you need me."

"Will do." It didn't escape Ryder's notice that Sal was leaving him alone with the new horse. Well, sort of alone anyway. A mixture of pride and concern—because it had been so long since he'd been in charge of a horse—filled him. Yet, the pride at Sal's obvious trust in his abilities overpowered the hesitancy.

Ryder spent the rest of the day between getting to know the horses and learning the intricacies of working the ranch again. By 2:30, when Sal called it a day, Ryder was sweaty, caked in mud, and tired. But still he felt good. It was a relief to use his body after so long sitting at a desk.

"Great work," Sal said as Ryder was downing the remaining water from his bottle.

"Thanks. I enjoyed it more than I expected."

"I hope you still feel the same tomorrow."

Yeah, that was one part of the desk-to-ranch transition Ryder wasn't quite prepared for. "I'll be okay."

The warmth radiating from Sal's smile competed with the sun. "No doubt there. Just...not positive you'll wake up *enjoying* it."

"Heh, fair enough." Ryder slung his bag over his shoulder. "I'll see you tomorrow at six?"

"Yeah, uh, would you like to come by tonight after dinner? We could watch a movie or…"

Netflix and chill? the demonic part of his brain filled in. It was quickly shut down by the shrewd part. *Sal is taking pity on you. He's probably got a boyfriend in town. Not that you'd deserve him, anyway.* Though the hours ahead stretched empty before him, Ryder said, "Should we be spending time together outside of work? I wouldn't want to cause problems for the other employees." Despite the darkened lenses shadowing Sal's eyes, his confusion was written into the rest of his features. The heavy silence weighed Ryder down. *Shit. I didn't want to offend him. He doesn't care enough to be offended.* "What?"

"I'm trying to figure out if you're rejecting me because you don't want to reconnect or if you're honestly putting professional interests first."

"It's not the first one," Ryder rushed out. "The latter is a factor since I need the job and I'm sure you have rules about employee/manager relationships… Not that I think you are suggesting a relationship because that—"

Sal cut him off by leaning in and pressing their lips together. It wasn't a long or terribly deep kiss, but it was enough to take Ryder's breath away. When he pulled back, Sal rested his forehead against Ryder's and locked gazes with him over the rim of his glasses. "I actually *was* thinking of an eventual relationship."

"You don't even know me anymore. You have no idea…" *What I've done.*

"So, tell me. Show me." Sal tucked a strand of Ryder's hair behind his ear.

The temptation to do just that was so strong that Ryder almost blurted the whole terrible, horrible story out. *It would solve several problems. I wouldn't need to worry about alienating other employees due to perceived favoritism because Sal would be too disgusted to talk to me. But, goddamn, that kiss felt better than anything has for a long time. How selfish would I be to want to hold on to the illusion that it might happen again?* "I want to." The whispered words left Ryder's lips before he realized he had committed to saying them.

"I hear a 'but.'"

Ryder swallowed around the lump that had taken up residence in his throat. "It's a lot right now. Everything is changing. My life today looks nothing like what it did two weeks ago." God, had it only been ten days since he walked into his house from his Thursday night poker game to find his world under water? "I need to find my place again before becoming romantically involved." He raised one corner of his mouth. "Hell, you've barely liked me for twenty-four hours." He wanted to cry when Sal put distance between them, never mind that that was exactly what Ryder was telling him he needed.

"Ry—"

He shook his head, quieting Sal because if Sal kept talking, it wouldn't take much to convince Ryder to jump in with both feet. "I really need a friend, and I need to know that whatever you want from me, you want from who I am now, as opposed to who I was."

The dejection in Sal's eyes wilted away. "I respect that. But do me a favor and try not to shut me out."

"Why would I? Friends don't do that to each other." With that, he gave Sal a quick hug and left with Elle. He feared that if he didn't, he would take it all back.

RYDER CALLED THE sitter, Katie, a local college student who Ryder had connected with through one of his colleagues a couple of years ago, as he did every Thursday, to remind her that he'd be home late that evening—8:00 instead of his usual 5:30 to 6:00. He had no reason to reconfirm with her every week aside from his own overprotectiveness.

After he received her customary reassurance that Gabby would be ready for bed when he arrived, Ryder ended the call and followed his coworkers out of the office to the local pub. Ryder never drank with them. No, his thrill came from the poker cards, and the anticipation of maybe getting enough good hands to settle his debt with the loan shark, known to everyone simply as "Boss." A walking cliché if Ryder ever heard one, but whatever.

The cards whizzed in front of his eyes. Queen, Jack, two of clubs. Then the images blurred. Chip piles rose and fell. Like any other Thursday, his alarm went off at 7:30, announcing his last round. And like every other Thursday for the past three years, his coworkers mocked him for his early departure. None of them had children. Few even had serious partners, or pets, for that matter. Nothing that would draw them away from work or fun.

But unlike every other Thursday, blue and red flashing lights welcomed him into his neighborhood.

RYDER SHOT UP in bed with his hand over his heart. "At least I woke up before the real nightmare started," he said to his room, empty save for Elle, who remained sleeping in her crate.

Chapter Seven

SAL STOOD WITH the equine vet the next day while he looked over Brie. Brie had had no additional digestive symptoms between yesterday and today, but he'd kept the vet appointment, anyway, just to be sure. "Well, what do you think?"

"I think you need to switch her food to one more supportive of her pregnancy."

"She's pregnant?" Sal tried not to let the shock show in his voice, but he may well have been unsuccessful, judging by the amusement written in the doctor's features.

"Were you not breeding her?"

"No, I planned to wait another year for her."

"We make plans and God laughs." The vet offered Sal a reassuring smile, but it faded. "Did you want to discuss terminating?"

Terminating...? It took Sal's coffee a moment to help make the connection. "Oh, God, no. Of course not. I was only waiting to see if she got bigger as she aged."

"Ah, I think she'll be fine. Some people breed fillies."

"Some people are dumb." The words left his mouth before reason could stop them. Sal drank his coffee faster in hopes of the liquid caffeine providing a better brain-mouth filter.

Luckily, the vet laughed. "Now, isn't that the truest statement out there?" He ripped off a paper from his notebook. "I assume you know how to perform proper prenatal care?"

Been doing this for long enough. "Yes, she's the third mare who is currently pregnant." *Which you should know since you're the one in charge of their care.*

"Right. Many patients, you know. I'll expect to see you in a couple weeks, unless you run into problems before then."

"Yes, thank you, Doctor." Sal saw the vet to his car and brought Brie back to her stall. "No reason to keep you away from your friends, girl. Pregnancy is not contagious." He stroked her cheek and offered her an apple, which she gobbled up.

After locking her stall gate, Sal made a notation on her chart. He whipped around when something hit the back of his calf. "Good morning, Miss Elle," he said as he crouched to scratch behind her ears.

"Sorry about her. She got away from me." Ryder jogged toward them, the sun illuminating his silhouette, creating an image so appealing Sal had to bite the inside of his cheek to keep from reacting.

"Really hard to complain about a visit from a happy puppy." Sal straightened. "Brie is expecting a foal."

Ryder stopped walking. "Is this good?"

"Not planned, but better than colic." Then again, almost everything was better than colic.

"Ain't that the truth?"

When Ryder shifted from one foot to the other, the sun's new angle illuminated a darkness under his eyes. Sal opened his mouth to ask but closed it before the words could come out. Had Ryder wanted to discuss it, he would have brought it up. But a friend would ask if he was okay. *And that's what we decided to be yesterday—friends.* Sal had kicked himself for most of last night for coming on too strong. *I'm not even sure what I was thinking. Ryder's right. No matter how much we want to, we can't erase the last six years. Yeah, but...I'm right too. We've known each other our whole lives. Almost a quarter of a century if we disregard the time between now and the fight. All our formative years have to count more than the comparatively short time apart. But nevertheless, it doesn't matter where logic falls until Ryder is ready—or decides he wants it. Possible he'll want to start fresh with someone new when the time comes.* Sal hated the ache the thought created in his chest every time he allowed it to permeate his brain.

"Sal?" Ryder waved a hand in front of his face.

He blinked. "Yeah, sorry. I zoned out. What were you saying?"

"I asked which other mares were pregnant."

Sal grabbed the hanging clipboard with the basic information about all the horses and leaned toward Ryder. "Milly and Star. We notate pregnancy with an adult and child stick figure."

"Those are human stick figures," Ryder mock protested.

"Those take less time to draw than horses." After returning the clipboard to its rightful place, he asked, "Is the rest of the crew being helpful?"

Ryder paused long enough for Sal to get his answer. "I'm trying not to pester them with too many questions."

"In other words, they're giving you a hard time."

"I believe they're concerned about losing their positions." Sal's confusion must have translated to his expression because Ryder explained, "They don't think they needed additional help, so... Where are you going?"

"To set them straight. This is not acceptable." Sal strode so fast in the direction of the other stable that Ryder had to jog to keep up.

"Are you sure—?"

"Yes." Sal stopped to face him. "I would tell them the same thing regardless of who the new employee was. No kind of bullying is acceptable on this ranch."

"I wouldn't call it—"

"Bullying? I would."

"Could be hazing the new guy."

"Still a problem." As much as Sal wanted to take a hard line and rip into them as a group, the concern on Ryder's features and his tense body language softened his resolve. "I'm going to approach Les and talk to him. He'll pass the message along."

Ryder released an exhale. "Thanks. I'm heading to change a few of the horses' shoes."

Sal watched him walk away with Elle trotting along at his side. When Ryder disappeared into the stable, Sal turned to see Leslie standing in front of him. "Jesus Christ, Les. Don't sneak up on me like that."

"Sorry, boss. Didn't realize I was." He jutted his chin toward the stable Ryder disappeared into. "Yankee's eager."

Yankee... It took Sal a moment to connect the words to their meaning. *My coffee needs to work, like an hour ago.* "Ryder? He's not a Yankee."

"Got a New York accent if I ever heard one."

Does he? Sal replayed his recent conversations with Ryder in his head. Maybe his Southern drawl wasn't as strong as it was before he left for college, but neither was Sal's. "Not that it should matter—"

"All due respect, course it matters. They do things different up North. Gonna take more training to get him up to speed."

Sal inhaled, let it out slowly. "First of all, from what I saw while I was working with him yesterday, he doesn't have far to go. Second, he is not a Yankee. He lived in New York for a couple of years, but he grew up down the road. Seems to me that you're more a transplant than him." Leslie, a man in his midforties, had moved here from South Carolina last year. Sal allowed three beats to pass, enough time for Les to narrow his eyes, but not enough to come up with a suitable retort. "Unless Ryder starts asking questions that take significant time from your day... No, actually, not even then. If you have legitimate concerns about his performance or skills, come to me and I'll handle it. I'm not kidding around. Tell the rest of the guys the same thing."

"Yes, boss." Leslie turned on his heel and headed toward the run.

Sal rolled his shoulders on his way to check on the hay bundlers.

Chapter Eight

BY SEVEN THAT evening, Sal had showered and changed his clothes three times. He finally settled on formfitting jeans and a red button-down top with nice boots. As he mussed his short hair with gel, he rolled his eyes at himself in the mirror. "Could I be more vain? Really, what the fuck does it matter what I'm wearing? No one there is going to care." The muttered words were hollow, though, because Sal wanted someone to care.

"Sal!" Jason called from the bottom of the steps. "Are you about finished with your makeup?"

"Fuck off!"

"Salvatore! I never."

Sal groaned at the sound of his grandmother's voice. He grabbed his phone, wallet, and keys from the chest of drawers, stuffed them in his pocket, and headed downstairs. "So, he's allowed to make fun of me, but I can't respond?" Sal kissed Grams's cheek.

"You're the big brother. You must set a good example for Jason."

"He's twenty-five! We're long past the point where my example would mean anything to him."

"You know that's not true. He'll always look up to you." Grams recited her part of their oft-repeated conversation.

"Hey, I'm right here, you know." Jason pretended to be put out because that was his role in the exchange. "Grams brought over meatballs."

"Thanks, Grams, you didn't have to do that." Sal noted three place settings at the table. "Where's Pops?"

"He went to get lamb from the butcher. One of the farmhands gave him a recipe for gyros that he wants me to make over the weekend."

"I'm sure you'll be up to the task." Sal scooped spaghetti onto plates for himself and his grandmother, then placed them down at their respective seats.

"You hardly took any! You're a growing boy."

A laugh Sal failed to contain burst through his lips. "I'm hardly growing."

"Unless you count the middle," Jason interjected. That time, Grams slapped the back of his head.

"Anyway." Sal couldn't keep the amusement from his voice. "I'm going out with my friends tonight, and we usually split an appetizer."

She nodded thoughtfully as she ate before turning her attention to Jason. "Why aren't you going?"

Jason stuffed more food in his mouth, probably to buy himself extra time in answering. "Because it'll be like a date for Sal. Ow!" He glared at his older brother. "Did you just kick me?"

"Yeah, I did. Don't pin this on Ryder. Number one, we're friends. Number two, you've never had an issue with him before."

"I don't have an issue with him now—doesn't mean I want to hang around on your first date in years."

"Number three—" Sal raised his voice. "—I ask you to come to the pub every week, and you always have an excuse to stay home."

Grams set down her fork and zeroed in on Jason again. "Is that true?"

Jason gaped. "I tell you he has a date, and you want to discuss my socialization habits?"

"They don't sound like habits to me, more like avoidance." She paused. "But I suppose that avoiding things can be a habit as well."

Sal smirked at his brother. *Serves him right.* A glance at the oven clock had him cursing under his breath. "I gotta go. Ryder will be here any minute."

After loading his supper plates and glass into the dishwasher, Sal kissed his grandmother's cheek. "Thanks again, Grams. I'll stop by and see you and Pops tomorrow." The sweat slicking his palms made the knob hard to grasp. He wiped his hands on his jeans, swung the door open, and walked out to the front porch. The house was from a bygone era where neighbors sat on porches to socialize, or court, according to his grandparents. As he reached for his phone to check the time, Ryder pulled up in his mom's four-door hatchback. For the first time since Ryder had been back, Sal questioned why Ryder didn't have his own car. *Probably didn't need one in the city.*

"Hey," Ryder greeted when Sal reached the car. "How was your...?" He looked at the clock on the dash. "Four hours?"

Sal chuckled. "Uneventful. Yours?"

"Same," Ryder answered as he pulled onto the two-lane road.

"This is the first time I've seen you without Elle. How's she handling being home without you?"

"She seemed okay when I left, but time will tell if she drives Ma crazy." The grin that twitched at the corners of Ryder's mouth was heartwarming to Sal. It reminded him of the trouble the two of them used to get into back in the day.

But it's not back in the day anymore. It's now. Ryder insists he's changed. Yet, the more Sal studied him from the passenger seat, the less he believed that to be true. "Tell me about your life up North."

"What about it?"

"Did you end up working on Wall Street?"

"For a while." Ryder scratched the back of his head. "The hours weren't conducive to raising a child, so I got a job in risk management with an insurance company."

Sal blinked. "Is that as boring as it sounds?"

"Oh, no, it's far *more* boring than it sounds." The laugh eased some of the tension in Ryder's shoulders. "Honestly, it was fine. I was good at it and it paid well. Had it been more exciting, I would have devoted more time to it than I already did, which would have defeated the purpose of changing jobs to begin with."

No matter how hard he tried, Sal could not picture Ryder as a parent. *Maybe that means he's right, that we don't know each other as well as I thought.* "So, you don't miss it? Your job, I mean?"

Ryder chewed his bottom lip for a moment but shook his head. "There's not much about it to miss."

"Except the money. I imagine we don't pay as well."

"Don't need it as much down here. You could buy a five-bedroom house with an acre in back for the price of a year's rent in the city."

Sal remembered well the heart attack he'd had when looking at real estate with Ryder. They had been planning to live in New York so Ryder could work a few years on Wall Street. Luckily, they hadn't signed anything before Felicia had dropped the baby bomb. *Gabby. The baby's name was Gabby,* Sal reminded himself, even though they weren't discussing her.

"What about you? Heard you went to Raleigh after graduation. Do you miss that?"

"Yes, I do." Sal spun his phone in his lap. "I miss that a lot."

Sympathy glistened in Ryder's gaze when he glanced away from the road. "What were you doing there?"

"Working for an ad agency. In two years, I had been promoted twice, to team leader. My team headed campaigns for national brands like Hershey's and Budweiser. They actually put me on that campaign because my boss told Budweiser that I 'knew horses.'"

"Right, and they've got those Clydesdales in their ads! Did you actually have to work with them at all?"

"No!" Sal ran his fingers through his hard, spiked hair. "I did get the chance to meet them, which was cool." He worked to keep the wistfulness out of his voice.

Three silent beats passed between them. "Did you ever think of going back?"

"Think about it? Sure. Wouldn't—couldn't, really."

"Because of Jason?"

"Jason, my grandparents, the farm, the workers... I...can't."

Ryder pulled the car into the pub parking lot and faced Sal. "You could. Many people would sell the land, use the profits to pay for a nursing home for your grandparents, and maybe bring Jason up to the city."

"You really think I'd do that?" Sal fought to keep the indignation and offense out of his voice.

"Clearly not, and I admire you for that. My only point is that there were other options."

"None either of us would've taken." Sal stared out the window. "Don't get me wrong. I'm not unhappy with my life now. Just..."

"I get it."

When he met Ryder's gaze, Sal understood the truth of the sentiment. *Good, because I sure as fuck don't have the words.* "Thanks." He motioned toward the building with his head. "Better get in there before they start speculating." There was no need to specify who *they* were.

"You say that as though they ever stop," Ryder muttered as he opened the car door.

Chapter Nine

RYDER ROLLED HIS shoulders back in an effort to lose the remaining tension. The last time he was here it did not go as planned—not that he had a plan, but few people would call the previous Friday's events a successful outing. Would people make assumptions since he drove in with Sal? Probably, but Ryder couldn't bring himself to care about their opinions.

Out of nowhere, a hand clenched his forearm and tugged. He struggled against his instinct to jerk away long enough to identify it as a female grasp.

"Cat, you can't just go around grabbing people," Sal told her over the music.

"Not like either of you would hear me if I called your names." Her bright blue eyes sparkled. "Anyway, you're late."

"No, we aren't. It's 7:57," Ryder corrected, but she didn't answer as she led them to their table.

"Anyone who's here after her is late." Sal leaned in close to whisper to Ryder, who fought a shiver against his hot breath.

Ryder didn't bother arguing. Everyone else just accepted it as fact, so who was he to raise opposition? The pub was packed again. These weren't the average drunkards though. The tables were divided into sections with red, blue, yellow, and green cards marking the different teams, and another section for the spectators. "We're red?" he asked no one in particular.

"Every month," a guy Ryder remembered as Clay said.

"It's usually down to us and the green team at the end," Sal added. "Since I was the last one to walk in the door, I get the first round of drinks. What do you want?"

"Just get a pitcher of pop and a pitcher of beer. Don't make it complicated, Sal," Cat said. After Sal left the table, Cat turned to Ryder. "So...you two came together."

It wasn't a question, so Ryder didn't bother affirming. "Figured only one of us should have to stay sober."

The smugness on her face annoyed Ryder far more than it should have. He greeted the others at the table whom he remembered from last week and introduced himself to those he didn't. Leaning back in his chair, Ryder cast his gaze around the room searching for... Damn. Wanker from last week was here. And on the green team. *At least I don't have to pretend to get along with him for the sake of the game.*

"Why're you staring daggers at that guy?" Sal asked as he sat next to Ryder in the now cramped booth.

Ryder debated his answer internally. The truth might be seen as drama from the others on their team, but they might have witnessed some of the interaction from the previous visit and could call him out if he lied. He pressed his mouth to Sal's ear and whispered, "He's the asshole I told you about who got aggressive when I rejected him." He shook his head in response to Sal's sudden tension. "Don't bother, please. It's fine. He's not worth the trouble." *Neither am I.* As strongly as Ryder believed the thought, he knew nothing good would come from sharing it. He straightened when the night's MC called everyone to attention.

The yellow and blue teams were disqualified in the first three rounds. In the break between the third and fourth round, Ryder asked the table, "If the teams are the same every month, and every month the blue and yellow teams are the first ones out, why don't the teams trade players?"

"Because those of us on the red and green teams enjoy winning."

"Though it looks like green is gonna take this one," Cat commented.

"Don't say that. You don't know what the categories for the last two rounds will be," Sal said, taking a swig of his beer.

"Oh, we're gonna take it, pansies," one of the guys from the other team—thankfully not Wanker—said.

"Dude, back to your table." Lilly pointed to the other section. "We want to beat you because we're better, not because your stupid ass got disqualified."

The man sneered, but walked away without further comment.

"Good one, Lil." Her husband kissed her cheek.

"Baby and I want our celebratory cake."

"There's cake if you win?" Ryder asked.

"For me, there is." Lilly grinned. "Winning team gets the 'pot' from entry fees. Only about twenty-five dollars once you divide it up, but that's enough to splurge on cake."

Ryder nodded as though the logic made perfect sense to him. It wasn't worth arguing that if she could afford an entrance fee a five-dollar piece of cake shouldn't be too hefty. *Not my business.*

"All right, ladies and gents, the fourth-round topic is stocks," the MC announced.

Oh, good. I can help. Ryder had felt fairly useless when the questions centered on recent pop culture. He had spent the last six years watching children's shows, so while he knew who the Kardashians were, he couldn't name the brands they represented nor the year Kim's sex tape debuted.

"First question. True or false: You should buy stocks when prices are the highest."

Ryder scribbled "FALSE" on the index card and placed it in the middle of the table.

"Are you sure?" Cat asked.

"Positive." *I did this for a living. Does she know that?* Ryder couldn't remember if he told her, but in this town, he didn't have to.

"How do you know it's a good investment?" she hissed across the table.

"I will gladly explain the intricacies of trading to you after we win."

Sal passed the card to the MC, who added points to their score and subtracted them from the green team. The rest of the round passed in much the same fashion. By the end, red had a two-hundred-point lead.

During the break between rounds, Ryder's team offered pats on the back. He shifted in the seat. He had to pee, but he was not looking forward to going to the bathroom alone again. Nor could he ask any of his friends to join him because—weird. Ryder disregarded the fleeting thought that sometimes women did have it easier because the feminist in him knew those times were few and far between.

The next round was facts about states. The base knowledge between the two teams seemed nearly equal, but the red team's lead from the previous round helped cement their win. By the time the game was over, the second pitcher of beer had been finished, making for a louder than necessary celebration. Ryder had long since stopped drinking his pop to avoid further inflating his bladder.

Sal leaned over. "Ready to head out after we collect our winnings?"

"Are you sure? I don't have a curfew."

The heat in Sal's eyes simultaneously scared and thrilled Ryder. "I've about had my fill of crowds. And pretty soon the drunkest members of the other team are going to argue with the MC about the fairness of the point allocation." He rolled his eyes, bringing a smile to Ryder, despite the pressure in his abdomen.

"Works for me." Ryder figured out their share of the appetizers and drinks, and they paid it out of their winnings. He left a larger-than-necessary tip, so he had just enough for gas on the way home. He spied Sal studying him, but Sal didn't ask, so Ryder didn't explain. How could he tell Sal that "winning" money was not positive for him? That it could lead to him seeking out more opportunities? Ryder couldn't, so he didn't try.

They said their goodbyes and headed for the car. The movement of walking increased the pain from his overstuffed bladder. "I have to stop for gas."

"Okay. I'm in no rush." Sal buckled his seat belt and leaned back in the passenger seat. "There's a place up here with a twenty-four-hour mart. Nice clean bathrooms."

"How did you…?"

"You've been crossing and uncrossing your legs for the past half hour."

"Only thirty minutes? Felt like at least double that." Ryder considered being embarrassed that someone else had picked up on his need, but didn't bother.

He pulled into the lot and tried to hand Sal his ten, but Sal shook his head. "I got it. You bought gas on the way here. I can fill it for the way back."

That would leave me with cash. Shit! There is no way to explain that aversion which isn't weird sounding. "You got the drinks. We're even." Ryder grabbed the door handle. "I'll be back," he said over his shoulder, but he did not stop to check Sal's reaction—both because he wasn't sure he wanted to know and because his lower abdomen burned too heavily to care.

Dashing through the store, Ryder noted the sales clerk was busy with another customer and sent up a prayer of thanks to anyone listening. Normally, he would have gone into a stall, but the sound of water rushing from the faucet where another patron washed their hands inspired him to stop in front of the first urinal he reached. *Goddamn, this can't be healthy.*

When he was finally empty, he tucked himself into his pants, washed his hands, and headed out to the car, where he found Sal pumping gas. "I can do that."

"As can I." Sal eyed him. "If you won't let me pay and you won't let me work, I believe that would make me a kept man, and I don't think I'm okay with that."

Ryder snorted. "Except the fact that you're my boss. So, you'd only be temporarily kept, if that."

"Meh, minor detail." He gave the pump two extra squeezes and opened the passenger side door.

It occurred to Ryder to ask Sal to drive since Sal really hadn't drunk much, but he wanted to keep his word, and he had agreed to be the designated driver. As he climbed behind the wheel, his cell rang in his pocket. "Hold on a sec, Ma." Ryder pulled away from the pump and into a parking spot and put the phone to his ear. "What's up?"

"Are you on the road?" His mom hated when he talked on the phone and drove, even to her.

"No, Sal and I are just about to pull out of a gas station."

"Oh...did you have fun?" The edge to her voice made Ryder question the point of the conversation.

"Yeah, we enjoyed ourselves. Won the game." He let a few beats pass. "Is something wrong?"

"Elle dug her way under the fence into the woods. Your father is searching for her..." She kept talking, but Ryder couldn't make sense of the words.

"Hold on, Ma." Ryder muted the phone and looked at Sal. "Did the county ever take care of the bear traps?"

"Said they did."

"Shit." Ryder shoved the car into gear and passed Sal his phone. "Please tell my mom I'm on my way and Dad should be careful of the traps."

"What's—?"

"Please!" Ryder vaguely acknowledged Sal speaking to Ma but trained his focus on the road in front of him. When Sal hung up and set the phone on the console between them, Ryder said, "I can drop you off on the way, but—"

"You gotta know me better than that, Ry." Sal almost sounded offended. "The only reason we should stop at my place is if you don't have shotguns."

Shotguns for wild animals or...if we find Elle fatally wounded...and have to end her suffering. The thought burned his eyes and created a lump in his throat. Sal reached over and grasped his hand, slowing his thoughts to ones he could make sense of.

RYDER AND SAL reached Ryder's farm in record time. Ryder again sent a prayer of thanks to a god he could never be convinced gave a damn about him, even more so since he lost Gabby. Sal had kept contact with Ryder throughout the ride, which helped his nerves, but unsurprisingly, not even that anchor could steady his heart when he arrived at his farm. Ryder's family did have plenty of guns—almost everyone in the county did.

If asked, Ryder wouldn't have been able to explain how he and Sal got from the car to the back door armed with hiking boots, rifles, lighted hats, and cell phones. "I don't like that my dad is out there alone," he said to Sal. Never mind that his father was plenty active and healthy; no one, especially someone reaching the tail end of middle age, should be walking the woods by themselves at night.

"I'm fine!" his father called as he emerged from the edge of the woods. "I know this land as well as I know my wife's body."

"There's a visual I could have done without," Ryder said as he adjusted the chin buckle on the lighted hat.

"Where do you think you came from, boy?"

I try not to think about it. Ryder opened his mouth to respond, but Sal cut him off.

"Did you find anything, Vic?"

"No, but I didn't get too far. We might have to wait until morning."

"That's not going to happen," Ryder said. He slung the strap of the rifle across one shoulder.

"We'll be careful," Sal assured him.

"Call if you find anything." Dad patted Ryder's shoulder, but Ryder barely felt the contact. He must have given sufficient agreement, though, because his dad walked down toward the house.

"Any sense in searching the property in front of the fence?" Ryder asked, crouching to inspect the puppy-sized hole underneath it.

"I think if she was here your parents would've found her by now."

"That was my thought, but...would've been easier."

Sal offered a sympathetic nod and motioned him forward. The first acre of forest was still their property, but Ryder wasn't too concerned with trespassing on the neighbor's land if needed. They would understand and be more likely to aid in the search than to make an issue out of it—especially if they knew the trespasser was human, so Ryder was careful to make noise as he and Sal walked.

Ryder winced when a coyote howled in the distance. *Distance being the key word*, he reminded himself. *They can't hurt us or the animals we love from far away. Not to say there aren't some closer... Stop. That is the opposite of helpful.* He considered trying to argue to himself that he shouldn't be so attached to Elle after only a week, but that was pointless. He'd loved her from the moment he saw her separated from her dog family. There was no doubt in his mind about that. Some people in this part of the country treated animals like machinery—necessary for work, but not much else. Ryder never could—even the ones who mainly did work. Sal was the same way. It was one of the things that brought him and Ryder together when they were younger.

Sal used the tip of his rifle to clear brush from either side of the path. When he noticed Ryder watching him, he said, "Checking for traps."

"Thought the county said they took care of those?" Ryder's heart plummeted.

"County also said they were gonna fix the roads, but that pothole on Spruce has busted many a tire."

Which means even if we find her... Snapping metal cut his thought off. "Fuck!"

"Hey." Sal placed his palm on Ryder's upper back after engaging the light on his rifle. "It's gonna be okay."

"You don't know that." The platitude was nice, but useless once he saw and heard the teeth of the trap Sal had uncovered up close.

"You're right, but until we have reason to think otherwise, I'm gonna believe it." Though if Sal's tone was anything to go by, that wasn't entirely true. "I'll light the ground and you uncover as we walk."

Probably wants to give me a distraction. Which wasn't a horrible idea if it could work. Every few feet, Ryder would stop and call her name, hoping with everything in him that she would come barreling from behind a tree. "Do you remember when we were riding Clarence together for the first time? I think we were like fourteen?"

"Christ, we were so dumb."

"The dumbest ever," Ryder agreed and Sal laughed. Clarence, a then newly domesticated stallion, had arrived at Sal's family's ranch a couple months prior to the ride. Sal and Ryder were warned that the stallion was still unpredictable, but being fourteen-year-old boys, they thought they knew better. Had they been half as intelligent as they believed themselves to be, they would have backed off when the horse refused to accept a saddle. But, no, the two of them decided to ride Clarence bareback. Luckily for them, Sal's father had been close enough to lasso the horse before things got too out of control. Neither Ryder nor Sal sat for a week for putting themselves in that kind of danger, and Sal's dad promised them that if they ever pulled something like that again he'd leave them to take their chances with animals.

Sal halted so suddenly Ryder collided with his outstretched arm. "Stay here."

"What? Where are you going?" Ryder asked once Sal dropped his arm and lowered the rifle light to the ground in front of him.

"'Bout ten feet that way. Don't move."

"Why? What's—?"

"*Please.*" The imploring authority in Sal's voice kept Ryder rooted in place as he watched his friend shuffle through the leaves and dirt and crouch. "Shit." Sal's whispered word churned Ryder's gut.

"Is it...?" He swallowed. "Is she...?"

Anguish twisted Sal's features as he climbed to his feet. "I'm sorry, Ry." When Ryder stepped forward, Sal grabbed his arms to block his way and keep him steady. "There's no reason for you to see that."

"You're sure it's her?" Ryder cursed his squeaky voice.

"Sure as I can be in this light. I'll come up tomorrow and confirm."

"I should—"

"Torture yourself? Why?" Sal shook his head. "No. There's no point."

The roiling in Ryder's stomach increased. He pushed away from Sal and hung his head, resting his palms on his thighs. *Inhale. Exhale*, he chanted to himself, his stinging eyes shut tight. Half a minute later, the acid in Ryder's stomach started to settle. Unfortunately, when he opened his eyes, the first thing he saw was a black, furry tail. Ryder barely had enough time to turn away from the tail—and presumably the rest of the body—before he emptied his stomach of the previous day's food and drink. *Yet another being I love was killed because I wasn't home to watch her.*

It wasn't until the vomiting had turned to dry heaves that Ryder felt Sal's hand on his back. Had it been there the whole time? "Sorry."

Sal blinked and nudged him back to the path toward home. "I'm ignoring that."

"What?"

"You apologizing. I'm sure you have what is surely a ridiculous reason—like embarrassment for showing emotion or some shit. But I've already justified that with more of a response than I should have."

"You shouldn't be around me," Ryder whispered. At Sal's skeptical silence, he barreled on, "No one should be around me. I kill—"

"You didn't do that!" Sal widened his eyes. "The asshole who set the illegal traps did it. Hell, the county workers who lied about getting all the traps are more to blame than you."

Ryder's phone rang for the second time with his mother's ringtone. "Ma, we're coming back. She didn't make it." The words came out weaker than he intended.

"I don't know who you found, but a nice young man brought Elle home."

"What? She's there?" He stopped Sal. "Ma said someone brought her home."

Sal's eyebrows shot up. "Then why are we standing here?"

"You said that looked like Elle."

"I said in the light it did, but that could have been any black German shepherd." Sal nudged Ryder along.

After a brief hesitation, Ryder followed the path. *Is it possible? Can I trust it? What if Ma made the same error as Sal?* Ryder blinked hard in hopes of banishing the thoughts from his brain. Speculation would do no good.

As they neared the property line, Sal stopped him again. "Ry, you gotta know that sometimes terrible things happen to people who don't deserve it. Innocent children have deadly diseases, animals are treated cruelly...parents die in house fires." Ryder's chest constricted at the last example. The one describing how Sal's parents were taken from him. "You didn't blame Jason and I for not being home when it happened, did you?"

"Of course not. You were children. They wouldn't have wanted you to be there." Ryder, Sal, and Jason were in town with Ryder's parents, getting seeds for the coming crops, when the fire started. By the time they arrived home, the house was in shambles and the police delivered the bad news about their parents.

"Then why would the reverse have been true tonight...or in the past?"

The muscles of Ryder's back constricted. "Because it *is* the reverse. Elle is my responsibility." He paused for a breath. "So was Gabby. You don't know what happened, and when I'm ready to talk about it, I will." Ryder turned on his heel and made his way home while Sal followed a pace or two behind him the rest of the way. The night had such a great beginning and middle, but the end turned into a fucking roller coaster of emotions. Ryder waited for Sal to come closer before opening the gate. Last thing they needed was for one of the animals to get out and start this cycle all over again.

Again, Ryder lost time. He didn't remember the time between crossing over the fence line and opening the back door. But it must have happened because the next thing he processed was Elle colliding into his legs. "You have no idea how happy I am to see you, girl." He lifted her up to let her lick his face.

"You can't keep doing that, Ry," Dad said. "She's going to weigh almost as much as you soon."

"I think tonight is an extenuating circumstance." But he set her down. It was then that he became aware of the other people in the room. Ma sat at the table with Dad and a pale, blond man about his age while Sal leaned against the counter and eyed the newcomer with an unusual amount of suspicion.

"Ryder, I'd like you to meet Luke Bradly," Dad said. "He brought Elle home."

Ryder shook hands with Luke. "Thank you so much. How did you find her?"

"We recently moved in next door"—next door being a half mile away, as was typical in this part of the county—

"and our fence isn't in the best of shape. So, the little minx here was able to sneak in through a missing board. When I realized she wasn't feral, I asked the Grays if they knew her. They did not, but said you breed shepherds. So, here we are."

God, I am so lucky he isn't afraid of dogs, and that he took the time to realize she was a dog. In the dark, pointy-eared dog breeds could easily be mistaken for foxes. "I can't thank you enough for bringing her home."

"It's no trouble at all. I'll have to introduce you to my brood."

"Maybe when I come over to help with your fence."

Luke smiled. "That's right nice, but you don't have to trouble yourself."

There was something off about Luke's accent, but Ryder couldn't identify what it was. "What are neighbors for?" He returned the smile. "I'm off tomorrow, but I work Sunday."

"One day should suffice. Probably. I don't know too much about repairs."

"We'll figure it out," Ryder said.

"Who's 'we'?" Sal asked, the first words Ryder had registered from him since they walked into the house.

"Beg pardon?" Luke tilted his head to the side.

"You said '*we* moved here recently.' Who's 'we'?"

"My dad and I came here to start over after my mum passed." Luke rose, but motioned for Ryder's parents to stay seated. "Vic, Ma'am, it was a pleasure to meet you. You have a beautiful home." He shook Ryder's hand again. "See you around nine tomorrow?"

"Eight would be better, so we're not working when the sun is highest."

Luke's smile returned and widened. "See? I have so much to learn." He turned toward the door and his lips tightened. "Salvatore."

"Lucas." The two of them exchanged stiff nods, and Luke left through the back door.

"Do you know him?" Ma asked Sal.

"Used to." Sal cleared his throat. "Ry, can you give me a ride home?"

"Sure..." Ryder shrugged at his mom's questioning expression, clipped Elle's leash on, and walked out with Sal.

They made it to the car in silence, but as soon as Ryder turned the ignition, Sal asked, "Do you trust me?"

Ryder screwed up his face. "Is this about Gabby? I told—"

Sal shook his head. "This is nothing I want you to tell me. I'm asking if you trust me enough to listen to what I say."

"Of course, I do." He absentmindedly scratched Elle when she pawed at him.

"That guy is bad news." Sal released a breath. "He and I went out for a while when I was in the city. I don't know the full extent of what he's involved with, but I doubt it was legal." He, too, started petting Elle, which sent her tail thudding against the seat.

A spark of jealousy filled Ryder, and, yes, he knew how stupid such a reaction was. He could hardly have expected Sal to turn into a monk while they were apart. But once he got past the unreasonable emotion, he replayed Sal's last sentence. "You're afraid he's going to hurt someone in the neighborhood? The animals?"

"Any? All of the above?" He lifted his shoulder. "Just be careful. Lucas is a very practiced liar, and a chameleon. He can fit in anywhere."

Ryder ground his bottom lip. Looking at Elle, he wanted to be nothing but grateful to her savior, but Sal wasn't the type of person to gossip—even about ex-lovers. "You knew him in Raleigh? So, he's from the South?"

"Far as I knew." The corners of Sal's mouth twitched upward. The first sign of amusement Ryder had seen from him since Ma had called them on the road. "I agree with you about his accent. I have no idea where it comes from," Sal said, possibly in response to Ryder's incredulous expression.

"Sure as fuck wouldn't pass the Leslie test." Ryder squeezed Sal's leg. "Thanks for the warning. I'll keep my guard up when I help tomorrow."

"And try not to give him anything he could use against you. Maybe I'm wrong to worry. Maybe he has changed, but a guard is still good."

Ryder nodded and drove him home. As much as he wanted to kiss him good night—fuck, did he ever—he knew nothing good could come of it. Not yet.

He drove home to find his parents in bed. Relief that he didn't have to make small talk filled him. The adrenaline seeped out of him and was replaced with fatigue as he and Elle completed her leashed walk around the yard. "Come on, baby girl. Let's head to bed." After the first night, she hadn't given him problems with sleeping in her crate, though he suspected it wasn't her favorite resting spot.

Ryder debated if he would go to bed or shower, but the desire to wash away the lingering specks of panic pushed him into the bathroom. By the time he finished, he was happy he made the choice, even more so because his fatigue had risen to the level where he felt certain he would fall asleep as soon as his head hit the pillow. However, the flashing light on his phone drew his attention. His stomach churned at the sight of the words on the screen. *Text from a restricted number.*

Glad she's okay. Would hate for anything to happen to another bitch you love. I'll be in touch about ways you can win the remainder of your debt.

Chapter Ten

SAL FILLED THE horses' feed buckets in the stables early the next morning. He tried hard not to think about the fact that as he worked Luke was cozying up to Ryder. Not that Sal had any legitimate claims on Ryder, of course. But he wouldn't want any of his friends to get mixed up with the likes of Luke. *Yeah, that's all it is.*

"Hey!" Cat called as she walked toward him, seeming to be conscious of stepping into his line of sight. "Can I help?"

"You want to help collect manure?" He faced the horse so she didn't see his smirk.

She gave his shoulder a light push. "Looks to me like you're catering to the other end of the horse there."

"Well, I mean eventually..." Sal motioned to a bucket near the end of the row. "Grab it. I'll fill you up." He did as promised, then directed her how to feed them and who to stay away from. "Isn't Owen coming home from his tour today?"

"Last I heard."

"They wouldn't change this late without a good reason, would they?" Sal wasn't fond of her cynicism toward the armed forces. Both of his grandfathers had served with pride, and while it was never for him, he had nothing but respect for the men and women who put themselves in harm's way for their country. *Then again, I'm not the one waiting at home for my spouse's return.*

Cat shrugged. "You'd be shocked by what passes as a 'good reason' with these people, Sal. Sometimes they don't even tell the soldiers why they're being kept from their families longer because it's 'classified.'" She paused to stroke Trixie's mane. "I like this one."

"She's very special. An autistic girl comes to ride and care for her every day." Sal offered Trixie a sugar cube, which none of the horses refused.

"Does she own her?"

Sal bobbed his head from side to side. "Sort of? I own the horse currently, but her parents are on a payment plan. They couldn't afford to buy Trixie outright, but their daughter showed such improvement since working with her that they don't want to chance someone else getting her."

"With a payment plan, could you sell to a family with the money upfront and then give these parents their money back?"

"I guess in some twisted way, I could, but...God, shoot me if I'm ever desperate enough to use a technicality like that." Sal gave Trixie a parting pat and moved to the next stall.

"How are things going with Ryder?" Cat asked.

"Mostly good?" He immediately regretted answering in question form.

"Mostly?" Cat's eyes sparkled. "Looked pretty cozy to me last night."

Sal cast a glance around the stables to ensure the only other ears around were covered in fur. "We're starting as friends to get to know each other again. But it feels like more."

"Anything will because of your history." She filled the last feed bucket and faced him. "Is he always so quiet? I don't remember him being that way before."

He hadn't lost a child before. "Ryder's sad. I think whatever happened to his little girl messed him up."

Cat leaned on the wall between two stalls. "You don't know how she died?"

"Ry doesn't want to talk about it." *And I should respect that and change the subject, but...* "Do you know?"

"I've heard a couple of stories. The most often repeated is that she drowned in the tub."

Sal squinted at her. "A six-year-old?" He didn't know a lot about kids, but most of the six-year-olds he met could sit in a tub without drowning.

"Maybe she hit her head. Maybe the babysitter got mad... All I know for sure is that her daddy wasn't home when it happened."

"Shit. That's why he blames himself." Sal didn't bother to ask how she knew that for sure. Cat had her ways, and it was best not to question them.

"That'd be my guess. I don't believe he'd intentionally harm anyone, never mind his own child." She tucked a piece of hair that had fallen out of her ponytail behind her ear. "But then it's safe money that any parent whose child dies will blame themselves, at least a little."

"Probably right."

Cat opened her mouth, but before she could say more, her cell phone beeped. A grin spread as she read the message. "Owen's getting on the plane in Germany! Means they let him out of the war zone." She typed a message at warp speed and shoved her phone back in her pocket. "I should call May and see if she can fit me in for an appointment."

Sal chuckled. "Cat, I don't think your husband is going to care about your hairstyle when he comes home from Iraq."

Her smile took on an air of faux innocence. "Maybe not the hair on my head, but May also does bikini waxing, you know."

"Nope. I did not know that. And I could have spent the rest of my life very happily without that knowledge." He returned her smile and gave her a hug to soften the words. "Have fun." Sal waved to her as she sped across the field toward her car. "She's got a good heart underneath all the gossip and pink, Bishop." Sal addressed the young horse. *Can't entirely blame her for the gossip, since I did ask.* He blew out a breath.

Rustling noises came from Nelly's stall. "Jason?"

"Yeah?" Wood, stone, and distance muffled his brother's voice.

Petey ran out to meet Sal halfway between the two stables. After offering Petey the requisite amount of love, Sal walked with him the rest of the way to Nelly's stall. "Must be feeling all right."

"Never better." Jason barely spared him a glance as he fitted Nelly's saddle and bit on her. "Cat brought biscuits for us and Grams and Pops."

"She failed to mention that to me. I should be offended."

"Nah, you were surrounded by horses. Hard to think of food when presented by such majesty."

"Or it could be my good looks that distracted her."

Jason's snort turned into a laugh. "She knows you too well to be attracted to you, dude." He finished dressing Nelly and faced Sal. "Wanna get Bishop and ride with me?"

"I'll ride Brie. I don't think Bishop is ready."

"Isn't Brie pregnant?"

"Only a month or two," Sal answered. Experts said horses could be ridden until they were two months away from foaling. No sense in depriving mares of exercise prior to that. "Where did you want to go?" Sal asked when he realized Jason had followed him to Brie's stall.

Jason remained quiet for long enough that Sal turned to look at him. "I think we oughta look for traps. Before you squawk about doing things the proper way, keep in mind that we tried that last week and the county lied to us."

"Or they told the truth, but someone went up afterward." Despite his defense of the government employees, Sal continued saddling Brie. If nothing else, he wanted to find whatever the trap had gotten—be it a puppy or a bear cub or any number of small animals—and bury it along with the trap, so no one got hurt. "What are you doing with Petey?"

"Pops said he'd hang out with him."

"Oh, he's going to love that." Sal secured a small tool packet onto the saddle and mounted Brie.

"Petey will get over it." Jason's voice had lost its confident edge.

Sal sucked in a breath as he led Brie to Nelly's stall. "You sure it's a good idea to ride without Petey?"

Jason scowled. "Have you always been this much of a pain in the ass? I haven't had a seizure in like six weeks. I'll be fine."

At least he isn't going out alone, Sal soothed himself as he watched Jason flawlessly mount Nelly. *Why wouldn't he be flawless at it? God knows he had enough practice before the accident.* That seemed like another lifetime to Sal, but it had to be an even greater contrast for Jason.

Sal waited until his brother was situated, checked his rifle on his back, and indicated for the two mares to walk together. Luckily, they'd grown up around one another so they got along fine. "Keep her on the path when we reach the woods."

"Seriously, Sal? You're not actually going to nag the whole time, are you?"

"That would be boring." Sal held the rein loosely in one hand and stroked Brie with the other as they rode past the tree line. He relaxed when he saw how naturally Jason handled Nelly. "Let's head over in the direction of the Christensen property. That's where we found the closed trap."

Along the way, they spotted two open traps. Each time, Jason took a picture and noted their exact location. *Gotta love technology.* Ten years ago, they could not have been so precise in the reports. "Here. Stop." Sal dismounted and tied Brie to a nearby tree, then did the same for Nelly while Jason poured water for them.

Once the horses were content, Sal moved the leaves barely concealing the trap and the body with a stick. "What the hell?"

"What is it?" Jason appeared next to him. Before Sal could answer, he remarked, "There's no blood."

Sal retrieved his tools and released the puppy from the trap. He sent up a prayer for the soul of the baby who didn't get the life he should have and gently turned him over. He was being more reverent perhaps than necessary, but even if he didn't know the animal in question, he deserved respect after meeting what Sal could only assume was an awful end. "Fuck."

"He's not decomposed?" Jason held his arms out for the victim, and Sal passed the puppy to him. "Doesn't feel right. There should have been some change by now."

"Wrap him up in a blanket, and we'll bring him back to show Grams and Pops." Sal broke the trap, squirted antibacterial gel on his hands, and started back toward home with a gut roiling from confusion.

Chapter Eleven

BY THE TIME Ryder headed over to Luke's place, he had already run at dawn, packed the hole under the fence, and eaten breakfast. He considered leaving Elle home with his parents, but that seemed unnecessary. After her disappearance last night, coupled with the ominous text he'd received, Ryder wasn't in a rush to let her out of his sight. That would, of course, change if Luke's dogs were unkind to her.

"Morning, neighbor!" Luke waved as Ryder stepped out of his car.

"Good morning." Ryder cringed at the man's fashionable Western attire. Skintight jeans, a ruffled shirt, and pointed cowboy boots was not the best working outfit. *He'll learn soon enough. Or I can be nice and tell him...* "Are you open to feedback?"

"Already? God, how did I manage to screw up before we even started working?" The words were punctuated with a charming smile.

Ryder chuckled and approached the porch with Elle running at his side. "Those clothes would be great for a pub night, but not so much for getting messy work done—and it's all messy work."

"Fair enough. Come on in. You can meet my dad while I change."

"Where are your dogs?"

"Backyard. Figured that's the best place to introduce them to Elle."

At least he knows that much. Hey, just because he made a fashion misstep doesn't mean he won't be competent at everything else. In the middle of Ryder's warring consciences, Sal's voice whispered for him to be careful. *Maybe he has changed, but caution is still the best plan.* Luke's property was more modest than Ryder's or Sal's, which surprised Ryder after what Sal had said about his wealth. The house had a simple layout of a sitting room, kitchen, and stairs that presumably led to the bedrooms.

Ryder had to hide his shock when Luke introduced him to his father, Max. Max appeared to be the same age as Sal's grandfather, but in much worse shape. Whereas Pops still did minor chores on the farm, Max struggled to walk from one end of the room to another. It made Ryder wonder if an upstairs bedroom suited him.

"Better?" Luke asked, reappearing downstairs in looser jeans, a T-shirt, and trainers.

"Much, but I'd suggest investing in a pair of good work boots."

"Think I can manage that."

After they both said goodbye to Max, Luke led Ryder to the backyard, where they were greeted by two medium-sized mutts—Gomez and Morticia. Elle, bless her, went right up to them with her head held high. Ryder stood close in case he had to intervene.

"They're fine," Luke said. "Give them some space, or they'll assume something is wrong."

Ryder took a reluctant step back and let out a sigh of relief when the three tails started wagging.

"See? They're good. Remember, they met last night."

"I had actually put that harrowing experience out of my mind for a moment, so I appreciate you reminding me." He grinned as he watched the three dogs play.

"Oh, come on, it could have been worse."

"You have no idea how much worse I thought it was." He shivered as he recalled the feeling of finding the trap with the puppy's body in it and the panic brought on by the text message, which he still hadn't figured out. If they thought he was going to gamble again, they were out of their goddamn minds.

"Well, she's safe now, and I had an excuse to meet one of the only two other gay men in this town."

"Might be a couple more," Ryder said, thinking back to Wanker in the bar. His skin prickled at the realization that Luke had inched closer as they spoke. Ryder stepped in the direction of the shed. "Are your tools in here?"

"Yeah, I think we have some wood in there too."

Hope so if you want to fix a fence. Ryder deliberately ignored the twinge of disappointment in Luke's voice. "Let's see what you have." *Should have asked that before I came over to avoid needing to go home if we're short supplies. Oh, well, I suppose there are worse fates.* Luckily, when Luke unlocked the shed, Ryder saw an assortment of top-of-the-line tools—and guns, lots of guns. This shouldn't have shocked Ryder as much as it did. Everyone around here exercised their second-amendment right jubilantly. "Is that an AK-15?" he asked, working hard to keep the judgment from his tone.

"It is." Luke walked toward it, but Ryder picked up a loose piece of lumber.

"Don't worry about it. We should focus on the fence before the sun gets too high." Ryder was out the door before Luke could respond. He walked to the fence, but kept checking back to make sure that when Luke followed, he did so sans visible firearms. Which he knew was stupid and presumptuous. *I have no reason to believe that Luke would use his guns irresponsibly. But there also isn't a need to have machine guns outside of a war zone.* He zeroed his attention on the fence. "Looks like we need ten panels 'bout six feet each."

Luke nodded. "I'll bring the chainsaw and measuring tape. You wanna grab the wood?"

"Sure thing. Don't forget nails."

"Right." Luke and Ryder collected their supplies. They worked studiously, stopping only for Ryder to give directions, for forty-five minutes. As Ryder was nailing a piece in, Luke broke the quiet. "Ryder, do you have anything you regret in life?"

"Who doesn't?"

Luke didn't respond until Ryder faced him. "I'm guessing Sal warned you about me. About what I was like when we knew each other in the city." When Ryder tightened his mouth, Luke continued, "People change, and I'm here for a fresh start. I know I'll never convince him of that, but I'm hoping you understand the need to start over."

Ryder studied him for a long moment, then nodded. "I do, but as much as I'm happy to be neighborly, friendship would take time."

"Long as you aren't writing off the possibility. Because I'd like the chance to get to know you. And look"—he gestured to the dogs—"our animals are already taken with each other. Can't argue those instincts."

"No, you can't." *Should I ignore mine though? They haven't always led me well before...* "Did you say you wanted help with finding chickens to raise?"

"And maybe some cattle. I'm also thinking of hiring people who know about farming so I can grow vegetables..." Ryder's jaw dropped. "What? Too much?"

"Way too much. Cattle raising can be a full-time job in of itself. Not to mention, you would have to figure out why you were raising them. Meat? Show?" The haphazard idea hurt Ryder's brain. "I'd come up with a specific plan before you go buying any animals because once you have them you gotta raise them." It felt like a patronizing thing to say, but Luke just showed his pearly whites.

"I admit to getting overly excited sometimes. But I just want to learn everything I can about my new life, ya know? I have the capital to make it happen."

Make what happen? You don't even know what you want! Ryder opened his mouth to say something, but his phone chimed—from Luke's pocket.

"Whoops, thought I gave this back to you." He passed it over. "You dropped it by the shed."

Wouldn't I have felt that? But why would he lie? Ryder glanced at the screen to see a text from Sal.

Come over when you're done? I have something to show you.

Sure. Give me an hour.

"Everything okay?" Luke asked.

"Fine. Let's finish up here." Once they had arranged all the pieces of wood, Luke took out his wallet, but Ryder shook his head. "You saved my dog; I helped fix your fence. We're even."

Luke scrutinized him. "All right, but next time you help, I'm paying. I'd hate to be a charity case."

"I don't think that's a possibility for you." Ryder whistled, and Elle came bounding to him but missed and rammed headfirst into the fence. Ryder and Luke laughed.

"At least we know it's sturdy," Luke said.

"That we do." Ryder clipped Elle's leash on, waved to Gomez and Morticia, and bid Luke goodbye.

Once he reached home, Ryder found a text message from *Unknown Number* that he hadn't heard the signal for. His blood ran cold as he read the words.

Always nice to make new friends, isn't it?

Ryder's first instinct was that Luke sent it. *But...why?* Luke was either a fantastic actor or genuinely trying to start over. *Sal did say he was slick...which is even less reason to believe he sent this. A slick man would have been careful not to give himself away. Texts like this are too obvious. Or is that what he wants me to think...?*

Another chimed through a minute later.

I suggest you get in touch about paying your debt.

"Fuck."

Elle yipped from the back seat, bringing his attention to the present. "Sorry, girl." He scratched behind her ears and opened the door to go inside.

As promised, Ryder showed up an hour after he answered Sal's text. He had left himself just enough time for a shower, so he didn't come smelling of sweat and mud. Though after receiving that anonymous text, his shower was far less relaxing than he would have liked.

"Hey, there, Petey!" He bent down to scratch the block-headed dog, who responded with full-body wiggles before he noticed Elle. Apparently, Petey did not appreciate the scent of the other dogs on her because he worked quickly to clean it off.

"How was fence mending?" Sal asked from above him.

"Fucking hot." Ryder snorted at the sight of Sal's raised eyebrow. "You should see your face. Priceless."

"Jerk," Sal muttered and headed toward the quarantine stable. "Are you coming or just gonna stare at my ass?"

Ryder took a few quick strides to close the distance between them. "Latter tends to, eventually, lead to the former."

"Just by staring? Must have been a while." The happiness in Sal's words excused the teasing. Not that Ryder could have complained, anyway, since he'd set himself up for it.

"What did you have to show me?"

Once they reached the stable where the horses received medical care, Sal stopped in front of an empty stall—well, almost empty. On closer inspection, Ryder spotted a bundled blanket in the otherwise sanitized area. He followed Sal inside and squatted but didn't reach out to touch the fabric. "What is it?"

"Jason and I rode out to where you and I found the trap. The dog—"

"Is here?" Ryder straightened and backed away. "Why didn't you bury it or...?" *Leave it alone?* That sounded crueler than he meant it, but his confusion overpowered any sense of propriety in questioning.

"There was no blood. No decomposition." Ryder knitted his eyebrows together, and Sal lifted the bundle. "I showed Pops, and he thinks it's a taxidermy puppy."

"As in, it once was alive, but then professionally stuffed?"

Sal held the swaddled blanket out to Ryder, who hesitated. "Feel it, Ry."

When he finally took the puppy from Sal, Ryder eased the blanket from his face to find what could have been one of Elle's sleeping brothers but wasn't because they were all home safe with his parents. He had checked before he left. "Goddamn. That's...realistic." He handed it back to Sal. "You said he was caught in a trap?"

"Yeah. The question is, why? Who would go to that trouble? For what purpose?"

"To scare a hiker." The words left Ryder's lips before he could comprehend them. The text message he received last night flashed before his eyes. *To scare me*, he concluded. His head spun, but he mustered enough wherewithal to ease himself to the ground. *They found me. The bastards are coming after my neighbors, my dog, who's next?* His throat tightened as he begged for oxygen. But every breath was a struggle.

"Ryder!" Sal's frantic voice brought him crashing back to the smells of the farm mixing with his friend's distinct scent.

"Sorry. I..." *God, where to fucking start? Nowhere, unless you want to lose what little you've built.* "Haven't eaten since early this morning. Guess it affected me more than I thought."

Sal chewed his bottom lip, as though debating whether to believe Ryder. "Come on. Let's go inside. Grams brought over meatballs. I'll make grinders for lunch."

"I should—"

"Don't say you should go home because there's no way I'm letting you drive like this." Sal extended his hand to help Ryder to his feet.

Their touching palms sent a bolt of electricity through Ryder. "I could argue that you don't have to *let* me do anything."

"And I could phone your ma and tell her you're driving without all your senses in working order."

"Ouch. You're cold!"

"Or I care. Take your pick." Sal gave a half shrug but didn't release his hand. Ryder debated pulling away, objecting in principle, but the connection was too warm, too comforting, too...good to reject—even if he knew he should. Any number of people could see them if they were paying attention. Or gave a shit. But since Sal didn't seem concerned, Ryder pushed it to the back of his already cluttered mind.

When Sal and Ryder reached the back door, they found Petey and Elle sitting, waiting patiently to go in. "Ready for an air-conditioning break?" Ryder asked, stopping to pet them both.

"Sal?" Jason called from the other room.

"Yup, brought Ryder in too."

"Hey, Jay," Ryder said. He heard rustling, and Petey met Jason in the hallway.

"Sit, Ry." Sal gestured to a chair at the round table. "You have lunch yet, Jay?"

"No. You cooking?"

"Meatball grinders?"

"Perfect. Grams brought fresh bread." Jason brought over a white loaf wrapped in plastic and a sharp knife.

Each cut of the blade enhanced the scent wafting from the bread until Ryder's mouth watered. "I can already tell that's going to be heavenly. Why doesn't she sell her cooking?"

Sal shook his head. "I've been suggesting that for years, but she insists that selling would take the joy out of it."

"Probably right." Jason cut enough bread for three sandwiches, then put butter on an extra slice and passed half to Ryder, who mouthed *thanks*. With a nod, Jason continued, "The amount she'd have to bake to meet demand would be overwhelming."

"Christ, that's good." Ryder couldn't remember the last time he'd had homemade bread, much less homemade butter. "If she wanted to, she could sell the recipes to a restaurant or magazine."

Jason and Sal shared a hearty laugh. "She'd never allow that," Sal said. "She'd convince herself that someone would fuck it up."

"Hell, she barely trusts us with them," Jason added.

The conversation faded into the back of Ryder's mind as the text messages crept into the forefront. *Is it worth contacting them to set the record straight? No, there is no record. If there was, their whole business would fall apart. They operate under a "gentleman's agreement," according to Boss. But if I don't meet with them, the threats to my loved ones could increase.* His gaze swept around the room between the brothers, who were his oldest friends, to the innocent dogs who provided unconditional love, to the window, out of which he could see his childhood home that held his family. *None of them deserve to be hurt because of me. But if Boss has more demands, what could I offer him? Two weeks' worth of wages...*

"Ryder!" Jason waved a hand in front of Ryder's face. "Jesus, you're in your own world. Sal asked if you wanted cheese or just sauce."

"Um...cheese is good, thanks." He flicked his gaze to Sal's but quickly brought it back to his plate at the sight of Sal's concern. "Hold on a second. I have to make a call."

Ryder stepped outside and shakily pressed the fifth speed dial on his phone. One ring. Two rings. Three rings. "This is Boss. Leave a message."

"Boss, it's Cowboy." Thank God, the shaking didn't translate to Ryder's words. "Let's talk. Pick a time and place in Tryon. I'll be there." He ended the call, tucked his phone in his pocket, and walked back into the kitchen just as Sal was slipping the grinders onto plates. The three of them made light conversation as they ate their meal. Afterward, Ryder and Jason helped clean up since Sal cooked. It all felt...normal, which offered Ryder comfort against the turmoil in his brain. Once the kitchen was in order, Jason announced that he and Pete were going to visit Grams, leaving Sal and Ryder alone. Elle's snoring meant she couldn't be a distraction.

"You got somewhere to be?" Sal asked.

"No, why do you ask?"

Sal wrung out the dish rag and draped it over the faucet. "I don't know. You look like you're searching for an escape route."

Ryder shook his head. "I guess I'm trying to figure out what we're supposed to do."

"Supposed? What do you *want* to do?"

He laughed without humor. "Now, isn't that the million-dollar question?" Sal's wariness deepened. "Do you want to watch mindless television?"

"What if we listened to music and played poker?" Sal countered.

"No poker. No cards." Ryder cursed himself as the words tumbled out of his mouth unbidden. "I can't...I just can't." So much confusion decorated Sal's features, but Ryder again didn't know where to start, so he averted his gaze. "Maybe this is a bad idea," he whispered.

Somehow, Sal crossed the room and sat next to Ryder without him realizing it until his hands on Ryder's sent electricity throughout his body. "Ry, look at me, please."

Though he knew *that* was a bad idea, Ryder lifted his gaze to meet Sal's. The warmth in his touch reflected in his eyes.

"What happened?"

Ryder opened his mouth to lie, but closed it when he realized he couldn't. Not to Sal. Especially not to a direct question with a plea for honesty resonating from every part of him. "I can't play one game of poker for the same reason an alcoholic can't have one beer."

Understanding replaced the confusion on Sal's face. "I didn't know."

"Of course not. I'm working pretty hard to keep it quiet. My parents don't even know. That's why I'm living with them, actually."

"Because you lost all your money?"

"And then some." Ryder tried to look away. Tried to break the adhesive spell Sal had him under, but failed. Thankfully, he managed to stop short of telling him what that meant now. "I had to sell my house, car, stocks, everything of value to pay my debts."

Sal worked his bottom lip in much the same way Ryder imagined his mind was churning. "I'm sorry it was so difficult to get to where you are now, but...I'm glad you aren't dealing with it alone anymore." He paused. "Is there more to deal with?"

"Shouldn't be." That was true. If the asshole had honored their agreement, Ryder wouldn't have had to think about him again. "If there was, though, I promise not to drag you or Jason or my parents into it." Sal's horrified expression signaled that was the worst choice of words Ryder could have made.

"Aren't you listening? Honestly, Ryder, why would you believe that we, people who have cared about you for most of your life, would want you to go through something like that alone?"

This time, Ryder was able get to his feet. "Because I'm the one who fucked up. I'm the one who let this drive me away from my family." He inhaled sharply. *Go ahead. Tell him. Watch him run away. It's better for everyone, you know.* "If I didn't have this addiction, my daughter would still be here. I would have been home instead of playing cards with my coworkers. There would have been no babysitter to fall asleep." Ryder balled his hands into fists at his side. He should leave now. Save Sal the trouble of kicking him out. But, no, he'd started telling this story, and fuck it all, he was going to finish it.

"Every Thursday night, I would meet up for cards with coworkers. It was the only night I came home after six. I used the excuse of adding excitement to my life after I left Wall Street. The stakes increased over time as the group expanded beyond our office. Some of the people who joined had questionably high skills. But none of the original players minded. They made good money and had no responsibilities outside of work. I know I should have stopped. I should have thought about my mortgage and my daughter. And I did, but it felt good to win. I just...didn't win enough."

Ryder couldn't bear to see Sal's expression, so he kept his eyes closed tight. "When I called to confirm that the sitter would stay late, she hesitated, but agreed. I ignored the hesitation. Didn't even register it until she brought it up to the police later." He let out a shuddering breath. "We played. I had a decent night—game wise. Didn't see the money. Went right to chip at the interest in my loan."

"The collector was there?" Sal's voice was raw with... anticipation? Concern? Horror?

That's the one. He already knows how the story ends. Like Titanic. *The ship would sink regardless of the acting talent in the film.* "Always. He played and offered loans to people who ran out." Ryder could have described the smell of the room, the clothes he wore, hell, what the other players were wearing, but it would all be a stall tactic. "I stopped at 7:45, as I always did, so I could get home in time to tuck Gabriella into bed. I had to be home to do it, or she wouldn't sleep. No one wants to deal with an overtired six-year-old—not me nor her teachers." Ryder was well-aware he was rambling, but he couldn't slow his speech and he didn't want to get to the end of the story. "I drove home relieved that I hadn't really lost anything that night." An odd, humorless laugh left his mouth. "Isn't that rich? God, I had no idea."

"Ry..." The heat of Sal's breath singed Ryder's skin.

Ryder put his hand out to stop Sal from getting closer. "Not yet. Please." If Sal touched him now, Ryder would break down, and he wanted, no, needed, to get this story out. "When I pulled onto my street everything—trees, roads, sidewalks, houses—was colored by red and blue flashing lights. My first concern was for my elderly neighbors. But...the emergency vehicles weren't parked by their home. They were on the street outside mine. Because the rest of the street was filled, I told myself. One of my neighbors was having a very bad night, and it would be terribly selfish to worry about my family when my daughter was probably having her bedtime snack." *God, I am setting myself up for a nightmare tonight. Not that I don't deserve it...* "From here, my memory gets sketchy. The door wasn't locked. I had been all ready to lecture the babysitter about that. It was a decent neighborhood, but we weren't in the South." The joke fell as flat as Ryder expected it would. He couldn't perform the correct inflection for humor right now if his life depended on it.

"She sat in the living room alone, her hanging head concealing her swollen eyes. 'I'm sorry. I'm sorry.' She kept repeating it, no matter what I asked. I tried to construct some non-awful explanation but came up blank. The cops must have heard us talking or opening the door or walking... I don't know, but two officers appeared from my bedroom, where I heard other voices. They led me to sit at the kitchen table, and someone else took the sitter out of the house. I asked repeatedly to see my daughter, but the male cop told me I had to listen to them before I could go back. I could barely hear what they said, much less listen to it. Words hit me—*Gabriella, seizure, bath, sitter*. My brain couldn't catch up. Couldn't make sense of the story. Until he said, 'EMTs are attempting lifesaving procedures.' My world stopped.

"Someone yelled 'Clear!' from the bedroom. Despite the burly policeman trying to stop me, I barreled in to find a semicircle of EMTs kneeling on the floor with my girl in the center. Her naked, bluish-gray body looked so small. Cold. I wanted to wrap her up in the warmest blanket in the house and heat the life back into her." This time, when Sal pulled Ryder into his arms, he didn't resist. He relished the warmth. Clung to it. "It took days before I could wrap my head around what happened. I had to decide what to do with her remains. On autopilot, I buried her in the local cemetery because...what else do you do?" Somehow, Sal had managed to get Ryder to sit on the living room couch with him. Ryder didn't remember moving, but he was glad to not need to hold himself up. Though he still couldn't convince himself to look Sal in the face. "That felt so weird. And stupid, I quickly realized. Why would I want her there when I had to be here? I couldn't process. Could barely feel anything." Ryder shrugged. "I guess it should be weird."

"What?" Sal asked.

"Children dying. That's not something you want to get used to."

"No, it isn't."

A moment of silence stretched between them. Not uncomfortable, exactly, but Ryder felt it should be filled. *Why is he still holding me? Why hasn't he kicked me out?*

"I'm sorry, Ry, but I don't get it. I don't understand how you could blame yourself for that tragedy."

"I wasn't there. I was off feeding my addiction. Having fun, if it can be called that." Ryder stroked Elle, who had jumped up on the couch on his side opposite the one leaning against Sal. Dogs knew so much. "Hell, what if I had given in to her request for a dog earlier? He or she could have been in the bathroom and alerted the sitter when Gabby had her seizure."

"What if they didn't?" Ryder screwed up his face, so Sal clarified, "What if the dog you brought home wasn't Lassie? What if they didn't see the seizure? Or if they did, they didn't know what to do? Would you blame them?"

Ryder recognized the trap Sal was setting. "It's different."

"How?"

"Because it's not their job. Children are parents' responsibility."

"And you acted responsibly that night. You had a sitter you knew and trusted staying with your daughter." Sal cupped Ryder's chin and tilted it up until their gazes met. "I know I'm not going to convince you not to blame yourself right now, but I want you to listen to me when I say that I don't blame you, and neither would anyone else who hears the story."

Ryder desperately wanted to believe what Sal said was true. But even if the first part was, he couldn't speak for everyone, and plenty of people would pin it on Ryder for not doing enough; of that he was certain. "Thanks." And he hoped Sal didn't ask him to specify what he was thanking him *for*, because Ryder didn't think he had the words.

"Promise me, if this shark wants more from you, you won't try to handle it on your own."

Ryder focused more attention than required on petting Elle. "I promise if they want more than I can handle, I will let you know." Sal opened his mouth, but Ryder placed his finger on Sal's lips. "No, Sal, these people are dangerous. I won't drag you or anyone else I care about into this fucking nonsense if there's any other way." A growl rumbled from low in Sal's throat, causing an unexpected smile to spread over Ryder's face. "You don't scare me." That was one of the sexier noises Sal made. Though Ryder would prefer he had inspired it for a different reason, but...not much he could do about that.

"You *do* frustrate me."

"Yeah, well, what else is new?"

Sal glanced between the spot where their bodies were pressed together and Ryder's face. "Is this okay? I'm not winning at the 'just friends' thing, am I?"

Ryder considered. If Sal wanted to take him on after knowing how fucked up Ryder was, who was he to stop him? In answer, he leaned over and pressed their lips together for a long, searing kiss.

Chapter Twelve

RYDER AND SAL made an effort to conceal their relationship from the rest of the employees, for Ryder's sake. They still weren't huge fans but had laid off the overt bullying. Ryder had been playing phone tag with the shark—rather the shark's people. The shark had better things to do than make appointments to settle already settled debts. He was too busy doing...whatever it was he did to make the money he lent out in the first place. *God, I'm stupid to get involved with something so shady. At least I'm trying to get out of it. That counts for something, right?*

"Hey, Ry," Jason said as he jogged up next to him, "Sal is talking to the vet about one of the pregnant mares. Can you handle supervising Trixie, Marianna, and her parents?"

"Sure?"

"What are you confused about?"

"If the child's parents are there, what am I supervising? Is she going to ride her?" Ryder's pulse picked up speed. He hadn't yet taken on the lessons without supervision and was in no hurry to do so.

"I don't know. She says not today, but sometimes she changes her mind after Trixie calms her down. I have to go meet potential boarders. The parents know what to do. It's just better for everyone to have staff on hand."

"Okay..." If Jason noticed Ryder's hesitation, he didn't acknowledge it. *Why would he? The answer is going to be the same regardless.*

On his way to Trixie's stall, Ryder's phone rang. *Unknown number. Shit!* "Hello?"

"Three p.m. Mac's. Look for a red scarf. Don't be late." The rough, disguised voice ended the call before Ryder could object.

His cell phone screen read 12:10. *I still have more than two hours before I have to leave, but that's an hour prior to when I'm scheduled to go home. Fuck!* Ryder pushed on to Trixie's stall. He did a double take when he spotted two women standing with a little girl. "Hi, I'm Ryder."

The taller of the two women extended her hand. "I'm June. This is my wife, Nancy."

The three adults shook hands, and Nancy gestured to the biracial little girl, who brushed Trixie in slow motions. "This is Marianna. She's having a bad day today," Nancy said in way of warning. She lowered herself to Marianna's level. "Can you say hi to Ryder?"

Ryder wanted to tell Nancy not to worry about it. That he understood bad days for children with autism could make it difficult to speak, or even look at strangers, but he didn't want to interfere with their parenting. This certainly was a different world down here than the one he'd left. While he and Sal weren't good at being closeted, to hear a woman with a Southern accent call her partner *wife* sounded foreign. And wonderful.

Marianna flicked her gaze in Ryder's general direction. "Hi," she whispered.

"Hello, Marianna," Ryder said. "It's very nice to meet you." Her lips twitched upward, and she focused on Trixie while her mothers praised her. Ryder petted the opposite side of the horse. "What have y'all done with Trixie so far today?" He had no idea how Trixie's care tasks were allocated. Sal and Jason treated Trixie as a special case, so who performed her care varied by the day.

"We just got here," June answered. "As far as I know, Trixie has had breakfast and was let out to pasture, but her stall didn't need to be mucked, since we did it yesterday. Is that right?"

"Yes, we use an every-other-day mucking schedule, unless there's a problem, obviously." He watched Nancy correct Marianna's method and wondered what exactly he was there for. These parents knew what they were doing with both the horse and their daughter. Ryder wouldn't have been surprised if at least one of them had grown up in the equestrian world.

"Why don't we take her out and enjoy her for a bit?" The mothers exchanged relieved looks and agreed. Marianna and her mothers went about selecting a blanket and saddle for Trixie while Ryder stood back to watch. He had decided to let the family handle the horse, unless they asked him to step in. As much as it made him feel useless, they seemed to have it well in hand.

Once Marianna was settled on Trixie with her special riding helmet, Ryder gave Nancy, who stood closest to her, suggestions for small adjustments on Marianna's posture. From the run where Trixie trod along, Ryder spotted Sal coming out of the stable. "June, I have to ask Sal something real quick. I'm going to have Karen stay with you in case you need anything." Ryder gestured for his coworker, who was between tasks, to come over.

"We'd be fine alone."

"I know you would, but we like to be safe."

When Karen reached them, Ryder asked to stay with the family for a few minutes. After receiving her agreement, Ryder jogged over to Sal. "Do you have a minute?"

"I think I could spare one." Sal tugged him into an empty stall, away from prying eyes, and pressed their lips together.

Though not what he'd intended when he approached, Ryder easily melted into the kiss. Their lips fit as well together as their bodies. Ryder explored Sal's mouth, scraping his tongue. But when Sal nibbled his bottom lip, Ryder had to pull away. "Hey, now! I have to go back to the clients."

"Mm, pants are thick enough not to cause a problem." Sal smirked. "What'd ya need?"

Only one need came to mind—the one that the thick pants were not doing a great job of hiding. Ryder dug past the image of the sun glistening off Sal's dark hair to find what he needed to ask him. "Can I leave at two today? I need to go into town for an appointment."

A beat passed, then two as Sal studied him. "Am I not supposed to ask what the appointment is for?"

"I'd really rather you didn't." *I don't want to lie.* Of course, Sal could deny his request to leave early, but that would just mean that Ryder would skip his shower. He leaned closer. "I promise I'm not cheating on you." Technically, they hadn't discussed being exclusive, or even putting a name to their relationship. *Partners? Friends who make out? It feels more than the latter, but the former might be rushing it?*

Sal scowled. "That's not my concern, and you know it." He blew out a heavy breath. "Yeah, Ry, you can leave early." He scrubbed his hand along his face. "Will you at least come by after and let me know you're safe?"

The concern in Sal's chocolate eyes touched Ryder. "I'll be fine, but, yes, I'll come by. Maybe I'll bring pizza."

With a resigned kiss to Ryder's forehead, Sal agreed.

RYDER ASKED HIS dad to look after Elle while he went into town. Dad wasn't concerned about why Ryder was going as long as he returned with coffee beans. Ma would have had twenty questions prepared, but luckily, his mother was making house calls today. The rest of Ryder's shift had flown by, as ninety-odd minutes will tend to when you're engaged in what you're doing.

"Hey there, neighbor!" Luke called.

"Hi, Luke. I'd love to chat, but I need to get into town for an appointment."

Weirdly, Luke's features brightened. "Would I be able to hitch a ride with you? My car wouldn't start, so the mechanic had to come tow it this morning. They said it will be a couple days. I wouldn't mind being housebound, but my father is about to run out of his prescriptions, so I need to get to the pharmacy." When Ryder didn't answer right away, Luke added, "If it's too much trouble to ride with you, could you give me the number of the local taxi company? Uber isn't available this far out."

Ryder ground his bottom lip. The taxi would cost more than a day's wages. "I don't know how long I'll be gone."

"I'm in no hurry. And I'm happy to pay for gas." The plea in Luke's gaze won Ryder over.

"Hop in." He unlocked the passenger door and waited for Luke to climb in and put his seat belt on. "What pharmacy are you going to?" *Probably should have asked that first...*

"The CVS on the main drag."

Ryder did a quick mental calculation. He could drop Luke off at CVS, then head over to Mac's without losing much time. They were on the same street, seven blocks apart. Luckily for him, Mac's had a parking lot. He tapped a beat into the steering wheel as he drove.

"You okay?" Luke asked.

"What? Sure." *How convincing.* "Just seeing someone I haven't for a while, and I'm not sure how it will go. You know how that is."

"Do I ever."

Ryder was intrigued by the inflection in Luke's response. *If he's thinking of Sal, what did he hope for? Did he move down here for Sal?* If so, Sal's reception couldn't have been more disappointing. The thought should have made Ryder jealous, but the situation was just too weird, and Sal uncharacteristically cold for it to raise his radar. Except to heed Sal's warning to be careful. *But I'm not really doing that, either, being alone in a car with him and whatnot. Just because he was a bad boyfriend, that doesn't make him a dangerous human being.* "How is the farm planning going?"

Luke gave a weak laugh. "Requiring way more work than I anticipated."

"Yeah, it's more complex than people think. Have you spoken to the Daniels about chickens?" Ryder asked, referencing the local chicken breeders.

"Mm, I meant to talk to you about that. It's a great place to send your enemies."

"What?" Ryder was at once incredulous and hysterical.

"He wouldn't stop talking! About chickens! And their personalities! They're chickens!"

Ryder almost had to pull over from how hard his laughter shook his body. "Do yourself a favor, pretend all animals you encounter here are dogs. You might not see the personality in the livestock, but you'd be offended if people disregarded your pets' individuality, wouldn't you?"

"But..." Luke seemed to be grasping for words. "Wouldn't that make you too attached? I could never kill my dogs for meat."

"Not everyone kills the animals. Many live out their lives on the farm." Ryder changed lanes as he spoke. "My ma, for example, won't kill any uninjured or healthy animals, either on her farm or in her vet practice. You'd be amazed and disgusted if you knew how many people try to put down their pets just because of age." Vets often saw the very worst of people, and Ma was no different in her practice.

"That, I believe. But, as a general rule, aren't the cows and chickens raised for food as opposed to companionship?"

"Yes, but ethical farmers still treat their livestock well, and with that comes a degree of attachment." Ryder wasn't sure where to go from there—how to make the attitude clearer. So, he stopped talking.

"I guess it's a whole different mindset here than what I'm used to."

"Truer words, my friend." Ryder offered a smile. He went to turn on the radio, but then remembered his father never got it fixed.

"How long were you in New York?" Luke asked.

Ryder had a burning desire to return to their conversation about livestock. "Since I graduated college, about seven years ago." He shifted in his seat. *Luke's making conversation, nothing more.* "What about you? Your family always live in Raleigh?"

"For three generations."

Then why would your dad want to come here for his retirement? The change was jarring enough for Ryder who had been gone for less than a decade, but what would inspire a family who never lived here to give up the comforts of city life? Not that Tryon was a backward town, and it was close enough to Asheville to experience different things if you wanted variety, but still, nothing compared to Raleigh or New York.

"We sold our family business around the time my dad started going downhill," Luke started, as though he had read Ryder's mind. "I was sort of lost without something specific to do every day. And we had enough money to start over, so I thought, why not do something completely different? Besides, we were told the fresh air would be good for my dad."

"So...you just happened to move down the road from your ex-boyfriend?" Ryder couldn't stop himself from asking.

"Honestly? Yes. I had heard talk of him going back home because we ran in the same social circles, but I had no idea where he lived." Luke cleared his throat. "I'm not looking to get him back, if that's what you're worried about."

Ryder had to snicker. "I might have been worried about it had there not been a solid wall of tension between you two." He turned down the main drag. The CVS sign came into view less than a minute later. "I'll be at Mac's, couple blocks down," he said as he pulled into the drugstore parking lot. "I should be round to pick you up in thirty minutes." Long time to stay in a drugstore, but it beat walking back.

"I can come to you. Promise to stay out of your conversation with your friend."

Ryder debated internally. Boss wouldn't be happy if he found out Ryder didn't come alone, even though he technically would, at least to the café. *But how would anyone know if Luke doesn't approach me in there?* "Whatever you want. There are also some shops between the two places, if you wanted to explore. Just, uh, text me where you'll be." Ryder tapped his nerves out onto the steering wheel. *I have to stop. Whoever Boss sends will sense weakness.*

"Will do." Luke paused halfway out the car door. "Good luck. I hope the meeting goes the best it can." He was gone before Ryder had a chance to respond.

That's actually not a bad way to phrase it. With a fortifying breath, Ryder drove from one parking lot to the other through the neighborhood streets. He scanned Mac's lot for...what? A shady-looking van? Ridiculous. Ryder knew better than that. These people were smart enough to blend in. *Shit. Still sitting here.* On the count of three, Ryder opened his door and strode into the café before he could overthink it any more than he already had.

The bright lights of the café contrasted with Ryder's mood, which his nerves had thoroughly soured. A glance around the place told him he had beaten the guy here.

"Hi, Ryder! You can sit anywhere, and I'll bring you a menu," the server called.

"Thanks, Louise." As she followed him to the booth, he added, "I'm actually meeting someone in the next few minutes."

"Not a problem. I'll send them right over to you and start you with a water."

Ryder thanked her again and flipped open the menu, more for something to do with his hands than interest in getting food. He wasn't sure if he could eat or if whoever showed up would want to. *Still, I have to order something. Bad manners to take up space at a place of business and not spend money.*

"Ryder?" Cat's voice caused a layer of sweat to congeal on his forehead. "I thought that was you."

"Hey, Cat. What are you doing here?" *Should've known I'd run into people I knew around here.*

"Oh, I was supposed to meet a prospective puppy parent here—we meet in public the first time—don't want crazies knowing where I live, but they canceled at the last minute. What are you up to today?"

"I'm...meeting an old friend." Ryder kept one eye on the door and one on her.

"Oh? Who?"

Shit. "Uh, you don't know them." He chuckled in response to her raised eyebrow. "They're from college. We're casual friends." *So casual I can't even tell you their name—or gender, really, but since I've only dealt with one woman in the "business," I'll assume I'm looking for a man.*

"Hmm, sometimes, those are nice. Not everyone has to know your secrets."

"Secrets? Are those allowed in this town?"

Cat's laugh was high. "No, I suppose we aren't big into privacy here, are we?" She flipped her long hair back. "Well, I won't keep you. Enjoy your visit. Hope to see you tomorrow."

Tomorrow? Shit, pub night. Does Sal go every Friday? Not that I have to do everything he does, but... She must have taken his silence for agreement because they said their goodbyes. As Cat headed out, a flash of red material around her neck caught the light. But she had disappeared around the corner so fast that he hadn't gotten a good look.

The clock read ten past three. Sometimes these assholes came late to fuck with people. That's how this thing often felt—like a giant goddamn game. *It* is *a fucking game, at least to them.* After another five minutes passed, Ryder ordered French fries. He was getting more agitated by the minute. When the door opened at half past, Ryder craned his neck, only to see Luke walk in.

Luke waved, but ducked into the table closest to the door.

Ryder played with his phone in his pocket. Took it out, stared at the screen, tucked it away again. Thirty minutes was pushing it, even for their games. No messages. No missed calls. *Fuck!* Ryder took it out again and jolted when it vibrated and lit up in his hand. Ryder held his finger up to the waitress in a silent promise that he'd return and scooted out the side door. "Where are you?" he hissed in greeting.

"Bad timing," the disguised voice on the other end said. "I'll call you with instructions later." The line went dead.

Ryder gaped at his phone. *What the fuck...?* A growl escaped his throat as he shook his head and went back inside. Blessedly, the waitress bought the fake smile he wore while he settled his bill, or at least she didn't bother to ask. Either was fine with him. "You ready to go?" he asked Luke, praying the man didn't have food on the way.

"Yeah. Didn't your friend show up?" He signaled for the check, which the waitress brought. After Luke paid in cash, adding a generous tip, Ryder walked with him toward the door.

"No. He couldn't make it."

"Sorry to hear that. Do you think you'll get to see him before he leaves town?"

"Hope so," Ryder answered as they got into the truck. It was the right thing to say, and truth be told, he'd rather be prepared to meet than get a surprise. Though he couldn't discount both happening. "I have to stop at the store for my dad. Do you need anything else while we're in town?" Ryder asked once he arrived at the store.

"I'm good, thanks. I'll wait for you in the car," Luke answered.

"I'll be fast," Ryder said, despite Luke giving no indication that he was in a rush. He grabbed milk and coffee, then ran out to the truck. "Now, we can hit the road."

The ride back was filled with small talk, and though it took until they were halfway there for Ryder to relax, he was grateful for the companionship. The idea of being alone with his thoughts did not appeal to him in the least.

Chapter Thirteen

AT DINNER WITH their grandparents that night, Pops turned to Sal. "How are things going with Ryder?"

Sal blinked at him. "He's doing well with the horses and clients. Hard worker."

Pops scoffed and waved the answer off. "I meant between the two of you, and don't you dare insult me by asking how I know there's something going on. I have eyes."

"It's fine."

"Just fine?"

Taking a drink bought Sal some time, but his grandmother cut in. "Leave the boy alone. It isn't like we're waiting for great-grandkids."

"I just don't want to see him get hurt is all."

"It's new, Pops, but we're doing okay. I'm not worried that he's going to hurt me." *Himself, maybe, but not me. Not if he could help it.*

"So, you know why he was driving around town with the new guy?"

"What new guy?" Jason asked.

"The one who moved into the house next to his. Blond guy. His car was parked outside of the Christensens' place."

The sip Sal had just taken went down the wrong pipe, sending him into a coughing fit. *Holy shit! Luke and Ryder went into town together? Is that the reason he didn't want to tell me what kind of appointment he had?*

Grams hit Pops's arm with the back of her hand. "Why are you causing problems?"

"I'm trying to look out for our grandson. He deserves to know the truth if he didn't already, which he clearly did not. I'd want to know if you were alone in a car with another man."

"I'd be a fool to tell you. The last one who gave me a ride home found himself with a bullet hole in his shoulder."

"That was an accident! Sixty years ago! The idiot was prowling around the woods without a reflective vest on during hunting season. Course he's going to get shot." Pops glared at Grams.

"Good thing your aim is as bad as your cooking or you would have gotten more than a slap on the wrist."

Sal glanced across the way at Jason, who cleared his throat. "Ryder had an appointment in town this afternoon. I'm sure it had something to do with that. No hunting neighbors, Pops." Despite verbally addressing his grandfather, Jason stared at Sal when he said it.

Forty-five minutes later, once his grandparents were safe at their home, Sal paced the length of his downstairs.

"I don't think he was trying to get you riled up," Jason said when he came out of the bathroom.

"Pops or Ryder?"

"Either, probably, but I was referring to Pops." Jason leaned against the kitchen doorway. "Would you stop? You're stressing Petey out."

Petey barked once at Sal, who crouched to pet him. "Sorry, boy." He took a deep breath. On his exhale, he straightened to his full height. "What was Ryder thinking? I told him Luke was bad news."

"Did you tell him why, or did you just want him to take your word for it?"

Sal scratched his head. "I told him that Luke was manipulative and that we broke up when I found out about his drug problem."

Jason's mouth formed a tight line. "Maybe Ryder isn't as concerned with what people put into their bodies as you are."

"Jay..." Sal started to object, but Jason visibly forced himself to relax.

"It's at least worth considering that Luke has changed, or Ryder isn't worried, but you should talk to him before you freak out." Jason paused. "Actually, calm down first, then talk to him. That's what you'd tell me to do."

If you had relationships. But Sal didn't say that. Now wasn't the time to bring up a very real concern he had for his brother. "You're right. I'll be back."

Jason jumped in front of him and blocked his path to the door. "What are you going to do?"

"We need to have a conversation."

"But *we* just established that you needed to calm down before that conversation happens. You aren't thinking rationally."

"And I'm not going to until I get answers."

Their stares locked. Jason was the first to break it. "Make sure you're prepared to listen and believe those answers. Pops means well, but he can only know what he sees." Jason stepped out of his way.

Sal nodded and plucked his keys from the door. Since their grandparents ate dinner early, Sal didn't have to worry about disturbing anyone too late. He slowed the car as he approached Ryder's house, but hit the gas instead of brake when he reached the driveway. Without giving his actions too much thought, Sal drove past the wooden fence separating the Christensen property from their neighbor's. He parked in front of the recently vacant house and strode up the uneven sidewalk to the front door, which was open, leaving only a screen between Sal and a sparsely furnished living room. Two dogs ran to the door to bark.

"Luke!" he heard from inside. "Someone's coming to the house."

"Okay, Dad," Luke answered, and water shut off. His shoulders sagged when he caught sight of Sal. "Give me a minute."

"I thought people just walked into their neighbors' homes in the country. That's what they do on TV," Luke's dad said. Sal couldn't see the man, despite hearing the conversation clearly.

"You're the one who told me not to believe what I see on television. Besides, I'm guessing that's for friends or at least people you trust. And if you don't have dogs threatening to bite visitors' faces off."

Is he implying that he doesn't trust me? That's fucking rich. Sal counted to ten twice before Luke squeezed outside past the dogs. "Hi, Luke," Sal greeted. For an inexplicable reason, being the one to speak first made him feel like he had the upper hand.

"Hi. I must say, you weren't who I was expecting to find."

"You were hoping for my boyfriend, perhaps?"

Luke rubbed his face. "Sal...I don't want to fight with you."

"I'm not..." He replayed the short conversation to himself. "Okay, maybe I started off more aggressively than necessary." He took a breath. "Can we talk?"

The porch light illuminated Luke's features as his mind worked. Luke never did hide his emotions well, which made important discussions easier when they were together. Unless, of course, it happened to be a time when Luke had shut himself off. "It'll be quieter out here."

With a nod, Sal took one of the plastic chairs on the porch while Luke lowered himself into the other. So many questions buzzed through Sal's mind that he didn't know where to start. He finally settled on, "Why are you here?"

"My dad sold his business for a pretty sum and wanted to take his retirement in the country. Since he can't live on his own, I came with him. Figured starting over would be good for both of us."

"That sounds...practiced. Like you give everyone the same answer."

"That's what happens when you tell the truth."

And you would know how? Stop with the antagonism. It won't get you answers. "But why this specific rural town? Why the one where I grew up?"

"I don't know of any others without leaving the state. We wanted to stay close enough to my dad's doctors, but far enough away from the insanity of the city to find peace. Yes, a Google search would have helped, but I assumed it was big enough that we wouldn't be fucking neighbors." Luke released a long, slow breath. "And besides," he said more quietly, "I liked the stories you told about being out with your boyfriend. It was a refreshing contrast to the stereotypical rural life. But, again, I didn't think I'd be living next door to him."

Sal took in everything Luke said. The words made sense, as did their delivery. But were they the truth? Or the whole truth? "How do you like it?"

"It's...taking some getting used to. Though Dad loves it. The air. The people. The animals. Everything. I'm honestly shocked."

"Why?"

Luke leaned back in the chair and gazed up at the sky. "I don't know if you remember me talking about my family—"

I don't know if I what I remember is true, was Sal's first thought. Not only did he question Luke's reliability, but also the reliability of his own memory.

"But I wasn't brought up like this," Luke continued. "Typical story of upper society family. Parents worked all the time. I had nannies. Grew up, worked in Daddy's company..." He waved it off as though bored of his own story.

Probably is. Luke and Sal had met at a networking event for young professionals in advertising. They had hit it off, but Luke partied way more than Sal could stomach.

After a pause, Luke went on, "Then Dad had a stroke. And another. As much as he had plans to die at his desk, he could barely move the right side of his body for months. We decided to sell the company and start over." He gestured to the area around them. "Can't get much more different than this."

A pang of emotion Sal couldn't name hit him in the chest. He nudged his glasses up his nose. "That explains why your dad is here, but—"

"I followed because I wasn't okay with the idea of strangers caring for him. My biggest mistake in all of this was thinking that it would be easier to run a farm than a company." Sal's eyes widened, and his jaw dropped. Luke laughed. "Yeah, that's what I'm learning. I had visions of planting vegetables in the spring, making sure they got enough water, then harvesting them in fall. Maybe I would bring in some animals for side money."

Animals...side money...oh, dear God. I don't even like this guy, and I want to set him straight. "Didn't you do any research before moving?"

"Apparently not the right kind." He rolled his eyes. "Don't get me wrong. We have money. I just need to figure a new plan to build a life here."

Sal quieted again. Back to the point of the visit. "What about Ryder? My grandfather said he saw you driving into town with him."

Luke narrowed his gaze. "What did Ryder say about that?"

"I'm asking you."

"If you're worried about your relationship—"

"I'm worried about Ryder. He's been through some shit lately, and you were into some fucked-up things in the city." Sal tossed a pebble from one hand to the other.

"So you don't trust him."

The calmness of the statement boiled Sal's blood. The next time he caught the stone in his hand, he chucked it into yard. "Goddamn it! It isn't about trust. He doesn't need the stress of a temptation." Did that sound any better?

"I don't remember you having such a hair-trigger temper. You might want to talk to someone about that."

Before or after I clock you? Sal stood to lean against the railing, putting distance between them so he didn't do something he'd regret.

"I don't have to tell you this, but I will, because I think it will make both our lives easier," Luke said. "My car wouldn't start, and I saw Ryder going into town so I asked if I could come along. I picked up prescriptions; he had an appointment that didn't pan out. That's it. I'll be honest, I could use friends in this town. Ryder seems like a nice guy, but if you don't trust him—"

"Stop saying that." Sal pinched the bridge of his nose and counted to five. "Did you bring the drugs with you?"

The heat of Luke's stare burned through the slight chill of the evening. "That was never what you thought."

"Are you delusional? Or do you think I am? It has to be one of those because the amount of drugs I saw at your apartment is way more than necessary for a casual coke user."

Luke growled and propelled himself to his feet. Sal refused to take a step back even as the other man advanced toward him. "I told you once, and I'll tell you again, it is not what you think." He raised his hand. "Don't you think that if I could have explained when you were walking out the door, I would have?"

Sal massaged his temple. "Whatever it was can't be good or legal."

"Are those the same thing?"

Oh, Jesus Christ, I forgot about his love for philosophy. "In the context of things that they send SWAT teams in to handle, yes." He paused, then faced Luke. The fading light illuminated the hard lines of his face. "I guess that's also the answer to my question. You brought the shit with you. How could you put your father in danger that way?"

"No one—least of all my father—is in danger because of me. I know you don't believe me, but they weren't back in Raleigh either." Luke exhaled long and slow. "The only drugs I use or possess are prescription. I truly am attempting to start over. Can you please not make it more difficult for me to do so?"

Sal believed Luke. He wasn't sure how he felt about this, never mind how he *should* feel. But the words rang true. "I won't stand in your way."

"Will you shut down rumors if you hear them? I know enough to be wary of small-town gossip."

Shutting down requires defending him. Can I do that? What if he's lying? The final question felt forced to Sal. Luke didn't look like he was lying. Not that lying had a surefire expression. Sal could only hope he had developed the skills to read people. "I'll tell people to give you a chance to prove yourself. Just...don't make us regret it."

"Thank you." Sal nodded, but before he could open his mouth to say more, Luke asked, "What can you tell me about Catherine Jacobs?"

"The better question is, what can Cat tell you about everyone else? The answer, by the way, is everything. Why? What did you hear?" *Who would talk about Cat? Ryder? That would be odd...*

"Oh, nothing. She dropped off a welcome basket to my dad while I was out today. He said he had never seen someone so cheery on a Thursday afternoon."

A badly hidden laugh turned snort fought its way past Sal's lips. "Yeah, that's our Cat. She's the great social organizer."

"Oh? Is that what she does? Event planning?"

Sal scratched his head. "No? Maybe? I don't know if Cat does any paid work. But she's involved in every aspect of the community. She's old money and her husband is in the navy." *What is with my verbal diarrhea? Must be tired.* "Anyway, I'm gonna head out." He silently debated the length of olive branch he was willing to extend to Luke. *Ryder obviously trusts him. That's gotta count for something.* "I'm assuming your dad can be left alone for a few hours, since you left this afternoon?"

"Yes, why?" *Was that suspicion in Luke's tone?*

If Sal took half a second to consider it, the question did come out oddly, especially given his prior accusations. "A group of us get together on Friday night at the local pub. Might be a good place to meet people." *Who aren't my boyfriend.* He didn't add that because it would reopen the idea that he didn't trust Ryder, and Sal didn't feel like defending himself again.

Luke blinked. "That's really nice of you. As long as my dad is feeling okay, I'll get a ride there."

Sal nodded again, still not feeling settled. "I'll see you later, then." With that, he walked down the stairs.

"Sal?" Luke called. When Sal turned around, Luke said, "Thanks."

"Sure. Hey, for the good of everyone, please hold off on getting animals until you talk to people who've done it. You really need to know what you're getting into there."

"Okay. I'll ask around." Luke waved goodbye and Sal got into his car.

As he sat behind the wheel, he took out his phone and texted Ryder.

You busy?
Nope. Want me to come by?
I'll pick you up.

The phone dinged a reply, but Sal drove to Ryder's without giving it another glance.

Ryder was waiting for him on his porch steps when Sal pulled into his driveway. "No Elle?" Sal asked when Ryder approached the car.

"She was dead to the world after running around after dinner." He leaned over for a kiss once he got in the car, which Sal happily obliged. They had been more openly affectionate with each other when alone, but were still careful around others. Ryder had relaxed a lot with Sal since he confessed what happened the night of his daughter's death, and Sal couldn't have been happier about it. "What did you want to do?" Ryder laughed at the smirk tugging on Sal's lips. "If we're going to make out, it has to be elsewhere. We aren't teenagers."

Sal thought back to their teen years and the many horses who'd had to share their stalls with hormonal boys. He shifted in his seat. "Are your parents still up?"

Ryder squinted at him. "What do you want to do? I have a feeling that whatever it is it can't be done here."

A sigh stopped just short of leaving Sal's mouth. "I don't know. I haven't planned it out, but I'd like some time alone with you." He licked his suddenly dry lips. "Asked if your parents were awake because I was going to see if you wanted to come home with me for the night. But I didn't know if you wanted to explain to them where you were going, and if you came, you'd have to grab Elle."

"You want me to sleep with you, but you haven't thought through what you want to do?" Ryder asked.

Sal shrugged and averted his gaze. "Not like I'd be the only one making that decision, Ry. You know me better than to think I'd pressure you into doing something you didn't want or weren't ready for." He couldn't identify where the increased drive to have Ryder in his bed—if only for sleep—came from, but God, was it strong. Just craving intimacy. Touch.

Ryder watched him in contemplative silence before slowly nodding. "I can't wait to get my own place. Give me a minute and I'll grab a bag and Elle."

"Don't forget to leave a note."

"Yes, Dad." Ryder rolled his eyes as he stepped out of the car and hustled up the walkway to the house again.

Jerk. As soon as Ryder had disappeared behind the door, Sal had second thoughts about the proposition. Despite the fact that they had known each other forever, their relationship was new. *I have to trust him to set his boundaries.* As soon as that conclusion solidified in Sal's mind, another concern cropped up. *Did he say "get his own place"? Where? Is he job-searching too?* The idea sent waves of panic through his body. *Why would he be looking for a new job when he's doing so well? Because he has a degree and experience in a field that pays a lot more than I ever could?* The answer did nothing to quell Sal's nerves.

The screen door closing cut into Sal's thoughts. He watched Ryder talking to Elle as they walked to the car. Ryder carried his duffel bag on his shoulder and the portable dog crate in the opposite hand. *Right. Elle is young enough to still be crated at night. Shit, this is more complicated than I anticipated at first.* "Hi, girl." He scratched the puppy head that popped up from the back seat to give him love as though it had been weeks, not hours, since she had seen him. "Will she be okay in that crate overnight?"

"Uh, we'll see. She should be, but she's only used this one for short periods of time." Ryder buckled his belt and gently nudged Elle to the back. "Lie down. Good girl. We aren't going far."

"Did you talk to your parents?" Sal asked as he reversed out of the driveway. It felt like the height of laziness to drive back and forth to Ryder's house without cargo to haul around.

"Ma was on the phone with one of her patients' humans. So, I wrote her a note."

"That's one way to not deal with an interrogation."

"Mm, she'll text me if she has something to say."

That was the damn truth. Sal often found himself glad that Grams and Pops weren't privy to the joys of texting. "She do that a lot?"

Ryder scratched his head. "Not unless there's a reason. Pick stuff up at the store, be safe, yada, yada." He said it with a faint smile and not a hint of resentment. "Does Jason know I'm coming?"

"Uh, no." Sal glanced over to see Ryder's raised brow. "What? When has he ever cared?" *He'll likely be thrilled I'm working off some of my earlier tension.* Sal kept that to himself because it sounded a whole lot like pressure, which he had promised not to do.

A moment of quiet passed, then Ryder grinned. "The last time I stayed here overnight was before college."

"Damn, that's right." They'd slept at their own houses when they came home because they weren't home for long and they lived together at school. "Well, Jason and I don't have bunk beds anymore."

"No?" The word came out through a laugh. "I swear your grandparents got them so we wouldn't fool around."

"That's the reason Jason and I shared a room."

"I suspected as much, at least after you had been living there a while."

When Sal and Jason moved in with their grandparents after their parents died, Pops and Grams thought they would grieve easier if they slept close to one another. Sal couldn't say they were wrong, but after a couple of months, they both started itching to clear out one of the storage rooms, though Pops always had a reason they couldn't. It wasn't until Sal left for school that Jason found out why. Despite accepting his sexuality unquestioningly, his grandparents weren't interested in giving him an opportunity to have sex with Ryder in their house. To be fair, they would have had similar rules had he been straight. What they didn't know, what none of them really understood, was that Ryder and Sal were on the asexual spectrum. They had tried to fool around when they were young, but it was never a driving need for them.

Once Sal and Ryder walked into the house, Jason waved from the couch. "Convince him to give you makeup sex?"

"Why would we need to make up?" Ryder glanced between Sal and Jason. "Did we fight?"

Sal glared at his brother. Of course, Jason would force the conversation. "No, I was just cranky when I left the house."

Jason gave him a look that feigned innocence, making Sal want to punch him even more. "Well, hopefully you can fix that crankiness, Ryder. You always did have the magic touch."

"Don't you have somewhere to be? Like hell?"

"Sal, chill," Ryder said. "He's fine."

But Jason stood. "Actually, I am going to see Ted for a bit."

Sal inclined his head. "I didn't realize you two were talking again." Ted and Jason had dated before the accident, but Jason rebuffed all of Ted's offers of support afterward.

"Yeah, it's sorta new." He grabbed his keys. "Don't wait up, or do, I don't know when I'll come back. Come on, Petey." A pointless call if Sal ever heard one. That dog was rarely far from Jason, especially when Jason indicated he was leaving.

Sal glanced at the night sky and opened his mouth, but closed it when Ryder gave a small shake of his head. Ryder was right. Sal had to trust Jason to know his limits. Didn't mean he had to like it.

"Have fun," Ryder said.

"Yup. You too." With a wave, Jason was out the door, Petey trailing behind him.

"What's your issue with him?" Ryder asked once the door had closed. He sank into the couch, but kept an eye on Elle who sniffed around the room.

"I told you before, his health is inconsistent. Want lemonade?"

"Fresh?"

"Is there any other acceptable kind?"

"Clearly not." Ryder scratched Elle's head after she completed her assessment of the space. "Oh, and please to the lemonade."

Sal raised his hand when Ryder started to get up. "I got it." He hustled into the kitchen and poured the yellow liquid into two glasses. Even knowing walking out of the room was merely a delay tactic did not limit his frustration when he came back and Ryder was poised to continue the discussion.

"Thanks. So, his health is inconsistent, I get that, but shouldn't he make the most of the good days?" Ryder studied him as he sipped his drink.

Sal held the glass to his lips several beats longer than necessary while he planned his response. "You aren't wrong," he conceded. "But if he has a seizure while he's driving, Petey isn't going to be able to do a damn thing for him."

"When was the last time he had a seizure?"

"Six months ago, as far as I know." *This is better than him asking me to explain my earlier crankiness,* Sal reminded himself. Though that may be coming too. He set his glass on the coffee table and faced Ryder. "I'm not pretending to be rational here, Ry. I lost that ability when I watched Nelly buck him off her back and then sat in the waiting room of the hospital while they operated on him for twelve hours." He rolled his shoulders back. "But I'm trying."

Ryder rested his hand on Sal's cheek. "I know you are. And I don't have a way to make it easier. Jay has always been tough. I can't imagine he takes well to babying, even when he needs it."

Sal relaxed against the warmth of Ryder's hand. "He doesn't, which is part of the problem. Forget babying, he pushes himself to crisis level before he ever asks for help."

Their gazes met. Ryder tugged him closer until Sal leaned his forehead against Ryder's. An adjusted angle would bring their lips together, which seemed like a far superior use of their mouths. "You can't distract me," Ryder whispered.

"Oh, can't I?" Sal assumed a challenge, slid his hand to the back of Ryder's head, and brushed his lips over Ryder's, who darted his tongue out and tightened his arms around Sal's neck.

"Not fair," Ryder breathed.

"Never promised fair." To prove his point, Sal broke the kiss to trail to his way to Ryder's earlobe.

"Jesus Christ, Sal!" The growl came from a place so deep within Ryder that Sal wondered if even he was still familiar with it. Ryder dug into Sal's back with the tips of his fingers.

One of the many reasons I'm happy to date men—less chance of long nails interfering with passion. Sal backed off and found the same fire in Ryder's eyes as was in his voice. "Why don't we take this upstairs?" Uncertainty flashed in his gaze. "We can still stop whenever you want," Sal reassured him. "But upstairs gives us more..."

"Everything," Ryder finished for him. He visibly swallowed. "Okay." He eyed Elle, who had curled up next to the unlit fireplace. "Let me set up her crate. We can move it upstairs with us later."

"She'll be all right. One of us will bring her up before we go to sleep." Sal climbed to his feet and extended his hand, which Ryder readily grasped. *Where's the hesitancy coming from? Should I offer to turn on a movie? Then again, having a movie playing hardly precludes other activities from happening.*

As he was about to ask, Ryder straightened his back and interlocked their fingers on the way up the stairs. "You're thinking too much," Ryder told him.

"Trying to figure you out." Sal kicked the door of his room partially closed, so they could hear if Elle started running around.

"Mm, how's that going for you?" A fire ignited in Ryder's gaze that Sal desperately wanted to stoke.

"I'd appreciate a little help." Sal took a step toward Ryder, silently cheering when he didn't back off. "What do you want, Ry? I'm getting mixed signals."

Remorse flicked across Ryder's features. "I'm not trying to lead you on. I just don't know. It's been so long," he said before Sal could address the emotion. "I can't pretend to be uncomplicated, though."

"You don't have to be." Sal eased him into an embrace. "I only need to know if you want me to stop or if there's something you're sure you aren't ready for."

Ryder scanned the room before looking back at Sal. "No sex. Not tonight."

"No problem. You lead." In an attempt to quell Ryder's uncertain expression, Sal captured his lips and allowed the kiss to heat naturally. He hadn't planned their activities. But God knew it wouldn't be worth it to pressure him into something he didn't want. What fun could that possibly be?

Breathless, Ryder put space between them. They held eye contact for a long moment, allowing silent emotions to pass through their gazes. "Is there anything *you* don't want?" Ryder asked.

Sal sucked in air, letting the fresh scents of the man in front of him mix with the earthy breeze from the open window. But at that moment, his vision, no, his world, focused on Ryder. "I'd rather not go bungee jumping tonight, but as long as it's limited to you and me in this room, I'm good."

"Oh, so I can push jumping off a cliff with a cord to later in the weekend?" Ryder's attempt at banter was counteracted by the desire in his eyes. With unsteady hands, he opened each snap of Sal's shirt. A movement of his shoulders had it dropping to the floor. The sudden cold erected his nipples against the tight fabric of his undershirt. Ryder took the opportunity to tweak them between his fingers.

Sal couldn't suppress the moan that the contact brought. "I wouldn't mind taking it off."

"No?" A smile played on Ryder's lips. "I wouldn't mind you taking it off either." He stepped back to give Sal enough room to remove his shirt.

Hands roamed as the kissing intensified. Ryder shuffled forward until the back of Sal's knees hit the bed. Taking that as an invitation, Sal fell to the mattress and pulled Ryder with him. Ryder disconnected their bodies only long enough to allow Sal to scoot up toward the pillows. Sal barely had time to get comfortable before Ryder trailed his lips down his neck to his navel and back up again. They matched their heavy, disjointed breathing.

Sal grabbed the sides of Ryder's face and tugged him for their lips to meet again. His pants tightened, but he was able to ignore it until Ryder thrust his hips to the beat of their dancing tongues.

"Fuck!" Sal cried out as the building tension created a warm, sticky sensation in his pants. *Did I really just orgasm without anyone touching my cock? How...?* "Goddamn," he whispered. He couldn't decide if he should be embarrassed or just impressed with Ryder's kissing skills. When his heart rate settled, he tilted Ryder's chin up and brushed his lips. "Can I help you out?"

"Thanks, but that was satisfying enough for me." Ryder drew lazy circles on Sal's lower abs.

And it more than likely *would* involve touching. As much as he wanted to bring Ryder pleasure, he was not going to push. Besides, the relaxation apparent on Ryder's features suggested he had been sated. "Let me clean up."

After shifting off his chest, Ryder swung his legs off the bed and grabbed his shirt. Before Sal could object, Ryder said, "I'll go let Elle outside. Then bring her up here."

"Would you...?" Sal let his voice fade as he thought better of the request.

"Check to see if Jason's around?" Ryder smiled. "Sure."

Sal removed the rest of his clothes and grabbed a washcloth for a quick clean but turned on the shower instead. Thorough trumped quick.

Chapter Fourteen

RYDER HURRIED DOWN the steps to find Elle dancing at the bottom. "Thank you for waiting, Miss Elle. You're such a good girl." He scratched her head on the way to the back door. No Petey, so probably no Jason. Ryder found the light switch as easily as he would in his own house, which would have made sense a decade ago, but... *Muscle memory is an odd thing*. "Okay, go pee," he told Elle as he stepped outside with her. The crops were blocked off so he didn't have to worry about where she went, yet he still kept one eye on her as he withdrew his phone. A message from an unknown number. "Fuck," he muttered, debating if he should check it.

Call tomorrow to reschedule.

Fuck you! he wanted to yell, but he wouldn't. The intended party couldn't hear and didn't care. They knew he'd do it. Everyone who had business with them fell in line. The consequences of not doing so were unstated, but ominous.

Elle barked at a figure moving across the property. "Elle, here, girl." Ryder added a whistle to get her attention. When she stayed frozen, Ryder advanced toward her and grabbed her collar. Still, she growled. "No." The figure had stopped moving. "Hello?" Ryder called.

"Does she bite?" Sal's grandfather's voice was barely audible across the distance, but it lowered Ryder's heart rate all the same.

"No, she's a puppy. I've got her." He considered asking Antonio to come into the light so Elle would settle down, but that somehow felt wrong. Instead, Ryder half dragged her to the back stoop. "Sit."

Antonio completed the journey across the land. Sure enough, when he reached the spotlight, Elle's tail started wagging. "She's a tiny thing."

"Yup, only a couple of months old. How are you, sir?"

The older man shrugged. "Still here. All I can ask for at my age. How about you? How'd your trip into town go today?"

Ryder inclined his head. Had Antonio been in town, or was Ryder's every move subject to the town gossip mill? "Fine. I had fries at Mac's. Nice place."

Antonio started to say something, but before he could, Petey exploded from the kitchen door. Ryder made Elle stand still for a minute, then released her to frolic with the pit bull.

"Hi, Pops, everything okay?" Jason asked. Ryder did a—hopefully discreet—double take when he noticed Jason sitting in his wheelchair.

"Your grams is out of vanilla, and she can't go to bed until she finishes her cake." The affection Antonio held for his wife shone through the mock exasperation. "So I thought I would ask if you boys had any before going to the grocery store."

"I think so. Come on in." Jason opened the door wider and regarded Ryder. "Let the dogs run out their energy. They'll be fine."

Ryder hesitated but walked into the house. He'd need to wait downstairs for Elle. *Oh, well, Sal will have to come fetch me if I'm not up by the time he's done with his shower.* He worked the inside of his cheeks to suppress the smile threatening to curve his lips at the thought of why Sal needed that shower. He blinked at the hand waving in front of his face. "Did you say something, Jay?"

"Man, what world are you in?"

"The one in my head. I don't recommend you visiting."

Jason half laughed, half scoffed. "Might not be safe. Anyway, the vanilla is on the top shelf. Would you please grab it for me?"

"Course." Ryder reached above his head and passed it down to Jason, who handed it to Antonio.

"Thanks, boys." Antonio glanced around the room. "Where's Sal?"

"I'm here." Sal meandered down the steps while pulling on a white shirt.

Wonder if he realizes how translucent it is. Wonder if he cares... After taking stock of the room, Ryder decided that it was unlikely Sal did.

"Are you getting ready for bed already?" Antonio asked.

"Isn't that the most responsible thing to do when you have to be up at dawn? Or did you think the farm was going to run itself?" Sal kept his tone light, teasing.

Antonio pretended to be put out. He gestured to Jason. "One sarcastic brother per family, please." He looked at the dogs outside, then back to the occupants of the room, though his gaze focused on Ryder. "Have fun, boys. Be careful."

Shit. Shit! What does he know? Nothing. He couldn't, right? Right. I'm paranoid. Ryder worked to keep his features neutral, despite the battle in his brain. The three of them wished him a good night, and Jason followed him out.

"Has he been in his chair since he got home?" Sal asked, stepping close enough that if Ryder leaned back an inch his back would be against Sal's hard chest.

"Uh, since I saw him couple minutes ago. I don't think he was here when I first came down, or at least he wasn't out in the common areas." *Why aren't you touching me?* Ryder asked silently. *Maybe he's worried his grandfather will return or he doesn't want Jason to see—*

Sal interrupted the thought by pulling Ryder to him. "It must be exhausting to think so hard all the time." He brushed their lips together.

Ryder let a moan escape. "You have no idea."

"Guys? Really?" Jason shut and locked the door behind himself and the dogs. "You've a room right upstairs."

"Waiting on you," Sal said.

Jason raised an eyebrow. "I have nothing to do with what goes on in that room."

Ryder laughed. "You two never change." He disentangled himself from Sal and ignored his pout to gather the supplies Elle would need for the night.

"How was Ted's?" Sal asked. "You didn't stay too long."

"Oh, my God. It's a fucking madhouse. I'm convinced he's intent on maintaining his frat boy image until he retires." Jason moved deftly around the kitchen, straightening things that had become disheveled throughout the day.

"Oh." Sal shifted from one bare foot to the other. "I thought you were going to be alone."

"You and me both. He's trying to get me to be more social." The eye roll was plain in Jason's words.

A few beats passed. Then Sal said, "Wouldn't be the worst thing in the world."

"Would you want to be ambushed by a party?"

"Would you have gone if he'd told you?" Ryder asked, still pressed against Sal.

Jason refilled the dogs' water, angling his body so he wasn't looking at them. "Not to that. Maybe if it was one or two other people, I would be more open to it."

"Why not tell him that?" Sal kept his voice light, as though he couldn't care one way or another how Jason handled it, but Ryder knew nothing could be further from the truth.

"Mm. Maybe." Jason grabbed a water and wheeled toward the kitchen doorway. When Petey saw the direction he was going, he finished licking Elle and trotted to him. "Oh, Ryder, your new hot neighbor was there."

"Luke?" Sal asked.

"You know him?"

Sal swallowed. "You could say that. How does Ted?"

Jason unscrewed the cap of the bottle and took a drink. "I didn't ask. He introduced me to Luke as 'the guy who bought the place next to the Christensens.' By that point, people were loud and bumping into each other, so I hightailed it out." He patted his lap pocket for his phone, then inserted the water bottle into his chair's cup holder. "Night, guys."

They wished him good night and watched as he wheeled into his room. "For the record," Ryder started, "I don't think he's that hot."

"No?"

"Nah." Ryder leaned up and kissed him. "I like my men darker."

The smile painting Sal's face melted Ryder's heart. "Good to know." A glance at the clock made them both cringe. "Let's go to bed. Five a.m. comes mighty fast."

"Yeah. Come on, Elle. Bedtime." Ryder grabbed the crate, and she led them upstairs. Feeling his bones creak as he set it up, Ryder muttered, "God, we're old."

"Can't argue that." Sal pulled the sheet down. "There's an extra toothbrush in the bathroom if you need it."

He dug out his toiletry bag and held it up. "Thanks, but I got it. I'll be right back." He padded to the bathroom where he changed into his pajama bottoms and spent too long debating a shirt. *After the make-out session we just had, I don't see how modesty is necessary.* The skin-to-skin contact was amazing. It might even center him enough so he got a few solid hours of shut-eye. *It's all about you, isn't it?* the devil in his brain sneered. *What if sleeping half naked makes Sal uncomfortable? He's too nice to tell you.* Ryder swallowed, tugged the shirt on, and finished using the bathroom.

When he came back to the bedroom, Sal was sitting bare chested with the blankets pooling on his lap. "What's with all those clothes? Planning on running away?"

"And where would I run? You employ me." Ryder took his shirt off again, feeling a sense of triumph over his brain devil.

Sal's features grew serious. "One has nothing to do with the other. You know that, right?"

Ryder checked that Elle had settled in her crate, then lay facing Sal. "They have a little to do with each other." Before Sal could react, Ryder pressed a finger to the man's lips. "Not like one is dependent on the other, but they are connected."

He seemed to contemplate this. "You would've had a job regardless of what happened tonight."

"Never doubted that for a minute." Ryder kissed him but pulled back when he felt Sal's hesitancy. "What's wrong?"

"I feel like I should tell you something." His chocolate-brown eyes bore into Ryder as though digging for a response.

"Okay?" Suddenly Ryder felt exposed, vulnerable, which didn't make sense since Sal was the one confessing, if it could be called that.

"I went to see Luke before I picked you up."

"But...you don't like Luke."

"No, though I'm willing to cut him a bit of slack after talking to him." Sal scooted down and mimicked Ryder's position of leaning on his elbow. "At dinner, my grandfather told me that he saw you driving with Luke, and I kind of lost my head."

Ryder snapped his eyes shut. Such a myriad of emotions raced through him that he didn't know where to start. Anger? Betrayal? Concern? "You didn't hit him, did you?"

"Ryder, look at me." Sal waited until he opened his eyes. "How many times have you seen me hit someone?"

"Twice."

"And both of those times I was standing up against bullying, right?"

Clear as day, the memories tumbled through Ryder's mind. In sixth grade, Sal, already the size of a high schooler, defended one of the girls a couple of jocks had cornered. Then in college, he beat the crap out of a guy who was kicking a puppy. That one tried to press charges, but dropped them when the cops told him they'd charge him with animal abuse. Luckily, that dog found a great home. If only there was a way to stop assholes like that from ever getting animals again. Ryder blinked his thoughts back to the present. "Right. Yeah. Just...seemed to fit the narrative."

Sal had the decency to look embarrassed. He reached out and ghosted across Ryder's cheek with his fingertips. "It's not what you think."

"No? I'm all ears." Ryder couldn't decide if his irritation should make him unaffected by the touch, but regardless, he was. *So, I should ask him to stop. Keep my head clear*. But that was the very thing he wanted.

"I don't want his lifestyle endangering you or the town."

"You mean the drugs?"

"That comes with a lot of baggage, Ry. And I never knew how deep into it he was."

Several beats of silence passed between them. Ryder wanted to tell Sal that he could take care of himself, but he no longer knew how true that was. *Doesn't matter. Sal has to believe it, or we'll never have an equal relationship*. But first, Ryder had to ask, "What did he say?"

"That I didn't understand. It was never what I thought." Sal flipped onto his back and blew out a breath. "I kind of believe him. How stupid is that?"

"Maybe it's smart. Paranoia doesn't help anyone." Ryder nudged Sal's face so they were looking at each other again. "I appreciate the spirit of what you're trying to do, but you have to trust me, including to be able to take care of myself."

Sal grasped Ryder's wrist and kissed his palm. "I'm sorry. I..." He shook his head. "There's no excuse. You're right." He leaned over for a kiss. "Let's get to sleep."

THE WEEK FLEW by for Ryder. The work came easier than he dared to hope for. Ryder was not as natural at giving lessons as other tasks he performed, but he was learning. The best part about those were having the opportunity to shadow Sal, thoughts of whom painted a smile on Ryder's face.

"What are you so happy about?" Sal asked, coming up next to him with Elle jumping alongside.

"Payday," Ryder answered automatically. Because what the hell else was he going to say? He tossed a stick for Elle to run after.

"Ah yes, the first payday after a stretch of unemployment."

He stopped to scrutinize Sal. "When would you have experienced that relief?"

Sal squinted. "You're right. I can't remember a time I wasn't working once I was physically able to do so."

Child labor laws were different for the farming community, and actors, Ryder had learned. CPS would have had a lot more work if they took every farmer's kid under sixteen who worked more than twenty hours a week. Not a practical expectation. Ryder felt Sal's stare boring into the side of his head opposite the sun, and he honestly couldn't say which was more intense. "Did you say something?"

"Are you coming to the pub tonight?"

Ryder tipped his sports bottle back and let the now warm water wet his throat. He made a face and set the bottle at his feet.

This time, Sal threw the stick for Elle. "Come on. What else are you going to do?

Ryder coughed. "You know that sounds good. Pub, I mean." He tugged on the stick Elle had brought back, but stopped when she growled. "Ask nice." He waited for quiet and tossed it in the other direction. "Want me to be the designated driver?"

"You don't want to drink?"

"Nah, I'd rather not risk running my mouth around Cat." Not to mention the possibility of trading one addiction for another. Ryder hadn't gone to rehab, but he spent a lot of time searching online for information about beating the habit and attended a few Gamblers Anonymous meetings in town and online.

"Wouldn't want that." Sal fixed his hat to better shade his eyes. "Pick me up at 7:30?"

"You got it." Ryder called Elle; then he and Sal walked in different directions.

Ryder brought Elle into his parents' house and found his dad at the kitchen table. "Hey, Dad. Where's Ma?" he asked as he removed his heavy boots.

"She's doing a house call. The McGregors's old dog is on the decline." His dad set down his paper. "What are you up to tonight?"

"Friday night pub," Ryder answered. "What about you?"

"That depends on how your mom feels when she gets home. If she isn't too down, we might try the new pizza place."

People think that vets get used to dealing with animals in all states of wellness, but the end is hard for everyone, especially for patients like Sparky, who she helped from a puppy. "That'll be a nice diversion."

"Mm." Victor studied Ryder. "How did Elle do on her first sleepover?

Subtle, Dad. "She was fine. Seems to like her portable crate." He glanced at the clock. "I'm going to take a shower. Hate to permanently ingrain this stink on me." Ryder didn't wait for his father to respond before going upstairs. *Really, though, what's he going to say? No, you can't shower?* Once he got to his room and shut the door, he extracted his cell from his pocket and stared at the screen. The message from last night was just beyond the lock screen. *I have to do it. It's the only way I can stop looking over my shoulder.*

With that thought, Ryder hit the speed dial button. One ring. Two rings. Three rings. *Beep.* "It's Cowboy. How about we try to meet in Asheville this time? I'm off Sunday this week and Saturday next. Let me know." He hung up. Technically, he was off Tuesday, as well, but he and Sal had a day date planned, and he didn't want to fuck that up by needing to work around meetings with goons.

"Ryder!" Dad called.

"What?" As Ryder answered, Elle darted into the room, almost knocking him over in the process.

"Didn't you hear her crying by your door?"

"No. Sorry."

"Apologize to her, not me. You didn't make me cry," he mumbled while walking away.

Ryder chuckled. "Sorry, girl." He bent to pet her but got a whiff of his own scent. "Wow, gotta fix that, hon." He shed his clothes and shucked them into the laundry basket. It crossed his mind to put her in her crate while he showered, but she had just been out and surely wouldn't make a mess in the timespan of a shower. *I hope.* Still, he kept it short.

By the time he came out, a message from Cat had appeared on his screen.

I might be late. Can you grab our usual table if you get there first?

Could I find the usual table without seeing the group? Why would she message me that request? He vaguely remembered the booth being toward the back, but more than that... Ryder towel-dried his hair and called Sal.

"Miss me already?" Sal answered the phone on the second ring.

"Yes, always. Cat sent me a weird text message."

"That she's going to be late? Yeah, she sent it to all of us."

"Oh. That makes more sense."

"Sort of. No one is going to take that table on Friday night."

"Not even the rival trivia team?"

Sal half snorted. "They wouldn't dare. And if someone was ballsy enough to try, there'd be enough people there to put them in their place. Nobody messes with Cat."

"Damn, Tryon's own mafia boss." Ryder rooted through his drawers until he found his underwear and socks. His shirt and jeans came from his closet, for Friday nights, anyway.

"What are you doing for dinner?" Sal asked.

Ryder balanced the phone between his shoulder and his ear as he struggled to dress, then remembered the speaker-phone option. "Can you hear me?" he asked after he set it on his bed.

"Am I on speaker?"

"Yeah, don't talk dirty."

"I'll try to restrain myself. Dinner?"

"Right." Ryder replayed the conversation with his father in his mind. "I'm not doing anything. My dad wants to take my mom out, but only if she feels up to it." He offered a truncated explanation, then added, "So, if they're out tonight, I have to stop back here before we go into town since Elle can't be on her own for that long." The other dogs were okay to be alone for longer because they could go out through the doggie door; plus, they were kept in the kitchen, so accidents weren't major problems.

"Whatever. Bring her with you and we'll drop her off. Unless...you want Jason to watch her."

Then I wouldn't need to come back here tonight was more than likely the rest of his thought. The idea did have merit. It was certainly easier to be at the job site when he woke up, but did he want to make a habit of that so soon into their relationship? What would the next steps look like if he did?

"Ry? You there?"

"Yeah, uh, I'm here. I wouldn't want to impose on Jason if he's going to Ted's or something."

Sal quieted. "It's up to you, but he doesn't mind, and I believe Ted's coming here."

"That...doesn't make him any less busy." Ryder paused to consider. "I'll talk to him at dinner and decide based on that."

"Cool. Dinner will be ready in about forty-five."

"We'll be there." He ended the call and grinned at Elle, who was watching him with her head tilted to the side. "No, baby girl, I have no idea what I'm doing. Been a long time since I've had a relationship." Though it did help that his last relationship was with the same man as the current one. Sort of. Then again, that might be making them more comfortable than they should be at this stage. *Speak for yourself*, the devil in his head protested. *You don't know what he's thinking or how he feels.*

But why would he want me to sleep over two nights in a week if he wasn't enjoying our budding relationship? Ryder shook the thoughts loose and changed out the dirty clothes in his duffel for clean ones. *If I'm going to make a habit of this, it might be worth talking to Sal about leaving a couple of items there. No. Way, way too soon.* "Come on, girl. Let's go see Sal and Petey."

As soon as Ryder opened the door, Elle bolted down the steps. "Whoa! Hi, Elle," Ma said.

Ryder descended the stairs. "Hey, Ma." He kissed her cheek. "How's Sparky?"

"Old." She sighed. "I hope they're willing to let him go before he's in too much pain."

"Is he okay now?"

"Aside from his arthritis, he seems to be. We'll see if it gets better." Ma eyed his bag. "Staying over again?"

"Maybe." Ryder offered what he hoped was a noncommittal shrug. "Easier than coming back less than eight hours after I get home."

"Hmm, easy isn't always better."

He opened his mouth to reply, but his father appeared in the kitchen doorway. "Loraine, leave the boy alone. He's almost thirty."

"That doesn't mean I want to see him get hurt."

"Ack." Victor flapped his hand. "You should know Salvatore better than that. He wouldn't hurt Ryder."

"Maybe not on purpose, but—"

"Hey! I'm right here." He waited until both his parents looked at him. "We're getting to know each other again."

"That takes time, dear."

"We know. I promise not to stop by the county clerk's office while we're in town." He kissed his mom's cheek again. "Now, I have to go or else I'll be late for dinner." On his way out, Ryder mouthed *thanks* to his dad, who offered a short nod. Since his parents might go out, he headed for the truck.

Chapter Fifteen

"COULD YOU LOOK more eager?" Jason asked, startling Sal, who had been staring out the window.

Sal scowled. "I don't want to put the rice in until he gets here."

"And the thirty seconds it takes him to get out of the car to come to the door will make a huge difference in cooking time?"

Tearing his gaze away from the picture window, he swept it over his brother. "You look awfully dressed up to watch superhero movies."

"Not all of us want to spend our time in sweats, even when we're at home."

Especially when you want to impress someone without looking like you're trying. But if that was the goal, Sal couldn't fault Jason's choice of nice jeans, a loose black tee, and new or at least clean Converse. "I don't mean to rag on you. I'm happy to see you putting in an effort again."

A light flush crept into Jason's cheeks. "Just tired of the same old."

"I'm proud of you." Sal would have liked to have seen Ted, but for some reason, Jason had been working to keep them separate. *Now, let's be a little more melodramatic, why don't we? It's a coincidence.*

Jason didn't get a chance to reply because Ryder's truck pulled onto their gravel driveway, making Sal glad he'd stepped away from the window. Though he'd never admit it to his brother, Jason was right. Waiting that diligently couldn't come across as anything except desperate. *Not that opening the door as soon as he knocks is any better...* Regardless of the optics, that's what Sal did. The smile on Ryder's face made Sal's heart jump. "Hey," they said at the same time.

Elle yipped, pulling them out of their admittedly dopey-looking spell. "Hi, girl. Come on in." He opened the door farther.

"Thanks. Sorry we're late."

Sal checked the time. "You aren't." He gestured toward the kitchen, indicating for Ryder to follow, which he, Jason, and the dogs did.

"Oh, okay, good." Ryder turned his attention to Jason as they walked. "What's going on?"

"You mean since I last saw you three hours ago? Not much. May have found the cure for cancer, but Sal claimed it was just moldy cheese and made me throw it out."

"So unreasonable."

"I know. You'd think he'd want to be millionaires."

Ryder properly greeted Petey in the kitchen and glanced at Sal. "Can I do anything?"

Sal confirmed the uncooked rice was situated correctly in the microwave. "Nope. We're good." The table had been set, and the chicken was warming. He took a deep breath to calm his nerves.

After they finished eating, Ryder insisted on helping to clean up. "Are you sure you don't mind if I leave her with you, Jay?" Ryder asked.

"Nah, as long as you don't mind if she goes into the crate if I know I'll be distracted."

"She'll be fine with that. She would have spent more time in the crate at home, I'm sure." Ryder thanked him and left with Sal.

"You won't feel bad for not saying goodbye and need to rush home halfway there, will you?" Sal teased as they got in the car.

"No, jerk. If I say goodbye, she gets anxious and is more likely to whine after I leave."

When they passed by Luke's house, Sal noted as he cleaned his glasses, "Luke's car's gone." He paused in his cleaning. "Did I tell you I invited him to join us tonight?"

Ryder's eyebrows shot up. "No. That slipped your mind when we were discussing him last night. Why?"

"Because he kept talking about wanting to meet people and the group is big enough that he might find friends."

"At which point, he wouldn't need to hang out with me?" Ryder kept his tone neutral, but Sal heard the accusation for what it was.

"That hadn't occurred to me." At Ryder's dubious expression, Sal emphasized, "Seriously." *Though now that you mention it, that wouldn't be a drawback.* "He sounded like he needed to be immersed with locals. If for no other reason than to learn the realities of farm life."

"Ugh, yes." Ryder scrubbed his hand across his forehead. "Damn city boy is going to find himself in way over his head."

"I told him that much, and I believe I suggested he talk to the breeders of the animals he wants to keep."

"Well, at least we know that no one around here will sell him livestock if he doesn't know what he's doing." Ryder quieted, then asked, "If he doesn't know anyone, how did he get invited to Ted's party?"

Sal put his glasses back on his face. "I don't know. Was Cat there?"

Ryder rubbed his chin. "Possibly. If I remember correctly, Owen and Ted were friends. So maybe she found out about the party and told him when she dropped off the welcome basket? Possibly?"

"Your guess is as good as mine." He pointed to a sign on the road. "Exit's coming up."

"Is it really? Is it in the same place it's been for the last twenty-eight years?" Ryder widened his eyes in what could only be mock surprise.

"I'm only trying to help! You haven't lived here in a while." Sal blew out a breath.

"I should drive past it just to make a point," Ryder muttered, but didn't. A few minutes later, he pulled into the pub lot. "Um, we weren't together last week."

"No?" Sal thought back. They probably wouldn't have considered themselves officially in a relationship until last Sunday. "Huh."

"How do you want to handle it?"

"What do you mean?"

Ryder cut the engine and faced him. "Do you want to tell people?"

Sal licked his lips in thought. "I don't think we need to make an announcement, but I wouldn't deny it. If someone starts flirting with you, I'd like you to be comfortable with me shutting that shit down."

"That's rather possessive of you, don't you think?" Ryder said, his tone unreadable.

A sense of confusion mixed with a touch of dread roiled in Sal's gut. "And you would be okay with the reverse?"

"Didn't say that. But you never expressed interest in being exclusive."

Sal stared at him. "You're joking, right?" *No*, he realized, *he's serious*. "Why would you think otherwise?" It was ludicrous. Unless Ryder had developed an affinity for dating more than one person...

"Just...didn't know if you wanted to keep your options open."

There it was. The insecurity in Ryder's voice rang louder than it had in weeks. Guilt washed through Sal for thinking the worst. He leaned over and kissed Ryder, then held his cheek. "Babe, I haven't wanted to be with another person for years. Even when I was mad at you and didn't understand what had happened. Even when I tried to be with other men, none of them did it for me like you."

Ryder pressed his lips to Sal's palm. "I'll try my best to live up to that devotion."

"You don't have to try. That's who you are. Who we are." Sal wished he could shake the resignation in Ryder's features, but he didn't know how. Time was the only way.

With one more kiss, Ryder reached for the door handle. "We better get in there. Don't want someone else to take the table."

"Ha! I'd actually enjoy that. It's the kind of drama I welcome." And there would be drama. They climbed out of the truck and walked to the pub door. "Hold on." Sal moved Ryder to the side while his transition lenses adjusted to the different lighting.

"Fuck, that guy needs to give it a rest," Ryder muttered.

"Who?" Sal followed Ryder's gaze to a blond guy who was chatting up a very uncomfortable-looking Luke. "Who is that?"

"The wanker I told you about. He apparently corners all the new men in town." Ryder lowered his voice and added, "He hit on me the first night I came. In the bathroom."

As he'd reminded Ryder earlier, Sal was not a man prone to violence, but he took the safety of his friends seriously. Not that Luke was a friend, but the idiot had messed with Ryder once, who was to say he wouldn't again? "Are you afraid of him?"

"Afraid? No. I'd like to avoid being alone with him."

A humorless laugh pushed its way past the lump of anger in Sal's throat. "That's not a concern for you. Let's try to rescue him." A small part of Sal questioned if perhaps Luke didn't want to be saved. That maybe the advances were welcome. But nothing about the other man's body language indicated that. Sal and Ryder weaved through the crowd to the bar where the pair sat.

As they came closer, another guy blocked Sal's path. "I suggest you go to your usual table and wait for your group."

What is this guy, a bodyguard? He's taking the wingman role way too far. "One of them is chatting with your friend over there."

"Then let them chat. Still a free country." Bodyguard stared over Sal's shoulder at Ryder, a hunger in his eyes.

"Hey." Sal's voice darkened. "I'm talking to you."

"Yeah, well, he's prettier."

He's trying to get me to react. I don't know how he knows about Ryder and me, but I won't give him the satisfaction. "Move. Now."

Bodyguard stepped into Sal's personal space. "Who's going to make me?"

"C, what the hell are you doing?" Wanker spun around on his barstool and addressed Bodyguard.

He glanced back. "Explaining to the cowboy here why he should stay out of business that isn't his."

"We aren't looking for looking for trouble," Ryder interjected. "Luke, our table is the one in the corner there."

Obvious relief washed over Luke's face as he stood up. "Nice to meet you, Beck."

"You too. Think about what I said."

"Oh, I will." The crowd parted enough for the three of them to get through to their table. They were the first ones there. "Thanks," Luke said to Sal and Ryder as they sat around the curved booth.

"That guy is an asshole," Ryder told him.

"Mm, yeah, he needs to find himself a gay bar."

The conversation was interrupted by the waitress bringing them a pitcher of water and enough glasses for the usual group. She promised to return once more people showed. When she'd left, Sal poured water and passed the cups around. "Good luck with that here. The safe space stickers are as good as it gets." Sal paused to look him over. "Speaking of, how did he know you were gay—or you?" He directed the end of the question to Ryder. Neither Luke nor Ryder were flamboyant or obvious.

"I never made it much of a secret." Ryder shrugged.

"But he's not a local."

"Gotta know someone around here." Ryder paused for a drink. "Like you said, this isn't exactly party central, so he wouldn't travel here for the scene."

"Still doesn't explain Luke."

Luke refilled his glass. "Cat knows." When he saw their raised eyebrows, Luke explained, "She was at the party last night. I turned down a woman. It got back to Cat, she asked me why, I told her..." He turned both hands palm up in an "I don't know" gesture. "Also, does anything *not* get back to Cat?"

"Not much, if I have anything to say about it." Cat walked up to the table with Owen in tow. Greetings were exchanged all around.

An hour later, their full group had assembled. Luke seemed to have moved past the encounter with Beck. *What kind of a name is that anyway?* "You aren't drinking much," Sal whispered to Ryder.

"I'm the DD, remember?" Ryder answered. Before Sal could remind him that soda had little chance of impairment, he added, "And I'd like to avoid the bathroom if possible."

Fresh annoyance at the jerk flared in Sal, but he tempered it down. "I could go with you."

"Yeah, that won't look suspicious at all." Ryder squeezed Sal's thigh under the table. "I appreciate the offer, but we don't want to draw attention to ourselves. I'm okay."

You shouldn't have to hold it because some asshole wants to fuck everything that moves, Sal wanted to scream. But he settled for a nod. Ryder was a big boy and could decide his bathroom habits for himself.

"Any chance of another deployment, Owen?" Sal asked.

"Always a chance. Though it would have to be a short one. Unless—"

"Unless *nothing*." Cat's voice was harder than anyone at the table was used to. They all stared at her, but she paid them no mind. "You're out at the end of the year."

"My contracted service is up. I told you some of sailors in other platoons have been stop-lossed."

"I don't understand how they can keep you past your agreed-upon service date."

"Because...they're the United States military, babe. They just can." Owen's effort to be patient was evident in his strained features, indicating that this was not the first time they'd had this conversation. She sucked her perfectly painted lips between her teeth.

Sal caught Owen's eye and mouthed *sorry*. Owen waved him off with a small smile.

The server brought a new microbrew pitcher and filled glasses around the table. "You driving?" Sal asked Luke.

"This is only my second." Luke nudged him.

"Besides, officer, he didn't even finish his first one," Lilly said.

"I'm just asking." Sal huffed out a breath, pretending to be exasperated. He had to admit, once he relaxed, the evening was enjoyable.

"Are you itching to leave?" Ryder asked.

"Not unless you are."

"Soon." Ryder watched Beck and his enforcer walk out the front door. "I am going to use the bathroom."

Luke and Sal emptied out of the booth to let him through. Once seated again, Cat reached over and smacked Sal's arm. Not hard enough to hurt, but still unnecessary. "What the hell?"

"When did you start dating Ryder?"

"This week sometime."

"You don't know your anniversary?" Lilly asked.

Sal rolled his eyes. "I don't think dating anniversaries count past high school graduation."

"What happened?" Cat demanded as though Lilly hadn't spoken. "You were friendly last week, but now you can hardly keep your hands off each other. Next, you'll be walking down the aisle in secret! We'll have to find out by looking at your wedding bands."

There's a leap if I've ever heard one. But pointing such things out to Cat was useless, so instead Sal said, "Unless we already did. Maybe we decided not to wear rings. Wouldn't want them to get damaged at work." In answer to her gasp, Sal took a swig of beer while staring at the table to hide his grin.

"You're a jerk."

"And you're a drama queen. Now that we've stated the obvious..." He set his glass on the tabletop and leveled his gaze with hers. "We're feeling each other out after a long time and a lot of misunderstandings. I'll let you know if it becomes more than that." *Maybe.* Sal was used to her feeling as though she was entitled to every detail about everyone around her, but this time, it rubbed him the wrong way. Owen adeptly changed the subject to the newest superhero movie.

By the time Ryder came back a few minutes later, Sal's irritation had reached a point beyond what beer could soothe. He scooted out of the booth before Ryder got to the table.

"You leaving already?" Owen asked.

"I just remembered we have a buyer coming early tomorrow," Sal answered. "We'll see you all next week." He waited while Ryder said his goodbyes, then the two of them made their way through the crowd and out the door. When the door shut, Sal turned to Ryder. "Sorry, I—"

"Sal! Ryder! Hold up," Luke called, jogging up behind them.

Ryder stepped off to the side of the parking lot, and Sal followed.

"Thanks for intercepting that asshole's advances. "

"Don't mention it." Sal offered a slight smile, not realizing until that moment how tired he was. *I'm getting old.* "Assholes like that need to be shut down before they spread whatever disease made them the way they are."

"Heh, yeah, I have a feeling there's more than one with that guy." Luke opened and closed his mouth several times before asking, "Do you know Jason's friends?"

It took a second for the question to puncture through the growing haze in Sal's brain. *Thank God I'm not driving.* "Sort of? I knew them years ago, but Jason has been largely out of the social scene for a while. Why?"

Again, Luke hesitated. "It's just that he oughta be careful with those parties."

"How'd you wind up there?" Ryder asked.

The question seemed to throw Luke for a beat. "Owen recognized me as the new guy Cat talked about at the grocery store, and he invited me to stop by and meet people." He paused, before adding, "Everyone's been super nice here, don't get me wrong, but people were engaging in...less-than-legal activities. I'd hate for your brother to get in trouble should they ever be found out."

"Thanks for the heads-up. I appreciate it." And he did. Luke was making it very difficult for Sal to hate him properly.

"No problem. No matter how old they get, you always want to protect younger brothers, or cousins, in my case."

"Yeah," Sal agreed. "Are you okay to drive home?"

"I am." Luke let out a laugh and walked a straight line. They all said good night and then went to their respective cars.

Ryder started the engine and turned to Sal while they waited for it to warm up. "She grill you as soon as I was out of earshot?"

"Pretty much."

"Figured that's why you were in such a hurry to leave." He put the car in gear and backed out. "Will you say anything to Jason?"

"Maybe. I am glad that he didn't stay long."

"So maybe whatever it was, he self-selected out."

Yes, that's the most reasonable explanation. Sal squeezed Ryder's thigh and leaned back to rest his eyes for the drive home.

Chapter Sixteen

"ONLY ONE MORE shoe change before you're done for the rest of your pregnancy. You're going to have such a pretty foal." Ryder spoke softly to Star as he lifted her foot. He waited for her to shift her considerable weight onto her other legs and then went about breaking the nails in her shoes. Yesterday, Sal had refreshed his memory on how to do this without hurting the horses. It amazed Ryder how quickly he remembered things.

As he cleaned the now bare hoof, a peculiar smell wafted into the stall. Vaguely familiar and yet...not one he'd expect to find in a stable. Once he ensured her hoof was clean, Ryder patted Star. "I'll be right back, girl." He checked the other horses, who were either lying down or eating, and none of their stalls had anything that would produce the odor. *But what is it? I know I've...* His brain shut down when he saw Jason leaning against the side of the stable, smoking a blunt. Ryder reached back and slammed the gate.

Jason almost dropped his blunt. "Shit, Ry. You nearly gave me a heart attack." He held the still smoking joint at his side. "Is Sal with you?"

Ryder glanced behind him to confirm that Sal had not followed. "No. Would it be a problem if he was?"

"Have you met my brother?" As the smoke ballooned from Jason's lips on an exhale, Ryder wondered how he could have mistaken the smell earlier. "He's too straitlaced to not give me massive amounts of shit."

"He'd be looking out for you, Jay." Ryder ground his lips between his teeth. "Sal doesn't want you to get hurt or in trouble."

The anger that flashed across Jason's features almost had Ryder taking a step back. "This is one of the only things that makes me hurt less." When the butt was down to a nub, Jason smeared the tip onto the stone walls of the stable.

"I get that, but—"

"No. I highly doubt you do. This morning, I woke up, mucked out a couple of stalls, exercised Nelly, and did a walk around to check on other horses for obvious problems. Know what I did Friday when I ran out of this? I slept way too late, then sat my ass in a chair and did math." The fire out, Jason wrapped the blunt in a tissue from his pocket, inserted it in a baggie, and stuffed the baggie in his jacket. "Those are my two options. I'll take today's morning, thank you very much."

North Carolina law still prohibited the sale, distribution, and possession of marijuana, though the government had decriminalized it. "I haven't lived here in a while, so I can't say for sure how things are anymore."

"I can. Depends on the time of month, the cop who catches you, what you're doing at the time—all the very relevant public safety factors." Jason whistled, and Petey came running from the other side of the stable. With an affectionate hand on Petey's head, Jason met Ryder's gaze. "Please don't tell him. He'll find out soon enough, I'm sure, but I'd prefer to hold off on the lecture as long as I can."

"It's not my business," Ryder said. "But you don't know what's in those plants if you're buying them off the street."

The anger faded to sadness. "Well, if you can think of a better way, I'm open." Jason let the silence hang in the air for several beats and nodded. "That's what I thought. I have to go change."

Ryder watched him walk over the hills toward the house until he couldn't make out more than the top of his head, then he went back to shoeing Star.

Chapter Seventeen

THE NEXT DAY after work, Ryder came back to his parents' house—he didn't feel as though he spent enough time there to call it home—much to both his and Sal's reluctance. Though he would have preferred to stay, he had chores to do on Sunday. Clean clothes kept clients happy. As he stripped off his shirt for bed that night, his cell dinged with a text alert. His stomach lurched at the restricted number on the screen.

Asheville Brewing Company 12 p.m. Look for the red scarf.

Goddamn red scarf again.
A minute later, another message came through.

Come alone.

What's the alternative, bringing my posse to get you to leave me alone? Much as he wanted to send that, Ryder stuck with responding, *K.*

He tossed the phone on his bed and flopped next to it. Then he made the mistake of glancing at Elle through the bars of her crate. "Don't give me that look, baby girl. Couple more months and you can ditch the crate at night. Believe me, I'd rather have you in bed with me, but we don't want an accident where we sleep, do we?"

The only response she gave was to lower her eyes to the floor. "Sorry, Miss Elle, Gabriella made me immune to that look." Ryder's chest constricted at the thought of Gabby and her gap-toothed smile. What he wouldn't give to see it combined with those begging eyes. If he could, just once more, he'd give in to whatever she was asking for a thousand times over. If only he could have done that day differently, knowing what he did. He'd have come straight home and never taken his eyes off her. The only solace he had was that her seizures had been undiagnosed. At the same time, he had to wonder, what kind of father missed such a thing? *Are there signs?*

A groan he wasn't aware he had been holding in escaped when he swung his legs off the side of the bed. *This is not conducive to sleep.* He padded to the bathroom and popped a Benadryl. Not a perfect solution, but it might let him rest. Maybe.

Rest turned out to be a poor descriptor for the nightmare-infused on-and-off sleep he participated in between 8:30 and 5:00 a.m. when Elle started whining. "I'm coming, love." He pulled on running shorts and a T-shirt and let her out of her crate. She bolted so fast she almost hit her head on the part-open door. Ryder chuckled. "All right, silly. We're getting there. Your daddy isn't as young as he once was."

Judging by the way her tail whipped from side to side as she barreled down the steps, she forgave his shortcomings. *Or she really needs to pee.* For his own peace of mind, he decided both could be true.

After letting her out the back door, Ryder kept his gaze on her while he fiddled with his cell phone, cursing the lag time. *Damn inconsistent cell reception. What did I expect in the country? I should be happy it ever works.*

"Good morning," Ma said from behind the screen door, jolting Ryder so much he dropped his phone. "I'm sorry. I didn't mean to frighten you."

"That's what happens when you sneak up on someone." He picked up his phone with one hand and pressed his hand to his chest with the other. When he glanced up to see Elle had finished her business and now just sniffed around the yard, he whistled for her. "Breakfast, girl?" In response, she ran into the house through the door Ma held open for them. "Thanks."

"No problem. What were you concentrating so hard on?"

Ryder's pulse remained in hyperdrive as he scooped out wet food for Elle. "Trying to look up directions to Asheville."

"Why Asheville?"

"Shopping," he said, possibly too quickly. "Sal's birthday is coming up, and I wanted to find something nice. Different."

"Mm, Asheville's good for that." If Ma was suspicious, her bright eyes gave no indication. "In fact, would you pick me up fabric? I'll write down the information and give you money."

"No problem."

"Thanks, dear. Now, do you have time to collect the eggs, or should I?"

"I don't have to leave until eight."

Her lips quirked upward. "Eight? That's conveniently close to church time."

"Isn't it?" He kissed her cheek. "I'll get those eggs. Come on, Elle." Ryder watched the puppy run outside and followed after her.

A text beeped through. Ryder was almost afraid to look, and his heart didn't slow until he saw Sal's name on the screen.

Still dedicated to doing chores on this beautiful day?

"Henrietta, he's trying to make me irresponsible," Ryder grumbled to the chicken who had left three brown eggs in her nest. "Thank you, pretty girl. You're so strong to give us all these babies." He stroked the chickens while he went down the line, talking to them.

Before Ryder could answer, Sal sent a picture of a saddled horse with the caption, *We could ride up to the lake with a picnic. Laundry can always wait.*

Ryder pressed the Call button. "You're a bad influence," he said once connected.

Sal laughed. "Good morning to you too."

"I can't complain so far. Sleep well?"

"Not as well as I would with you, but nothing worth bitching about. You?"

The wind rustled in the background, and Ryder could picture Sal walking around the ranch in the early morning sun. "Mm, same."

"Cure for that, you know."

"Well, maybe we'll see about enacting that cure a couple times a week." Ryder couldn't suppress the grin at the promise in the words. Never mind his brain's warnings of *too soon.* Logic and love weren't always compatible.

"Gonna hold you to that. So...ditch the laundry for the lake?"

"If only I could. My mom asked me to pick up fabric in Asheville for her." He thanked his lucky stars that she had given him the excuse so he didn't have to lie to Sal too. "I should be home by early afternoon if you wanted to do the picnic then."

"Silence hung in the air. "I'm guessing you don't want company on your expedition?"

A light sweat formed on Ryder's forehead. "I'd rather go and get back quick. I don't know if you realize this, but you have a tendency to distract me."

More silence. "I get that, I guess. What time do you think you'll be home?"

Indecision roiled in Ryder's gut. *Meeting at ten. If I'm lucky, it won't take more than thirty minutes. Lucky, right. More like if I plan to come out unscarred.* "Shouldn't be later than two."

"I can work with that." Sal's voice softened. "Any special picnic requests?"

"Nope. I trust you."

"Good. I'll see you around two, then. Give me a call if it's gonna be different."

"I will." *I love you* balanced on the tip of Ryder's tongue, but he caught himself before he said the words. Last thing he wanted was to freak Sal out. So they ended their call with conventional goodbyes.

"What do you think, Miss Elle? Is this enough?" He showed her the basket of eggs, and she responded by wagging her tail. "Wonderful 'cause that's all they have for us today." Ryder held the basket up when she tried to jump for it. "Nope. Gotta bring it in to Ma, but I bet if you're real nice to her, she'll share the scramblers with you." Scrambled eggs with bacon on a Sunday morning, another tradition Ryder was salvaging by settling with the shark. *Never mind that there shouldn't be anything to settle. This should have been over when I left.* More realizations that did him no good.

At 8:03, Ryder bid his dad goodbye while Ma distracted Elle. *She'll be fine for a few hours,* he reassured himself. Not that he had much of a choice. He sure as fuck wasn't going to risk taking her. The drive in the pickup was smooth—or as smooth as North Carolina roads allowed—and fast. He was only slowed down when he got behind an elderly couple on a one-lane road.

Asheville had been called many things—artsy, eccentric, fun, and in some parts, well-to-do, as evidenced by the baby grand piano at McDonald's. *Seriously. Maybe we should have met there.* Something about dealing with a loan shark with a piano in background brought a smile to Ryder's face. But no. The goons had to draw attention to themselves by choosing a damn brewery at 10:00 a.m. He couldn't even believe a brewery was open that early. *Maybe it's not. Maybe they called in a favor... Again, that seems like a waste, but what can I do? Not a damn thing, so it's not worth debating.*

Ryder had planned for traffic that never materialized, so he parked a few blocks away and browsed the windows of the shops along the main street. Everything except the cafés were closed until 11:00, which meant he would have to stop for the fabric after the "meeting."

A gust of wind prickled the hair on the back of his neck. Or Ryder assumed it was the wind until he turned around to find Luke getting out of his car a few feet away. "Are you stalking me?"

"Yes, and I am so bad at it that I make sure you see me every time." A grin spread across Luke's face. "What are you doing here?"

Same thing I was doing the last time we were in a town together. "Meeting a friend in a bit."

"I hope they show this time."

"You and me both." Ryder checked the clock on phone. Still had forty-five minutes. "What about you? What brings you to Asheville?"

"Shopping for artwork or something to decorate the house with. Kinda lacking in personality right now. I could have gone to downtown Tryon, but I heard Asheville had a different variety of stuff to choose from." Ryder snorted a laugh while Luke glanced around at the closed signs on the doors. "But it looks like I'll have to wait."

It took him less than half a minute to consider options. The thought of wandering and letting his mind go where it wished for the next three-quarters of an hour did not appeal to him. Though if Luke hadn't shown up, that's exactly what he would have done. "In the mood for breakfast?"

A flash of hesitation colored Luke's face. "I could eat."

"Sure?"

"Yeah, what's good?"

"Fuck if I know, but really, how much can they screw up pancakes?" With that agreement, they chose the emptiest café they could find and took seats at the high top against the picture window. A placement Ryder chose so he could spot a goon with a red scarf.

"What time are you meeting your friend?" Luke asked.

"Ten. Forty minutes is more than enough time to eat." Assuming the cook was efficient, but since Luke and Ryder were the only ones there, Ryder didn't foresee a problem. As if on cue, a middle-aged man walked over to take their orders. Luke wanted an omelet, and Ryder asked for an egg sandwich. He felt better if he could pick up and run. "Any progress on the farm?"

For the next twenty minutes, the two of them discussed the finer points of raising livestock while they ate their breakfasts.

At five to ten, Ryder glanced at the check and set enough cash for his portion and the tip. The butterflies started as soon as he found his feet. "You gonna stick around here until the shops open?" Ryder asked.

Luke scanned the rapidly filling room. "I don't think they'd appreciate me taking up the table for that long. I'll walk for a bit. Burn off some of my breakfast."

Yeah, like you need to worry about that. "Well, maybe I'll see you when I'm done." *You're stalling,* Ryder's conscience berated him. *Get it over with.*

"Sure. Text me if you want to meet up. You can show me the best home stores." Luke winced. "God, I could not sound more gay if I tried."

Ryder patted his shoulder. "See ya." He walked out, each step lowering the corners of his mouth until it formed a straight line. His increasing pulse couldn't decide between anger and fear. *Anger. Remember, they're fucking with you. Watching you. Think of the puppy in the trap you believed was Elle.* The words marched through his mind. His steps became harder as he turned the corner. Tunnel vision narrowed his sights to the brick building that held the brewery. One foot in front of the other closed the distance at a steady pace.

A hand grabbed his arm and yanked him between the two buildings. With his other hand on Ryder's chest, a hefty, masked mouth breather slammed his back against the bricks. "You think we're fucking stupid, Cowboy?" Mouth Breather snarled, his breath stinking of stale booze.

"What? No—" The hand on his chest moved up to his throat.

"The fuck you don't." Another masked man emerged from behind the trash cans. A single ray of sunlight made it through the symmetrical windows on either side of the building to glisten off the metal of a blade on his belt holster. Ryder had no doubt that the man cutting off his air supply had a matching weapon set, and he'd bet money he didn't have that the set included a gun.

A sheen of sweat formed on his forehead as the mouth breather glared directly into his eyes. Ryder used every ounce of his will that wasn't searching for oxygen to return the glare. He may have made some bad decisions, but he damn well knew enough not to show assholes like this weakness.

"We told you to come alone, Cowboy," the man in the back said, his voice raspy, as though he had smoked too many cigarettes over his useless life. "Let him talk." He gestured to the mouth breather, who inched his hand down to Ryder's collarbone.

Ryder pulled in as much air as he could muster before answering, "I did, but—"

"Bullshit!" Faster than Ryder could track, Mouth Breather drew his blade to Ryder's Adam's apple. "We saw you with the cop!"

What the fuck is he talking about? Ryder racked his brain, trying to remember if he had spoken to a police officer that morning. He came up blank. "Then you're hallucinating." Less than a second after the words left his mouth, Ryder realized how ill-advised they were. Apparently, though, his brain/mouth filter had checked out because he barreled on, "But if I was, do you really think slicing open my neck is the best way to go? Your fingerprints are all over my clothes now—"

"Shut up!" Mouth Breather punched the wall next to Ryder's head. "Here's what's going to happen. You're going to pay us the extra ten thousand by the end of the week—"

"I have no more debt to you or your boss. He told me we were good." Since Ryder's sense of self-preservation had apparently gone the way of the dodo bird, he added, "Unless, of course, your boss isn't a man of his word after all."

Ryder likely would have had more to say, because he clearly enjoyed the various colors of red the man's face turned beneath his mask. What other reason could he have for speaking? However, a gust of air followed by sharp pain sliced through the flesh of his abdomen right above his hip.

"You don't ever talk about Boss that way," Mouth Breather growled, the booze on his breath strong enough to make Ryder intoxicated. "Boss saves men like you. Where's your respect?"

"Maybe it's the same place as his money." The other man stepped closer. "We oughta help him find it."

Come on, fight-or-flight response! Pick! React! Please! But instead, Ryder's body froze as warm liquid collected at the top of his pants. He couldn't know for sure without looking, but the cut on his stomach didn't feel mortally deep.

Mouth Breather grabbed Ryder's forehead and slammed his skull against the bricks behind him. While Ryder had his eyes closed in reaction, the second man decked him with a left hook across the jaw.

Fuck! Thought they didn't leave visible marks. That's what I get for believing what TV gangsters say. They don't want to kill me. That does them no good. That much Ryder was almost positive of. "Okay...stop..." he croaked, cursing himself for the weakness in his voice. But his spinning head made it difficult to think clearly, never mind speak.

The goons let him go, and he slid down the wall to crumple on the ground.

The sudden loss of pain and pressure stole more of his breath. *Why? Just because I asked them to stop? What the fuck?*

"What's going on here?" a vaguely familiar feminine voice asked.

"Nothing, Miss Cat," the second man stammered. "We found this man. He'd been hurt. We were going to call the police, but he asked us not to."

Cat? It took Ryder a minute to process that they weren't referring to a small, fussy animal—because that's how fucked up his head was—but then he further identified the woman as his friend. And he couldn't decide if that was good or bad.

RYDER CLOSED HIS eyes for what felt like a minute, but when he opened them again, the sun had been replaced with an overhead light. The brick had become white walls. A groan bubbled up from his throat and popped out his mouth. *Hospital.*

"He's awake," Sal called out, then leaned over and took his hand. "Hey, you scared us."

"Who's 'us'? Where am I?" Ryder's voice grated.

Sal slipped an ice chip between Ryder's lips. "Who do you think *us* is? Me, your parents, Cat...everyone." He stilled Ryder's shoulder. "Stop moving until the nurse comes in. We're at the hospital in Asheville. You're lucky."

"Lucky?"

"Yeah. Thank God, Cat was there when you got mugged."

Mugged. Okay. That's the story we're going with. The more Ryder considered it, the truer it rang. They *were* trying to take money that wasn't theirs. "Did they catch the people who did it?"

"No, unfortunately. They ran after knocking you out with a drug."

Drug? Interesting. "Thought it was from them hitting my head."

"With the way you're talking," a nurse started as she walked in, "the pounding your head took doesn't seem to have done you a lot of harm." She strode over to his bedside and raised her hand. "How many fingers?"

"Two."

"Good. No double vision." The nurse made an annotation on her chart. She then went through a series of questions to determine his cognitive function. "I'm impressed. Your head took quite a beating."

"Eh, it's always been pretty hard. Takes a lot to rattle the contents inside." Not to say it didn't ache, but he wasn't sure what they had him on. "How long was I out?"

"Around two hours. Besides your head, your stomach had a cut about five inches long, which we stitched up for you. Like your partner here said, you were lucky. Nothing major was hit."

Ryder let that sink in. *Nothing major. No arteries. No organs. Couple of stitches, some painkillers, and I'll be good as new. Okay, that may be an exaggeration.* "What did they give me?" When he saw her confusion, he clarified, "What drug did they use to knock me out?"

"We found ketamine in your system and an injection site on the side of your stomach opposite the cut."

Tension radiated off Sal at the explanation. Ryder squeezed his hand and eased himself up straighter. He thrilled to find that the pain wasn't any greater after an initial shock. "Thanks. When can I go home?"

The nurse rolled her eyes and smiled indulgently. "Wow, it took you a full twenty minutes after you woke up to ask that question. That must be some sort of record!"

And yet you aren't answering. Stop, he berated himself. *Between her and the doctor, they probably saved your life. You can spare her a couple of minutes of teasing.* "Are my parents here?"

"They're in the waiting room. I can go get them," Sal offered, but Ryder grabbed for his arm.

"No, please. I mean, maybe this lovely lady will tell me I can hightail it home now, and they were just waiting for me to wake up." He attempted to flutter his lashes at the nurse, but suspected the seduction technique so often favored by women didn't translate as well for a drugged-up ginger man.

Her snickering laugh confirmed his suspicions. "You're a riot. I bet he's a laugh a minute at home."

That drew Sal's lips upward. "He thinks he is." Ryder stuck his tongue out at Sal, then focused back on the nurse.

"You'll have to watch for signs of concussion for the next few days and I wouldn't recommend too much strenuous work, but I doubt Dr. Shapirro will want to keep you overnight."

Relief flooded Ryder. "Thank you..." He squinted at her name tag. "Clarice."

She smiled again and patted his shoulder. "I'll bring the doctor in to see you."

Ryder thanked her again, then faced Sal. "Question: who drugged my mom to keep her out in the waiting room?"

"We've been switching on and off between who got to sit with you, since there's only room for one chair in the curtained space." Sal glanced at his phone. "I should probably let her know you woke up, huh?"

"Mm, only if you enjoy having the ability to pee standing up." Ryder massaged his forehead while Sal typed out a message. "What about the police? Don't they need to talk to me?"

"They were here, but got called away. Your mom promised to bring you by to give a statement after your discharge."

Of course, she did. Oh, well, it's not like I could get out of it anyway. Ryder started to say something else, but the curtain separating him from the other patients slid back to reveal his parents.

His mom stared daggers at Sal. "Did you really text me, 'He's awake, but the doctor is discharging him soon, so you don't have to come back?' Or am I misreading it?"

Sal had the good sense to look contrite as he stood to offer his seat. "I was only trying to save you extra walking..." He shut his mouth when her gaze intensified.

"I'm fine, Ma."

She whipped her glare toward him and strode three steps to his bedside. "Fine? Fine? Young men who are fine do not go to the emergency room."

"Well, I mean..." He attempted a bashful smile. "They might if they're visiting, or a hypochondriac."

Her skin turned as red as her hair. "Then they still aren't fine because mentally healthy people do not willingly go to the hospital."

"What about doctors?" Sal asked.

"Or nurses?" Ryder tried. "I would hope they're physically and mentally healthy. Otherwise—"

"That is enough from you two! I have half a mind to—"

"Loraine," Dad said, putting his arm around her shoulders. "Why don't we just be grateful that Ryder is well enough to joke around?"

She responded with a grumble under her breath but walked over and kissed Ryder's head. "Are you all right?"

"Yes, my head hurts, but I feel okay." He kept eye contact with her to show he was serious. He shifted on the bed. "Did Cat mention why she was in Asheville?"

"I think she said something about a festival later today. I have to be honest that I was too grateful she was there to be overly concerned about why," Ma answered. "You can ask her after your discharge. She and Luke are out in the waiting room."

Ryder scrunched his face. "Luke is here too?"

"Yeah," Sal said. "Weird that all three of you ended up in the same place on the same day."

Is that suspicion in his tone? No. Can't be. Curiosity would make more sense. But it does look odd. "I had no idea they'd be there when I left this morning."

Sal opened his mouth but shut it at Dr. Shapirro's appearance. Ryder shook the doctor's hand, then cooperated for his verbal and walking tests. Once satisfied that the worst of Ryder's problems stemmed from the drugs, Shapirro signed his discharge papers.

"Am I okay to go to work tomorrow?"

The doctor glanced at Ryder's file. "You work on a horse ranch, right?" He nodded, and the doctor shook his head. "It wouldn't be my recommendation, but if you're feeling up to it, I doubt I could stop you."

"I could stop him," Sal said.

"He's the boss," Ryder explained.

"I suggest he not do a lot of heavy lifting until his stitches come out on Friday. Lucky for you, the cut wasn't terribly deep, so the healing should be quick," Dr. Shapirro told Sal. "I don't see any reason he can't ride a gentle horse or perform other farm chores, if, and only if, your head is okay. You will do yourself no favors if you give yourself a concussion."

Ma narrowed her eyes at the man. "Dr. Shapirro, if you don't mind me saying so that sounds like a rather laissez faire attitude toward his recovery."

The doctor laughed. "Mrs. Christensen—"

"Dr. Christensen," she corrected.

He showed no signs of being fazed by her clarification. "I grew up on a ranch, my family are all ranchers, at least a third of my patients are ranchers, so I have gotten pretty good at determining what instructions they will follow. For young, otherwise healthy men like your son, that means the bare minimum that won't kill him." Dr. Shapirro faced Ryder. "Am I wrong?"

"No, you're right." *And you've got bigger balls than any of us in the room.* Ryder's thought was confirmed as he glanced at Sal and Dad, who had both shut their mouths tight and stared at the near-elderly doctor with a mix of awe and respect.

"That's what I thought." Dr. Shapirro tore off a prescription and went to hand it to Ryder but didn't let go of the paper. "Now, this is Tylenol with codeine. You cannot work or drive if you need to take it."

"I would have to be pretty close to dying to take it, Doctor, but thank you." *I may not even fill it.* True, but Ryder knew better than to argue against anything this magical, laid-back man said, lest he change his mind.

Dr. Shapirro released the prescription and stared Ryder in the eye. "Don't be a martyr. As stubborn as I know young men—particularly ranchers—to be, your family and friends would rather you take care of yourself to prevent long-term damage than repeat this visit because you insisted on doing too much too fast."

"I promise to be careful. Thank you, Dr. Shapirro." The doctor left to a chorus of the same sentiment and shut the curtain. *Yeah, they're right. It is* way *too cramped with everyone in here.* "Do I have clothes?"

"Yes, I brought you some sweatpants and a T-shirt from home." Ma dug a plastic bag out of her large purse and set it on the bed. "Do you need help?"

Ryder half coughed, half choked. *Oh, fuck, no.* "I think I'm okay, thanks."

"I'll stick around in case he does," Sal offered.

Ma opened her mouth, but Dad took her hand. "Why don't we go bring the car around, Loraine?" Her lips formed a straight line, but she followed.

Thank you, Ryder mouthed. His dad nodded and shut the curtain. "You think I'll ever be too old for that question to be inappropriate?"

"In your mother's eyes? No way. Especially not when you've been hurt. Something about seeing their kids sick or injured erases multiple decades for parents and grandparents." Sal hovered off to the side while Ryder untied the strings holding his hospital gown closed.

Ryder discarded the blanket along with the gown and replaced it with his clothes. His skin tingled under the heat of Sal's gaze. "I'm okay," he repeated as he stood.

Sal brought him into an embrace. "Do you have any idea how scared I was? Your parents got the call and drove over to take me with them. All we knew was that you had been stabbed and had a head injury from being mugged. In broad daylight. On Main Street in Asheville. I thought for sure it had to be a joke. I've never seen your dad drive so fast." He pulled away just enough to tilt Ryder's chin up. The blast of pain radiating from Sal's features was enough to break Ryder's heart.

"I'm sorry," Ryder whispered.

The corners of Sal's lips tugged up in the faintest of smiles. "You didn't do anything wrong, love—"

You don't understand. I've done almost everything wrong! The voice in Ryder's head drowned out the rest of what Sal told him. Much as he should have said it to warn

Sal, he couldn't make himself do it. Couldn't drive Sal away when he could barely hold his head up. Ryder realized Sal had stopped speaking and was watching him expectantly. "I'm sorry, what?"

"Lost ya for a second there." Sal glided his thumb over Ryder's cheek. "Will you be okay if I run to the bathroom? I'd take you with me, but—"

"That would draw a lot of unnecessary attention," Ryder finished.

"Especially since it's single person."

"Wouldn't want them to get the wrong idea." Ryder forced himself to take a step back. "Yes, I'll be fine. Have to wait for the wheelchair anyway." He rolled his eyes at the hospital protocol.

"Don't leave without me."

Like that's gonna happen. He could imagine the conversation with his parents that would have to take place, but stopped trying when it got too ridiculous. Almost as soon as Sal disappeared from sight, Cat rounded the corner. *Jesus, did he send in reinforcements?* Ryder's annoyance dissipated when he remembered that he needed to talk with her before he reached the police station.

"Oh, Ryder," Cat whimpered and surprised him by greeting him with a too-tight hug that left him gasping for air. "Sorry. Didn't mean to hurt you. Are you okay? Do you remember what happened?"

"Yes, and sort of." He tugged his shirt down past the waistband of his sweats, which he made sure lay beneath the stitches. "Some guys were giving me a hard time with their fists, and then you showed up. Started yelling at them... All goes blank from there." *Well. Not completely. They called her Miss Cat. Why? How would thugs like that know my small town's prom queen?*

"I happened to be walking by."

Liar.

"Just lucky, I guess." Cat glanced to the left, right, and out the window. Anywhere except at Ryder.

Ryder offered his best smile. He had to push through the increasing throbbing in his head. "I guess so. Thank you for stepping in. It must have been scary."

Cat shook her head. "Think nothing of it. I did nothing more than any decent person would have. I'm glad I walked by when I did."

"Me too. Crazy coincidence that."

Her gaze hardened in a flash but returned to its normal soft state before Ryder could react. "I don't believe in coincidence. I think you were right the first time. It was luck. That's exactly what I told the police too."

She held eye contact until he nodded. "Then I'll say the same." He wet his lips. "You would know better than me, being the one without the head injury and all."

"There's the hero of the day," Sal said as he came up behind her.

"Hush now. Enough of that." Cat fiddled with her purse, then stopped to look around. "Where is your transport?"

"Tending to patients who actually need to be here?" Ryder shrugged.

Cat slung the bag over her shoulder. "If that were true, getting you out should be a top priority. Hold on."

Ryder and Sal watched her strut to the nurses' station as though she owned the place. Sal leaned in close to Ryder's ear and whispered, "Do you think she carries Owen's balls with her, or are they mounted somewhere in their house?"

"I imagine they're displayed prominently at home. How else would he get a constant reminder of who's boss?"

In true Cat fashion, she showed up five minutes later with a frazzled orderly pushing a wheelchair. Ryder thought about telling him that he didn't need to follow them out, but then they'd need to bring the chair back somehow. So, he decided it wasn't wise and simply followed protocol.

Ma jumped out of the passenger seat to open the door and hover as Ryder maneuvered the three steps between the wheelchair and the back seat.

"I got it, Ma, thanks."

"Don't you get exasperated with me, young man. I'm your mother, and I will worry if I want to."

What a strange thing to want. No pain medication was so strong as to make him stupid enough to say that. That would have been a sure sign of a brain injury. He patted the front of his pants. *Empty. Right. I was "mugged."* "They took my phone and wallet, huh?"

"Nope." Sal produced both items from his pocket and passed them to Ryder. "According to Cat, they ran pretty fast when they saw her. Didn't have time to finish the mugging."

Ryder knitted his brows together as he opened his wallet. All his credit cards, cash, and driver's license were exactly where he left them. "What the fuck?" he whispered.

"That's what I said." Sal buckled his seat belt. "Kind of sucky criminals, if you ask me."

"Easier to catch that way," Dad said from the front. "Ryder, are you strapped in?"

"Yeah, I'm good." Confused as hell, though that wasn't worth reporting. So, he sat back and waited to arrive at the police station to tell the story he and Cat had agreed on.

Chapter Eighteen

BY MIDAFTERNOON, RYDER was passed out at his parents' house, and Sal was on his way back to his place to get his car and some overnight basics. Victor and Loraine had already given him permission to stay with Ryder, though Sal half suspected that had more to do with Loraine's fear that Ryder wouldn't ask them for help if he needed it. Which was most likely true. Not that he would ask Sal, but sleeping in the same room would give him an advantage.

When Sal opened the door of his house, he was immediately hit with the sense that something was off. "Jason?"

Instead of his brother, a twitchy Ted appeared from the kitchen with a wet cloth slung over his thick forearm. "Hey, Sal. Jay isn't feeling well."

"What's wrong with him?" Sal advanced toward the bedroom, but Ted blocked his way.

"He's got a fever and is pretty out of it. I'm taking care of him."

Sal scrutinized the man in front of him. The first question that popped into his mind was, *why*? Why would Ted be the one helping Jason to reduce his fever? Why hadn't anyone called him? Most importantly, why was Ted blocking his way? "Excuse me." The politeness had an edge that Sal wouldn't feel guilty about.

"You don't need to worry. I got him."

"Ted." Sal worked hard to keep the impatience from his voice, but he was not in the mood to play games. "Did he ask you to keep me out?"

"No, but, um, he's not fully dressed."

"Right. Listen, I'm sure your intentions are good, but I highly doubt he cares about that." Sal didn't have to doubt. He'd lived with his brother long enough to be sure, especially since he was Jason's main caregiver after his accident. No, it was far more important for Sal to know he was okay.

The guy still didn't budge. "I...Sal, he's really out of it. I would rather he be of more sound mind before letting someone else in."

Sound mind...? From a fever? The hell is going on? "Move before I kick you out of the house." Sal didn't wait for Ted to clear a path for him. He could have walked around him, but Sal found some satisfaction in bumping his shoulder. After cracking Jason's bedroom door, he slipped inside. Instantly, he was assaulted by the stench of urine. *Either Petey had an accident—which he hasn't in years— or... Oh, God, please, no...* Sal shuffled silently to bed, where Jason lay bundled up with every blanket he owned. He glanced around the room to find it empty, except for Ted hovering by the door. "Where's Petey?"

"I put him in the basement because he made a lot of noise when Jason's headache was at its worst."

Sal clenched his fists. *Deep breath in and out.* When he had calmed enough to release the tension in his hands, Sal checked Jason's breathing and pulse, then got to his feet. Sal motioned Ted out of the room and shut the door. "Do you know why he has Petey?"

"Seizure alert dog, right?"

"Mm-hmm. And how do you think he goes about alerting us to oncoming seizures?"

"By...shit."

"Yeah, shit." This was Jason's first seizure in six months, and Ted had prevented him from getting help because the dog's barking annoyed him. Sal pinched the bridge of his nose. The thought process would do nothing for his blood pressure. "Where did he have the seizure? Were you there?"

Ted gestured to the bedroom. "We were lying on the floor watching TV, and he just started shaking. Then he wet himself and fell asleep."

"And then you did what?"

"I took his clothes off so he didn't have to lay in it and put him in bed."

One, two, three... Sal counted his breaths up to ten, hoping to rein in his anger. "You didn't think to call me or 911?"

"He was fine. I knew you were busy, and sitting in the ER wouldn't have helped him." Sal's raised hand cut him off.

"Go let Petey out of the basement. I'm going to wake Jason."

"He needs his rest—"

"Not nearly as much as I need to make sure he didn't suffer long-term neurological effects," Sal growled.

"But—"

"Do you want to help or make it worse? I promise you I am only interested in his safety."

"What's the worst that could have happened?"

Sal narrowed his eyes. Had Ted not looked genuinely nervous, he would have been a lot harsher in his response. "Seizures can lead to stroke or concussion if he hits his head on something. If Petey asks to go out, let him, but don't come back to the bedroom without him." He turned on his heel before Ted could ask more questions.

This time, when he went in the room, Sal left the door open. The light from the hallway illuminated Jason's tanned skin. Sal waited with bated breath until, thankfully, Jason mumbled and tried to shift away. "Jay, I need you to open your eyes for me." He took special care to soften his voice. It wasn't Jason's fault his friend was an idiot, and now did not seem like the best time to point it out.

"Bright," he said into the pillow.

"Yeah, I know, but I—" Petey cut off his explanation by running into the room and jumping on the bed.

"Hey, buddy." For Petey, Jason woodenly rolled onto his back. "I'm okay." Sal didn't know if he was trying to reassure Petey or him.

"You're awake." Ted didn't approach. In fact, he stayed close enough to the door to make a run for it.

"How could I not be when this lug let the sunshine in?" His voice sounded as though it passed through a cheese grater to get the words out.

"I tried to keep him out, but—"

"But his actions were making me nervous, so I had to see for myself that you weren't hurt."

"Hurt? Why would I...?" Jason inhaled deeply, sat up too quickly, and turned on the light. Sal reached out a hand to steady him as Jason's gaze zeroed in on the towel-covered wet spot on the carpet. "Shit! No, no, *no!*" He looked over at Ted. "I had a seizure?"

"You don't remember?"

"People rarely remember the experience, especially right away," Sal answered quietly, never taking his gaze off his brother. Which was good because, from what Sal had read, losing control wasn't something anyone would want to recall in the aftermath. Another scent mixed with the urine-drenched rug. "Was someone smoking in here?"

An emotion that looked a lot like panic flashed over Jason's face, but he glanced over Sal's shoulder. "Thanks for watching over me, Ted. I'll text you later."

"Uh, okay. Bye, Sal." He hustled out the door without waiting for a response.

"It's not a big deal." Jason started to stand, but Sal's hand on his shoulder was enough to keep him sitting.

"No? Then why'd he run like a bat out of hell?"

Jason released a gust of air and plopped back onto the pillows. "Because he knows how you get about shit like that."

"Like what? Expensive habits that will eventually kill you? S—"

"That's never been proven!"

Sal knitted his eyebrows together. "The hell are you talking about? Unless you're a tobacco rep, you damn well know that smoking is dangerous. But you're an adult and it's legal."

"Should be." Jason's words were so soft that Sal barely heard them.

Sal searched for words, but came up blank. Maybe the seizure did knock something loose in Jason's brain. "What did I miss?"

With one hand, Jason focused on scratching Petey while massaging his forehead with the heel of his other. He remained quiet for so long that Sal wasn't sure he would answer. "Marijuana isn't as dangerous as health class would have made you believe."

Sal dropped his hand from Jason's shoulder. "Wait. We're talking about smoking pot? Are you insane?"

A fierce growl emerged from Jason's throat. He whipped off the covers off and stalked over to the chair by the window to pull his pajama pants on. "Fine. I'm insane, but only if that word changed meanings. Only if insane now means being able to function at the same level as most adults."

"I...don't understand."

"No. You don't," he said as he stalked into the bathroom, emerging a moment later with cleaning supplies. "Notice how I've had more good days than bad lately? How I've been able to hold my own on the farm? Ride horses through the woods? That sure as fuck isn't because of the opiates the doctor prescribes too liberally."

"It's illegal, Jay."

"So is oral sex in four states! I bet if you went to Pennsylvania, you wouldn't be opposed to getting a blowjob."

A scowl creased Sal's face. "That's not the same, and you damn well know it."

"It's not that far off."

"When was the last time you heard of someone spending decades behind bars for having sex of any kind in private? Hell, public sex gets you less time than a certain amount of pot." Especially for a young biracial man like Jason. Sal had taken over petting Petey when Jason had gotten off the bed. So when Jason sat down again, Petey was in heaven, getting scratched from his two humans at once. If his happy pants and wiggles were anything to go by, the dog didn't pick up on the increased tension.

"I don't know, Sal." Jason's gaze was firm, unafraid, almost challenging. "I do know that it's a chance I'm willing to take."

"Why?"

"Seriously? Have you not been listening to me? What's the difference between here and Maryland?"

"State borders. Laws."

Jason rolled his eyes. "But nothing that changes what it does to me. For me. If I lived in one of thirty places in the US where a doctor could write a prescription, we wouldn't be having this conversation."

"No, and there are two reasons for that. One, you wouldn't be breaking the law, and two, you would know what you put into your body. I guarantee you that Ted doesn't know, unless he's the one growing it." Which would be an even bigger problem for Ted. At least, that's what Sal assumed. He'd never had a reason to analyze the drug code.

"He trusts the people he gets it from."

"Do you?" The silence dragged the seconds into minutes. *If he thinks I'm going away, he's got another think coming.*

"Don't see as I have much of a choice, do you?" Jason said finally.

Yes! Plenty of them. Find another drug—legal this time. But Sal didn't say that. He knew his brother well enough to know that it wouldn't do either of them any good. Jason had made up his mind. "If you get caught, it won't only hurt you. The county may take a closer look at our books or the codes."

"Neither of which have ever been a problem." Anger flared in Jason's words. "I've been able to do all parts of my job better since I started smoking. You just can't get past the idea that an unconventional solution is working better."

"No!" Sal got to his feet, but worked to keep his voice steady. "Yoga is an unconventional solution to pain. Acupuncture, chiropractic care, meditation...all fine unconventional options to try."

"All of which are unproven. I...can't go back to waking up every day wondering if I'll be able to walk. Not when the fix is so easy."

Not here. Not in this house. The implied threat hung on the tip of Sal's tongue, but he bit it back. As unhappy as he was about Jason's choice of treatment, he could never bring himself to ask him to leave his home. Hell, the property may have been in Sal's name, but it was remodeled for Jason. Sal patted Petey's head once more and climbed to his feet. "You gonna be okay? Steady?" An admittedly weird question since Sal had watched Jason walk to the bathroom. But one he felt compelled to ask.

"Yeah—"

"I'm going to Ryder's for the night."

"How's he feeling?" Jason shifted, seemingly unsure what to do with himself.

Sal shrugged one shoulder. "As well as can be expected after getting his head bashed." Which may have been overstating what happened, but technically, they did slam his head on the building they had him up against.

"Think there's more to the story than he's saying?"

"Don't know. Maybe he doesn't either. I gotta go. Be home in time for morning chores." Sal walked to the door, but couldn't push himself out until he added, "Jay, call me if you need me or you feel like you shouldn't be alone. I might have to sell my soul to convince Loraine that I can watch over Ryder here, but I...won't abandon you. No matter what."

"I know. Thanks."

With a nod, Sal walked out of the house and toward Ryder's.

Chapter Nineteen

LIKE A LASER, the rising sunrays forced Ryder's eyes open the next morning. He tried to stretch, but when he moved, his elbow came into contact with Sal's chest.

"Ugh," Sal groaned.

"Sorry." Ryder kissed the spot he had accidentally hit.

"Don't worry about it." He scooted over an inch, but that was all the space Ryder's twin bed allowed them.

Until last night, Ryder hadn't thought too hard about the size of his bed. It was at least long enough for him, and when he slept alone, the width didn't make a lot of difference. Then Sal slept over, and suddenly, Ryder wished he had taken his father up on the offer of digging the spare double out of the attic.

"It's only temporary," he had argued.

But then, he'd anticipated being the only one to sleep in it, and he had been interested in self-punishment at the time. So, yeah, they'd stay at Sal's or separately.

"How do you feel?"

"Sore, but I'll take a couple of pills before I decide how much work I can manage."

Sal barked out a quiet laugh. "Babe, you aren't working today. You barely slept last night—no, don't argue with me, I was here."

Damn. I tried so hard to keep still. Ryder hadn't meant to disturb Sal, but he couldn't find a comfortable position and he'd drunk too much water because the doctor had mentioned the importance of fluids to Ma. So, he was in the bathroom more than he had been since his college bingeing days. Not to mention that it took them a while to fall asleep, since Sal was so riled after his conversation with Jason. Ryder was selfishly glad that Jason hadn't mentioned that he had known about his smoking for weeks.

Sal lay on his side to face Ryder. "How about this? If you're feeling up to it, you can come over and distract me."

"Oh, that will make me wildly popular with my coworkers."

Sal groaned. "Fuck 'em."

"No, thanks." Ryder stuck his tongue out, and Sal slapped his arm lightly. He then answered Ryder's pout by brushing their lips together.

As if on cue, Sal's phone alarm started going off, which woke Elle. With a sigh, Sal rolled off the bed and walked to Ryder's dresser, where he'd left his cell the previous night. On the other side of the wall, Ryder's parents moved around their room. His ma no doubt getting ready for the day, while his dad debated if he needed to wake up yet. Ryder turned his attention back to Sal, who was reading something on his phone. "Jay text?"

"No. He's gonna see how long he can avoid me." The terseness radiated from his tone.

Definitely need to give Jay a batch of scones for not telling his brother my part, if it can be called that. Though if he had, Ryder had the perfectly acceptable excuse of "not my business" for not sharing.

"Can I let her out?" Sal asked, gesturing to Elle, who stared between them with huge brown eyes.

"Not until we're ready to take her downstairs to pee." Ryder pushed himself out of bed, making an effort not to wince, but it must not have worked because Sal pressed him back to a sitting position.

"I got her. You can go back to sleep."

"I don't think I can. I need food to take my medicine and that requires going downstairs, which in turn requires clothes, and after all that effort, I doubt I'll be able to sleep again." *At which point, I'll have to figure out a shower, but that will be another whole adventure.*

"I can bring you toast and water so—" Elle's whine interrupted Sal. "Yes, girl, you first. I promise."

Ryder opened his mouth to respond, but the sound of the doorbell—and the subsequent barking—cut him off. "What time is it?"

"Six fifteen." Sal passed Ryder the tee and cargo shorts on top of his dresser. "Do you need help?" Ryder couldn't be sure if Sal figured out how dumb the question was on his own, or if he sensed the glare Ryder focused on the floor. "Hey, better I ask than your mom, right?"

And she would have if given enough time. "Yes, and you should make sure she knows you asked too."

"So maybe she can relax enough to let you stay with me tonight?"

Ryder couldn't keep the scowl from his face. "She doesn't have to let me do anything. I'm—"

A knock on the bedroom door jolted Ryder to his feet. He confirmed that they were both dressed and nodded to Sal, who opened the door.

"Sorry to interrupt, boys, but, Ryder, there's a Detective Cranston from New York here to speak with you."

Cranston. Damn. There's a name I could have happily gone the rest of my life without hearing. "Give me a second, Dad. I need to brush my teeth and look semipresentable." The heat of Sal's stare burned into the side of Ryder's face, but he couldn't address it yet. More important to put socks and shoes on. Make it look like he had his life together.

"Should we call the lawyer?"

"Probably not, but that'll be my first question for her."

"I'll let Elle out. Your ma's making tea."

Because that's what you do in the South. No matter who comes to visit. Or what time they arrive. "Thanks, Dad. I'll be right down." His father left with the puppy and closed the door. "Detective Cranston was the officer assigned to Gabby's investigation," Ryder told Sal in explanation. He shook his head and pushed one foot in front of the other in the direction of the adjacent bathroom. *Can't make police wait, regardless of why they've come. Pee, brush teeth.* He repeated the plan in his mind until he was far enough along in the process to have confidence he wouldn't forget.

"Ry." Sal touched his arm after he had rinsed his mouth out. "Want me to stay?"

"Nah, you have chores."

"Nothing that can't wait if you need support."

Sal's furrowed brow broadcast concern that touched Ryder deep in his heart, compelling him to join their lips in a sweet, but heated kiss. "Thanks, but I got it. It's probably a case update she didn't want to share over the phone." Though Ryder couldn't come up with what that might be or why the case was even reopened at this point.

Their shared embrace may have lasted too long because a knock sounded at the door. "Ryder, honey, do you need help?" Ma asked.

Ryder pulled away from the warmth of Sal's arms and opened the door. "No, Ma, I'm fine." He and Sal stepped out of the room, almost tripping on the new golden Lab, who his parents had adopted to mother future puppies. But, as with all the breeder dogs, she'd be a spoiled pet first. "Hi, Missy. Taking cues from Carrie, I see." He scratched behind her ears quick, then followed Ma down the steps.

"I'm sorry we can't offer you breakfast, Sal," Ma started, but Sal waved the concern off.

"No worries, Loraine. It's a little early anyway."

"Ack. Not for people with roosters."

His chuckle strained when they reached the bottom of the steps. The living room was blocked from sight, but not sound in this position. "You'll call or text when you finish?"

Long as I don't have to leave with her for whatever reason. "I'll let you know how it goes." Ryder was glad they'd gotten their kiss out of the way upstairs since Ma's nerves ramped up his own. He settled on a parting nod to Sal, who looked as troubled as Ryder felt. *This is not going to work.* He turned on his heel and headed into the living room while his mom walked Sal out.

Detective Cranston climbed to her feet when Ryder entered the room. "Good morning, Ryder," she said as they shook hands.

"Seems a little early to be good, doesn't it, Detective?"

"Ryder!" Ma admonished from the doorway. "I apologize, Detective Cranston. He must have hit his head harder than we thought yesterday."

The detective, a middle-aged woman with cropped blonde hair, offered a smile that didn't reach her eyes. Maybe it never did. Ryder imagined those eyes had seen the worst of the world during her career. "That's perfectly understandable, Mrs. Christensen. I'm sorry for the hour, but the media picked up on a new development and I wanted to speak with Ryder before the stories started running."

New development? The case is closed, or it was. "So, I take it I don't need a lawyer?" Ryder asked.

"No, you're the victim here, Ryder." She scanned the room and fixed her gaze on Ryder. "Would you feel more comfortable if your parents stayed?"

Ryder considered, but ultimately said, "No, thanks. I don't want to make a bigger deal of it than it is."

Taking his cue, Dad crossed the room and directed Ma out the doorway. "We'll be in the kitchen if you change your mind."

"Thanks." Ryder waited for the swinging door to close. Still wouldn't block sound, but Ryder wasn't too concerned. Yet. He motioned for Cranston to sit, then took the couch opposite the chair she chose. "How can I help you?" Ryder was sure his mother would thump him for not going through the usual pleasantries of asking about the detective's husband, child, and Doberman, but that's why his mom wasn't there.

"The woman staying with your daughter the night of her passing has been shot."

Ryder's lips moved without sound, making him wonder how much he looked like a fish, which was possibly the most inappropriate thought he could have at the time. "I'm sorry to hear that," he said finally. "Is Katie…?" *Okay* would be a particularly stupid way to end that question.

"She's alive, but in critical condition, so we don't have the full story." Cranston leaned forward. "The reason I'm here is twofold. She had requested a meeting with me for the day after she was shot, but wouldn't give details, except to say that she remembered something else from that night."

Remembered? Had she struggled with her memory during the investigation? Ryder only recalled her falling asleep while Gabby was in the tub. But then, the two of them had been pretty hysterical at the time.

When he didn't say anything, Detective Cranston continued, "When the doctors ran her blood panel, it came back positive for ketamine."

"Wait. That's what they found in my blood last week." Ryder said the words without thinking.

"I know. That's why I'm here."

"I haven't seen her in months, if you're worried I gave her something. I have at least ten witnesses to confirm that I was nowhere near New York or—" He stopped the ramble when she shook her head.

"We aren't blaming you. We're concerned that the people responsible for yours and Katie's injuries may have had something to do with your daughter's death."

Ryder tried to let her words sink in, but his brain buzzed with static, drowning out their meaning. "You think someone killed Gabriella?" he asked slowly. A numbing shock coursed through his bloodstream, dampening the anger he knew lurked underneath.

"We have reason to suspect as much, yes. But we won't know until—"

"No. That isn't possible. They tested her for drugs during the autopsy and didn't find anything."

"No one thought to look for ketamine, in either her or Katie. I'm sorry. It just wasn't on their radar." She scrutinized him through her narrowed gaze.

Ryder had to close his eyes to escape it, in case she read something in him that he didn't yet know. He pressed his hand to his head. At that moment, he wanted nothing more than to turn back time and ask Sal to stay. *Well, if I'm going back in time, ten minutes seems like a cop-out. Think of all the problems I could solve if I went a little farther. Maybe I wouldn't start gambling. Maybe I never would have pushed Sal away. How much could I change without completely altering the course of my life and everyone else's?*

"Ryder?" Detective Cranston raised her voice and lightly tapped his knee. Ryder snapped his gaze to hers. "Did I lose you?"

"For a second, yes. Sorry." With a fortifying breath, he returned his focus to the conversation. "What was the last thing you said?"

"I asked if you would consent to us testing your daughter for traces of ketamine. Ketamine has been known to cause the type of seizures your daughter may have suffered that night." Cranston spoke carefully, as though worried saying the wrong thing would set him off.

He met her gaze. "So, you think whoever drugged Katie might be the same people who drugged me...and Gabriella? How?"

"After reviewing the traffic light cameras when we found the ketamine, we noted that someone delivered a pizza, which Katie had tried to refuse at first, but she eventually took it and shut the door. We believe either the person who ordered the pizza, or the one who delivered it, may have put drugs on it." Detective Cranston turned her hands over in an *I don't know* gesture in answer to Ryder's incredulous expression. "Ryder, we're trying. It may be grasping at straws, since the crimes happened states apart. But we'd be remiss if we didn't pursue it."

"Of course, but she's been gone more than a month. What would you test?"

"Her hair. It's actually more accurate than other tests, even on the living."

Ryder chewed his bottom lip but forced himself to stop when he tasted metal. The heat from the detective's gaze burned into the top of Ryder's head, but he couldn't look at her. "Yeah. You can do that." Energy buzzed through him. He rubbed his hands together in hopes of dissipating some, but that only revved him up more. Ryder climbed to his feet and paced. He ignored the continued heat as Cranston followed his movements with her eyes.

Finally, she broke the silence. "You understand that we can't make any promises, and this could be a shot in the dark..."

"I do. I'm not expecting miracles." *But what if I could nudge the investigation in the right direction? Could the little information I have make a difference?* Ryder stopped and faced her again. *Would outing myself help? What about my former coworkers who could be implicated?* All at once, he realized that it didn't make one bit of difference who else got in trouble. If those bastards had even the slightest chance of having a hand in Gabby's death, he would do whatever was necessary to see that they went down. "I might have somewhere for you to start. People—" *If you can call them that.* "—to question." With a shaky voice, he confessed about the money owed and the text messages he'd been getting. He diverted his gaze again as he spoke, too humiliated at how far it had gone and the consequences that resulted, but he heard her tapping furiously on a tablet.

Cranston straightened her back and squared their gazes. "You said they've been trying to reel you in down here, right?" Ryder nodded, and she continued, "How would you feel about working with us and the FBI to catch some of the people responsible?"

"FBI? What?" He blinked as he processed. "And how would I help?"

"The bureau has an undercover agent infiltrating this ring. If you accept their invitation to play, we can catch them with multiple crimes."

Suspected murder isn't enough? Ryder wanted to ask but didn't bother. Al Capone had been jailed for tax evasion. As Ryder understood it, once the cops got criminals in the system, they could further investigate the "real" crimes. "What do I have to do?"

A genuine smile spread across her face as she promised to be in touch with details as soon as she could. They shook hands, and Ryder let her out after she had said goodbye to his parents.

Once she was in her car, Ryder shut the door. As he turned around, Elle crashed into his thigh. He couldn't help but chuckle. "I'm sorry, baby, your schedule is all out of whack." He crouched to scratch her.

"You shouldn't make her so time dependent," Ma said.

Ryder tried not to roll his eyes. "Not sure I make her anything. I think dogs like routine." *And you want something to pick on.*

"Everything all right with the detective?" Dad asked.

With a final pat to Elle's head, Ryder stood. There was no way he could tell them everything, or even most of what he and Detective Cranston had discussed. At least not yet. Decent chance they'd hear about it later, along with everyone else. Ryder decided on the simplest explanation. "The babysitter who was staying with Gabby was shot, and the police have reason to believe it was connected to Gabby's death." He quickly raised his hand to stop his mother's question. "I can't say more than that right now. But when they exhume her for testing, Detective Cranston promised to have her cremated and brought down here." "Shipped" was the word Cranston had used, but he didn't like to think of his daughter that way and doubted his mother would either.

Ma sighed. "Yes, that is good news. I never liked having her so far away. Not in life. Not now."

Ryder turned his gaze to the ceiling and blinked in hopes of convincing the water pooling in his eyes not to fall. What could he possibly say to that? Of course, he knew his mom had always wanted him and Gabby here, or at least closer. Just like he knew his life would have been loads easier if he had found a job near his family. *Maybe I wouldn't be dealing with this. Maybe she wouldn't be gone. Okay, that is not keeping my emotions under control.* He took a shaky breath.

"Would you go collect the eggs for me, Ryder?" Dad asked. "I want an omelet."

"Sure." Ryder swiped at his face and mouthed *thank you* on his way past his parents to the yard, Elle and Missy trotting alongside him. He headed for the chickens on the far side of the house. They tended not to get as much attention. The fact that their coop was farthest away from the house was only a nice bonus.

Ryder texted Sal.

I'm not going to jail.

Well, that's good. Don't think you'd be happy as someone's bitch

What makes you think I'd be the bitch?

...aren't gingers always?

A few seconds later, another text popped up from Sal.

Are you coming over?

Ryder stared at the screen, debating where he'd get more peace. Ma would go to work soon, leaving Dad home, unless he had somewhere to be, but regardless, he wasn't likely to poke at Ryder nearly as much as Ma. At the same time, he wanted to see Sal between his boyfriend's chores without being too much of a distraction. He settled on compromise.

Why don't you let me know when you finish for the day? Then, assuming my head is okay, I'll walk over.

:(came through first, followed by, *Only walk if you feel up to it.*

If I don't, you'll come here?

I will gladly drive to pick you up and bring you back.

Implication being: we're not sleeping on your twin mattress again. Ryder briefly considered reminding him that they could sleep apart but concluded that he didn't want to do that. *Another compromise it is.*

We don't live together, you know.

The second he sent it, he wished he could take the words back. Compromise or not, he couldn't fathom a positive outcome of that message.

Ryder had enough time to collect all the eggs and distribute feed before Sal responded.

Why not?

Do you really want to discuss this over text?

No. But now I've got something to think about while I'm working with Bishop.

Don't think too hard. We don't know how he'd react to the smoke coming out of your ears.

He pressed Send, but quickly added a heart, then tucked his phone away, confident that whatever Sal replied wouldn't need Ryder's immediate attention.

"Well, girls, what do ya think? Should we go have omelets?" Missy tilted her head to the side, and Elle copied her. "Not hungry yet? How about fetch?" He had no clue if

Missy knew fetch, but judging by her thumping tail, she at least recognized the word. Damn his parents for keeping the grounds so clear. Made it harder than it should have been to find a stick. Ryder finally spotted one under an old oak tree.

The first time he tossed it, the stick didn't go far enough for Elle and Missy to even bother breaking out into a run. "Bring it back and I'll try again." His second attempt was more successful, if one could call tossing it on top of the fence, where it wedged between two pillars, successful. Ryder heaved a sigh as the girls went crazy barking at it. "I'm coming. I'm coming." *Like they can understand me.* Once there, relief filled him at the sight of a lone downed branch.

Ryder grabbed the wood but cursed at the realization that it wasn't quite long enough. "I bet if I asked the doctor, he would tell me that stick retrieval does not fall under the category of taking it easy," he muttered to no one in particular as he climbed onto the nearest rock. At that height, he had a clear view of Luke's kitchen.

While normally not one for spying on his neighbors, the woman with whom Luke was in deep conversation caught Ryder's attention. *Why the hell is he talking to Detective Cranston?* Of course, he was too far away to hear, and it most likely was no business of his, but that didn't stop his imagination from running wild.

"Ryder Victor William Christensen!" Ma screeched behind him.

Ryder caught himself on the wooden post. "Geez, Ma! Trying to kill me?" Once stable, he stepped onto the ground.

"More like you're trying to kill yourself. What were you thinking, climbing up there in your condition?"

Deep breath in. Now out. He repeated the chant several times as he tossed the stick for the dogs again. "I'm fine. Honest." He chose not to point out that while he shouldn't have been climbing rocks, the greater problem was her startling him into almost falling. Ryder kissed her cheek in hopes of easing her exasperated expression. "What time's your first appointment?"

"Seven thirty."

"Then shouldn't you—"

She cut him off with a wave of her hand, put her arm around his shoulders, and steered him back toward the house. "I know I hover too much, Ry, but you can't fault a mother for being concerned when her only child has had a litany of bad luck." She stopped a few paces from the kitchen door and faced him. The moisture pooling along the ridges of her eyes squeezed Ryder's heart. "You understand the pain of losing a child. Please don't put yourself in danger and risk us experiencing that heartache."

Ryder pulled her into his chest in a tight embrace. What could he say? *I wouldn't do that to you*? In a way, he had, though, hadn't he? By trying to handle the sharks on his own, he was putting himself in harm's path. *Better me than them.* Looking into his mom's watery eyes, however, he wasn't so sure. "I promise to be more careful."

With another hug, Ma released him. "Good. Grab the basket, and your father will make us eggs."

Chapter Twenty

A WEEK LATER, Sal checked his cell phone for at least the tenth time that day. *Five minutes since I last looked.* He held in a sigh. Ryder's dad had taken him to get the stitches out at noon because Sal couldn't get away to drive him. So, he stayed on the ranch with Elle, who had made friends with Sparkles, a newer horse that had taken a liking to Bishop.

"Clock moves faster when you're working," Jason said as he approached.

Sal widened his eyes. Jason hadn't initiated conversation with him all week. They spoke enough to run the house and the business, but other than that, silence. Sal tried not to get too excited about Jason reaching out. "I think it *feels* like it goes faster, but a minute is still sixty seconds, no matter what you're doing."

"And a watched pot will eventually boil, but the waiting is still more pleasant if you focus on something else," he answered.

"True. What are you up to tonight?" Sal walked with Jason to the far stables.

"I was thinking about going out, but none of the guys are returning my calls, so..." Jason shrugged. "Really, I'm not feeling all that great, so I might be better off staying home."

Sal chewed his bottom lip, contemplating how to respond. His initial instinct was to ask if the marijuana stopped helping, but it took a lot for Jason to admit he was hurting. Sal didn't want to risk coming off as critical. He'd done enough of that earlier in the week. "You want me to take over your lessons today?"

"Nah, I'm not that bad, but thanks."

The beeping of Sal's cell pulled him from the conversation. After extracting it from his pocket, he smiled at the text from Ryder.

Okay if I head over?

You'd better come get your lazy ass back to work.
Yes, sir.

"God, you two are pathetic," Jason muttered on his way into Sandy's stall. "Yes, beautiful girl, I said Ryder and Sal are pathetic."

"Love is pathetic now?" Sal checked her information on the clipboard. Sandy was a newer horse, and Sal was learning her particular needs. "Careful, she reacts if you approach from the right." The caution was worth verbalizing because it was the opposite for most horses. "I think maybe her vision's not great on that side."

"Born that way?"

"Far as I can tell." The three-year-old mare had a great bloodline. She shouldn't have been born with problems. Either a group of recessive genes were triggered, or her former human guardian didn't know how to care for her. The vet would make a determination when he came tomorrow to do his rounds.

"To answer your question, no. Love is not pathetic. But the way your eyelashes flutter and the goofy grin won't leave your face is a little sad."

"Happiness is sad?"

Jason scowled. "Don't you have something to do? Anyone else to annoy?"

Sal couldn't hold back his snicker. He had missed this. "Yes, actually, I do." With that, he left to change Bishop's shoes.

AFTER THE LAST client left for the day, Sal walked over to where Ryder was straightening up the practice space. *God, his ass is amazing in those jeans.* He licked his lips in appreciation of the taut denim stretched over Ryder's globes.

"Not smart to stare at your employees," Ryder commented without turning around. "In fact, some people would call that sexual harassment."

Sal cast a glance around the barn, relieved to see no one was close. Then again, Ryder probably wouldn't have said it if they were in danger of being overheard. "Can't be harassment if you don't object."

"Fair enough." Ryder rubbed the back of his neck, his features darkening.

"What would you think about skipping the pub night and having the picnic we missed last week?"

"Probably. Do we have time to make food and take it up there before we lose the light?"

Sal turned his gaze to the sky. Couldn't be later than 3:30. Never mind that he had a clock on his phone so he didn't have to guess. *Isn't worth checking. We're talking about light, not time.* "We will if go clean up now." He paused, then asked, "Wait. Why 'probably'?"

"Detective Cranston asked me to be on hand if she needed me over the next couple of days."

"Needed you? For what?" Sal stared and, when he didn't answer, pressed, "Ry?"

"I can't tell you more than that. I'm sorry." Ryder snaked his tongue out and ran it over his lips. Sal allowed the sensual movement to distract him and followed its journey with rapt attention. "Sal!" The impatience in Ryder's voice indicated that may not have been the first time he'd said his name.

"Your tongue is distracting me." *Which may have been intentional*, Sal realized as he opened the gate for Ryder, who walked through. "What'd you say?"

"I asked if you wanted to shower together or—"

Sal cut him off by pulling him into his chest and locking their lips. After a few heated seconds, he had to pull away to catch his breath. "The answer to that question is almost always yes. Especially when we don't have a time limit." With another glance around the ranch to ensure any lingering employees were otherwise occupied—though if they weren't it would have been far too late anyway—he took Ryder's hand and led him toward the house. They paused at the door for Ryder to whistle for Elle, who came bounding toward them.

Jason looked up when they entered the kitchen. "Hey, Grams brought her coleslaw over."

"Well, that's perfect timing. We're going for a picnic after we shower."

With a hand over his heart, Jason sighed. "That's one of the sweetest things I've ever heard. Next, you'll tell me you're going to teach Bible school on Sunday."

Ryder blinked. "How are those things connected?"

"He's mocking our old-fashioned fun," Sal clarified. No matter how many chaste picnics they went on, Sal highly doubted the local United Church of Christ wanted them to set the example for the church youth.

"Oh." Ryder shrugged. "I wasn't aware this town had much outside of picnics and drinking."

"Speaking of, I heard back from Ted, and he's going to a party. Said he or one of the guys would pick me up."

At least Jason's not trying to drive. Sal took comfort in that. "You're feeling up to it?"

Jason waved his hand. "I'll survive. May not stay long, but I should see people other than my family and those I employ. Or so I'm told."

Sal nodded because what else could he do? Much as he wanted to beg his brother to find better friends, Jason was too old and too headstrong to take such a suggestion well. "Have fun. Be careful."

"Always. And you two enjoy your ride to the lake."

"We will." Ryder tugged Sal toward the stairs. He waited until they reached the second floor to pull him into a hug. "No matter how noble your intentions, Jason has always been like the wild stallions. He'll do what he wants with or without your approval. But if it's any consolation, I believe he's getting better at judging for himself what's good. Ten years ago, he would have left blunts all over the house to make a point."

Sal buried his face in Ryder's neck, inhaling and exhaling the woodsy, yet salty scent of his skin. "You're right," he admitted.

"Happens once in a while." Ryder took a step back. "Come on. We better clean up so we can get dirty again."

Their shared shower was more enjoyable than the ones they would have taken separately, but it wasn't faster. Sal found he could not have cared less. As they dressed, Sal again became distracted by Ryder's body. His muscle tone had improved dramatically in the last few weeks. *Going from a desk job to working on a ranch will do that for you.*

"You're staring again."

"It's at least more appropriate here," Sal answered.

"Can't argue that." He straightened his T-shirt over his belt. "Think we can take Sparkles? We'll have an easier time controlling Elle if she's with us."

"Hmm, that sounds doable." Sal put on socks and grabbed his phone. Once he'd checked that he and Ryder had all their essentials, Sal led them downstairs.

Thirty minutes later, they had packed cold chicken sandwiches, coleslaw, and Loraine's sugar cookies. Ryder, Sal, and Elle made their way to the stables. Ryder saddled up Sparkles, who had been named by her previous guardian, and Sal opened Bishop's stall door. "Hey, buddy, want to go for a ride? I don't think you've seen the lake yet."

"Think he's ready?" Ryder asked.

Sal blew a breath out through his teeth. "I hope." He offered an apple slice, which Bishop took without complaint. Sparkles must have seen because she nipped at Sal's shirt.

"Hey, girl," Ryder reprimanded. "That's not nice."

"To be fair, neither is giving one a treat and not the other." Sal rectified this by giving both Sparkles and Elle apple slices. He then chose the saddle that Bishop tolerated best. Had he been riding one of the horses who had been with them longer, Sal may have ridden bareback, but he wouldn't chance it with such a new and relatively untrained stallion. "Got everything?" he asked Ryder as he swung his legs over Bishop's back and settled his feet into the stirrups.

"Even things we likely won't need," Ryder said, and Elle added a yip.

"Good boy." He smoothed his palm over Bishop's soft, silky mane.

"Talking to me or Bishop?"

Sal quirked his eyebrow but couldn't help a chuckle. "Bishop. You get snappy when I call you 'boy.'"

"Can you blame me?" Ryder clicked his tongue to get Sparkles moving. Elle followed close at her side. "Especially when you think about making out with me."

"How is it different than 'baby'?"

"It's not, but we don't use that term of endearment either."

He knew there was an argument to be made somewhere, but since he couldn't figure out what or even why, Sal stayed quiet. Life teemed in the woods around them. Birds sang, insects buzzed, the light wind rustled the trees. It was like many rides they'd taken growing up. Two horses and at least one dog trotting at a leisurely pace toward the lake. Except the years had changed the two of them. Sort of. But then again, not in any way that mattered, it seemed. It all felt natural. "Do you think you'll go back to finance?"

Ryder glanced over at him. "Maybe? Eventually?" He shrugged. "I've been pretty deep in survival mode the last couple of months, and likely will be until this investigation is settled."

"That could be next week."

"Could be today. Could be a year from now. My life is in a damn limbo until I hear otherwise." He lapsed into silence as he guided Sparkles left toward the clearing. A grunt from the horse had Elle galloping to keep up. "I doubt it will be today, though, considering I haven't heard from them all week."

"Your attackers? Why would you have?" Sal's question was met with a sharp intake of breath. "Ryder?"

Before he could answer, they arrived at the clearing. Ryder jumped down off Sparkles and tied her to the tree by the lake. He then removed the blanket from the pack on her saddle.

Sal eyed him but followed his example. He praised Bishop for the ride but kept Ryder in his peripheral vision. Neither said anything as they settled. *Does he think I'll drop the conversation? Really?* Sal decided to wait him out. If he knew his boyfriend at all—and he liked to think he did—he was overthinking his response.

Without looking at Sal, Ryder said, "My memory of the attack is spotty, but I do know the attackers weren't strangers, per se." He tossed a toy for Elle, who scampered after it. "The sharks who I had borrowed money from back in New York have been...watching me. They've sent cryptic text messages and may or may not have been responsible for the taxidermied puppy in the trap."

"How? Why? I thought you paid all the debts you owed them."

"So did I. But the boss apparently had other ideas." This time, Ryder threw the toy a little too hard, landing it in the shallow end of the lake. He jumped to his feet as Elle took off after it.

"She's fine, Ry," Sal said, but he watched, too, just in case. Elle barked at the water and danced around it until she dragged the ball onto dry land. Sal and Ryder clapped for her as she ran up with her head held high.

After praising her and giving her treats, Ryder tossed it again. "Before you ask, I met with them because I wanted to see if I could end it on my own. Maybe make a deal... I don't know. But obviously that's not what happened."

"You didn't tell that to the police." *Or me, but that's less relevant.*

"Cat had already given an account that would have contradicted it."

"She didn't know—"

Ryder faced him, something akin to anguish on his features.

"I think she knew more than she claimed." Ryder again fell silent. "I remember her there before I blacked out. She was talking to the thugs...or they were talking to her as though she had authority over them."

"No," was Sal's automatic response. Cat was a good-natured busybody. Sure, her gossip could get annoying, but she couldn't be involved in a criminal organization. That was preposterous. "Why would you say that?"

"Because that's what I remember. I'm probably wrong. The drug they gave me does cause memory loss..." Another shrug.

Sal wanted to deny it. Remind Ryder that it was Cat who'd reached out to him first. She'd encouraged their reconciliation. She would *never* get mixed up with such people. And yet. Something niggled at the back of Sal's mind. Cat did know more than she should. She had told Sal the story of Ryder's daughter before Ryder had spoken about it with anyone in town. "Damn," he muttered.

"I'm—"

Sal raised his hand to cut Ryder off. "Don't apologize for recounting your truth."

"My truth? Are there different versions of truth?"

I hope so. Sal turned his attention to their food. He handed a chicken sandwich to Ryder and took the other for himself. "There are different versions of memory. No two people see events the same way..." He scrubbed his hand down his face. "That's crap. I'm just...trying to process." He hated the weak-sounding excuse.

"There's more." Ryder exhaled slowly as he fiddled with his sandwich. "The detective has been trying to draw a parallel between the attack on me and the one on Katie."

It took Sal a minute to remember that Katie was Gabby's sitter, but once he did, he gave a nod.

"She said she was going to involve the FBI and local authorities, then—I'm sure there's no connection—immediately after our conversation, she went to see Luke."

Sal had to shut his eyes against the onslaught of neurons firing, threatening to short out his brain. "Goddamn."

"Yeah." Sal heard, rather than saw, Ryder take a bite of his sandwich. "You should eat."

"I should," he agreed, but still took his sweet time opening the baggie and extracting the sandwich. "Did you ask him about it later?"

"I haven't seen him, which is a little surprising, since I've run into him a couple times a week since he moved here."

"Maybe they're old friends."

"Maybe. Just...a lot of coincidences, ya know?"

"I'll say." After finishing half his sandwich, Sal turned and grasped Ryder's hands. "Is there anything else you aren't telling me?"

Ryder locked their gazes. "Nothing that I'm aware of."

"Will you promise me that you'll stop trying to handle this on your own? No more meetings with the sharks unless law enforcement is aware and tells you it's a good idea?"

Elle stuck her nose between them. Sal laughed. "No begging!" He tossed a piece of chicken to the side.

"That's a very effective way to get her to stop. Next, you'll try making her lay nicely at your feet during dinner." Ryder rested back on his elbows. "I don't want anyone else to get hurt."

Realizing they had switched topics, Sal joined him in the prone position. "I know, and while I admire your attempts to stop that, you'll have a lot more success if you work with professionals." *Since you haven't had much on your own.*

Another beat passed with Ryder staring up at the clear sky. "You're right. Yes, I promise."

Sal leaned down and kissed him. The contact was soft and sweet and passionate, all at the same time. He craved more touch. "Thank you."

Ryder answered with another kiss. When he pulled back, he glanced over Sal's shoulder. "Why don't we go for a swim?"

The corners of Sal's mouth twitched up. Much as he wanted to say yes, he had business to take care of. "First, I have to ask you something else. I want you with me, Ry. Not halfway. Not answering to your parents—"

"Especially not with my parents on the other side of the wall?" Ryder interrupted.

"Especially that." Sal fought hard not to look away from Ryder. The intensity of his gaze threatened to undo him. "We know we want to be together, why don't you move in?"

Emotions warred in Ryder's eyes. Fear, hope, desire, love, and hesitancy played out over his features. His touch on Sal's cheek cooled the fire of nerves rushing beneath his skin. "I want to, Sal. I do."

"But?"

"But I won't feel right doing it until I know it's safe. Until I'm sure that I'm not a liability to you, your family, or the ranch. Hell, I'm hardly comfortable living with my parents for the same reason, but I've selfishly chosen that over homelessness."

"Your parents would skin you alive if they found out you spent so much as a night homeless, and you know it." The sadistic part of him wanted to suggest Ryder say that to his mom, but not enough to deal with the consequences of that fallout.

"If they knew about it." Ryder brushed his hair out of his face. "Anyway, yes, assuming we can talk it out with Jason and he's okay with it, I'll move in with you when I know this drama is over."

Sal's chest warmed with the understanding that Ryder took Jason's presence for granted. Another man might try to push him out or move themselves. Which is why it never worked with anyone else. *Ryder gets me and my family.* "Okay, I'll settle for that."

"Good." Ryder bumped his shoulder and climbed to his feet. "You didn't have a choice." He slipped his shirt over his head, then glanced back at Sal. "Come on. I thought we were swimming."

Sal opened his mouth to argue that they didn't have suits, but then they had never brought them before either. He took his shirt off and unbuttoned his jeans. "You know if we're caught, we'll get in real trouble, don't you? Like the kind of trouble where we're put on a list and not allowed to live around children."

Ryder shed his pants and his socks and piled them on top of his shirt. "Fine. We'll keep our underwear on."

"Still might be indecent exposure for two thirty-year-old men." But that didn't stop him from adding to Ryder's clothes pile.

"Goddamn, Sal, you missed your calling as a cop." Ryder ran into the water at full speed. "Shit! How is this so cold?"

Sal laughed. "That's what you get for mocking me." He went down and eased his way into the water. "It's not that cold." When he was waist-deep, he took note of Elle running from the blanket to the water's edge and back again. "What do you think?" he asked Ryder. "Is it deep where you are?"

"Eh, we'll keep an eye on her if she wants to come in." Ryder whistled, and she danced as her paws got wet.

For the next hour or so, Sal and Ryder played with the puppy until she wore herself into needing a nap in the sun. The water had warmed to a more comfortable temperature, and they found themselves in each other's arms—kissing, touching, exploring. It was heavenly. Like no one could reach them there.

Sal almost convinced himself of that when his cell phone rang from the backpack. Elle barked at the vibration/noise combo, which disturbed her sleep.

"Should you get that?" Ryder asked when Sal didn't move.

"Yes." He sighed as he disentangled himself from Ryder. The ringing stopped, but started again after less than a minute's pause. "Hush, Elle," he said while he dried his hands enough to swipe the screen. He didn't recognize the number, but their persistence inspired him to answer anyway. "Hello?"

"Sal? It's Luke."

"Luke? How did you—?"

"It's not important right now." Luke's voice was rushed, almost panicked. "Is Ryder with you?"

"Yes." Sal eyed his boyfriend, who was jogging up to the blanket. "Why?"

A pause, then, "Because I might need him to back me up on something."

"What's going on?"

"Is Jason planning on going out with Ted tonight?"

Sal chewed his bottom lip to keep from losing his cool. He really hated this answering-questions-with-questions nonsense. "He was waiting for someone to pick him up when I left."

Luke gave a sharp inhale. "Can you ask him to stay home or go to the movies or fly a kite...anything except show up at the party?"

One beat passed. Then a second. "Are you going to make me ask why?"

"I would love to tell you, Sal, but I can't. Not yet. But—" He paused again. "—if it were my brother, I would not want him to go to that party."

Ryder tapped Sal on the arm and showed him his phone. The screen displayed a message from Detective Cranston asking Ryder to be at his house ready to be picked up at nine.

Sal rubbed his face against the onslaught of information. "What does Ryder have to do with this?"

"I can't tell you that yet, but Jason should not be anywhere near it."

Sal took a deep breath. He didn't like nor understand it, but the memory of Ryder noting Luke's connection to the detective compelled him to agree. "I'll talk to him, but will you tell me what's going on tomorrow?"

Another beat of silence. "You'll know soon enough. Trust me."

Because you've always given me good reason to do that. "'Kay, thanks for the heads-up. I'll talk to you soon." Sal ended the call and looked at Ryder, who was pulling on his dry clothes. "I think we need to get back. I don't know what's going on, but Luke seems to believe Jason would be in danger at the party tonight."

"Did you try calling him?" Ryder handed Sal his pants after Sal removed his wet underwear.

Sal was a little disappointed he didn't get a chance to watch Ryder dress. But then they would have gone back to kissing and they didn't have time for that. "Not yet. Figured I'd pack while I talk." Once dressed, he pressed Jason's speed-dial number on his phone. Predictably, he didn't answer. "Fuck."

"Leave a message?"

Sal arched his eyebrow. "How often do you check voice mail?"

"Fair point." Ryder hustled over to where they had "parked" the horses and secured the pack on Sparkles.

A sinking in Sal's gut almost stopped him from being able to mount Bishop. Would they get to Jason in time? What would they be saving him from if they did?

"Hey," Ryder said, just loud enough for Sal to hear, "he'll be okay. With any luck, Luke called us well in advance of whatever is going down."

"Yeah, but I hate not knowing." Sal steadied himself, but his heart rate didn't slow until he met Ryder's understanding gaze.

Chapter Twenty-One

THE RIDE BACK to the ranch was tenser and faster than the ride out. Ryder's mind flicked through scenarios like a photo album. Would there be a connection between whatever was happening at that party and the previous crimes? Ryder had reached out to Katie's dad, Greg, one of his former coworkers, earlier in the week to express his sympathy. Her dad was obviously distraught on multiple levels.

"What could she know that's worth attempted murder?" he had asked over the phone.

Ryder didn't know. But that was a dumb response, so he had said, "I'm sure between the detectives and the FBI, they'll figure it out."

Silence had radiated from the line for so long that Ryder thought he'd hung up. Then he had said, "What the hell does my honor student know that involves the FBI?"

Again, Ryder didn't have an answer. But Greg didn't expect one. They had made polite goodbyes after Greg promised to keep Ryder updated on any major changes to Katie's condition, which Ryder appreciated because he had assumed Greg blamed him, at least a little.

"What's going on in that head of yours?" Sal asked.

Honesty won the debate in Ryder's brain. He had strongly considered coming up with a believable lie. But what would that really accomplish? Nothing. "I was trying to decide if I thought this party could be related to the investigation."

"How could it be?"

"How could any of it be related?" Ryder countered. "Hell, we don't even know for sure that the crimes *are* connected. All we've got is circumstantial evidence at best."

"Can't argue that." Sal reached across the few inches separating them and squeezed his leg. "It'll be okay."

"Mm, I'll settle for it being over." Ryder offered the strongest smile he could muster and wondered how pathetic it looked. As they crested the hill overlooking the property, lightness filled Ryder's chest at the sight of Jason coming from his grandparents' cabin.

"Thank God," Sal breathed, following Ryder's gaze. He nudged Bishop with his heel, prompting him to pick up speed. "Jason!"

Elle chose that moment to bolt ahead and meet Petey, which encouraged Sparkles to go after her. Ryder tightened his grip on Sparkles' reins. "No, girl." He didn't have to pull hard to remind her not to get too excited. A thought occurred him as they got closer to Jason. "Have you thought about how you'll convince him to stay home tonight?"

"Would be easier if I knew the reason," Sal grumbled. "I planned to start by asking and seeing what sort of resistance he shows."

Ryder nodded. Jason made it easy for them by meeting them in the stable that housed Bishop and Sparkles. As they drew closer, the worry lines on Jason's face became clear.

"You're back early," Jason said.

"Yeah, I need to head out. I'm meeting a...friend from New York."

Sal looked at Ryder. "Will you be back tonight?"

Ryder shrugged. "Guess it depends on how it goes." He gave Sal a kiss and said goodbye to Jason.

Sal watched him walk out, his worry growing with each step of distance between them.

After a beat, Jason said, "That was weird."

Sal nodded. "This whole goddamn day is weird." He took a breath. "So that thing you were going to tonight..."

"What about it?"

Sal rubbed his hands together in thought. "Do you know what's going on?"

"Yeah, we're playing cards, and I'm going to win some money."

"I think it might be dangerous."

"What are you talking about?"

God, I wish I had information, so I can construct a logical argument. Sal faced his brother. "Please, Jay, it's not what you think. There's more going on than you know. Please, please stay home tonight." He held Jason's questioning gaze steady until he nodded.

Chapter Twenty-Two

RYDER'S BODY THRUMMED with energy as he waited for Detective Cranston to pick him up between his and Sal's houses. He didn't want to go all the way home to avoid explaining what was happening to his dad, and staying at Sal's ran the risk of Sal following him, something he wanted to avoid.

A white van rumbled down the road, drawing Ryder's gaze. His mouth dropped open at the sight of the man in the driver's seat.

"Hop in," Luke said in his weird Southern accent.

"I'm waiting for—" Ryder was silenced by Luke flashing his FBI badge. The static kicked up in his brain, rooting him to the sidewalk.

"Ryder, we need to go. Now." The authority in Luke's tone sent Ryder's feet into motion before his mind could process what was happening or why.

It wasn't until Ryder was seated next to Luke with his seat belt buckled that understanding started to fall into place. "You're the undercover FBI agent."

"Uh-huh. I've been trying to infiltrate these assholes for months now. The bureau sent me down here to get chummy. It's been slow going." Luke stared at the road as he spoke.

"So, everything about starting over was—?"

"Partially true. My dad and I did need a change, and I had some sway on which assignment I got."

"At least you aren't dependent on your farming skills for survival," Ryder muttered.

Luke laughed. "That's the goddamn truth." He sobered quickly. "Do you know the plan?"

Ryder glanced over and swallowed, wishing he had water to soothe his dry throat. "Detective Cranston told me to act like I have every time I played for the last five years."

A moment of heavy silence filled the car. "Will that fuck your recovery up?"

Ryder had been asking himself the same thing since Cranston had suggested it. He only came up with one consistent answer. "Not as much as seeing the motherfuckers after knowing what they did to Gabby." His breath came in short spurts as the tension in the car filled his soul, making his body rigid. Thoughts of his daughter's laughter contrasted with her still form flashed through his mind, heating his skin.

Luke clamped his hand down on Ryder's knee. "I know this is hard, but you have to leave the assholes to me. Focus on playing a convincing game. That's all."

You don't know shit. True as the thought was, Ryder knew Luke was right. "Will there be other agents there?"

"Yes, but I can't tell you who." Luke let out a breath as he pulled into a lot behind the warehouse on the outskirts of town. "In the glove compartment is a wire. Stick it under your shirt on your chest."

Ryder drew his eyebrows together as he extracted the recording device and followed Luke's instructions. "Thought these clipped to the outside of clothing."

"Then the criminals would know they were being recorded. People would die."

You mean "more people would die." Ryder didn't bother saying that either. He simply nodded and tucked his shirt into his pants. He swallowed again as he caught sight of Luke loading a Glock. *He's one of the good guys. I want him to be armed. The bad guys sure as hell will be.*

"Leave your phone in the glove box."

Ryder considered objecting for approximately ten seconds, but a glance at the easygoing man turned hard-nosed agent beside him made him think the better of it. Looking at the burly men flanking the door, though, Ryder had a strong urge to send a text message to his loved ones. But the heat of Luke's stare told him in no uncertain terms that they were out of time. Once his cell was secured, he exchanged a nod with Luke, who opened his door.

Ryder's nerves sparked with attention, taking in every sight, sound, and smell as he and Luke approached the door. Were the well-built men guarding the outside agents or part of the gang? *Treat everyone as though they're the enemy. Except don't kill them.* He repeated this mantra until they reached the door, and one of the guards let them in. The warehouse was decorated in 1920s speakeasy style with jazz music filtering through the speakers.

"Ryder! I didn't know you'd be here." Cat flicked her gaze between Ryder and Luke.

After taking a second to recover, Ryder said, "Yeah, last-minute decision."

She shifted from one foot to the other. "Well, good luck. We should have a nice turnout." Cat scurried away.

Luke watched her a little too long before glancing at Ryder. "Five card is at the second table. I'll be playing blackjack at the third. Someone will come around with drinks soon."

Ryder's palms sweated as he lowered himself into a chair at the round table. "Deal me in," he told the man with the cards without looking up.

"So glad you could join us, Cowboy," the rough voice of the thug dealer said.

Ryder finally raised his eyes to find one of the men who had jumped him in Asheville. A shiver skittered down his spine. "Believe you said I had a debt to pay. Gonna deal me in or what?"

"Hold your horses, Cowboy," a man behind him said in a thick northern accent. "Took you long enough to come to your senses."

A growl caught in Ryder's throat as his blood ran cold. He'd recognize that voice and that smell anywhere. It was the same thug who'd collected his money at Gabby's funeral. *Keep cool. Focus. On what? The fact that he likely helped kill my daughter? What the fuck else can I focus on?*

Cat glided over to the table. "Let's go, boys. There are other customers wanting to play." She patted Ryder's shoulder as she motioned for the northern thug to move along, which amazingly he did. The dealer slid five cards across the table to him as Jason's friend, Ted, took the seat next to him.

Chapter Twenty-Three

SAL WAS JOLTED from his forced concentration on the movie he and Jason were watching when his phone rang next to him. He paused the movie and answered without looking at the screen. "Hello?"

"Sal? It's Cat. Um. Do you know where Ryder is?"

He took a deep breath. She could probably get even less information than he had. "He had to see someone he knew from New York. Why? What do you need?"

Silence filled the line. "It isn't what I need. I think you should come down here. He's gonna be in trouble."

"What? Why?"

"I can't explain, but—"

"No one can fucking explain anything!" Sal growled. The logical part of his brain told him that he should stay put. Ryder was with the police or the FBI or...something. Unless he lied, which was sort of a possibility, though Sal didn't buy it. But the part of himself that had loved Ryder for more than a decade won out as he stood and walked toward the door where he left his shoes.

"No, we can't. I can only say that he's got cards in one hand and a scotch in the other."

That did it. "Text me the address." He hung up the phone without waiting for her agreement. He snatched up the keys while jamming his feet in his shoes.

"Where are you going?" Jason asked.

"Warehouse outside of town, apparently."

"You mean the place that I was absolutely not allowed to go tonight?"

"Guess so." Sal shrugged. "Ryder's in trouble. I don't have details except that you could get out of it and he couldn't. Why, I don't know." He zipped his black jacket and held his hand out to stop Jason from doing the same. "No way. You aren't coming."

"If you're putting yourself in danger, why can't I help?"

Sal scrutinized him for a long moment while pocketing the keys. "Because...I said so. And if you try to drive, I will call the police and have you taken in for reckless endangerment. Maybe they'd test you and add a DUI to the mix."

"Fuck you, asshole." Jason spat the words like daggers at him. "You wouldn't really."

"To keep you safe? Away from a God knows who fucking up our town? Yeah. I really would. I'd rather you be alive to hate me than risk—"

"What about the risk you're taking? What makes you think you'd be safer than me?" If looks could kill, Sal would be bleeding out on the floor.

I'm more careful than you. I have a better respect for consequences, and no desire to get my thrills by poking thugs. He didn't say any of those things. Instead he shrugged again. "I'm sorry, Jay. I'm just gonna grab Ryder and get out of there."

Sal left without waiting for Jason's response. It wasn't until he was in the car and halfway down the main road that the insanity of what he was doing hit him. He had no weapons more powerful than a shotgun, not to mention little knowledge on how to use them properly. If things were as bad as Ryder implied—and considering the harassment and assault he'd received over the past couple weeks, they likely were—Sal was damn near powerless to help. *Why would Cat call me, then? Maybe she knows something I don't?* He debated calling her back and asking her, but he pulled into the lot behind the brick building.

A man with too much muscle and too big of a gun slung over his shoulder opened a side door, letting a stream of jazz-blues music out. Sal inhaled and shut off his car. The guy caught Sal's gaze and motioned him over.

Sal held his breath as he exited the car. *Well, no point in being here if I'm not going in.*

"You gotta pay the full entrance fee, no matter when you show up, you know." The man turned cold eyes on Sal as he approached.

"Course. How much?" Sal worked to keep his voice even. He had a terrible feeling that the price of admission would be more than the forty dollars in his wallet.

"Drake, he's with me." Cat strutted out with her usual confident air.

Drake's eyes widened as he stepped back. "Why didn't you say so, sir? Please go on in."

"Thanks..." Sal followed Cat in but stopped her in the entranceway. "What the actual fuck is going on? Why am I here? What can I do? What can Ryder do?"

"I don't know what Ryder's doing here. Only that he's not supposed to be and he's going to get hurt, especially if he keeps drinking and gambling. He's pissing off the...dealers."

Sal squinted at her. She was definitely hiding something. *Of course she is. Everyone is!* "What the hell are you involved in, Cat?"

Cat blew out a sigh. "I can't tell you what you want to know. But you've known me long enough that you should be able to trust me when I say that you need to get Ryder out of here."

"Sal, when I said Jason shouldn't come tonight, I thought it was understood that you shouldn't either," Luke said from the doorway.

Sal's head spun. "Cat called and told me Ryder was in trouble. Why are *you* here?"

Luke opened his mouth, but before he could say anything, a crash that sounded like a flipping table came from the other room. "Shit!" Luke rushed into the larger room, followed closely by Cat and Sal a few paces behind her. "Ryder, no!" Luke said.

It took Sal a good thirty seconds to see what Luke was seeing—Ryder pressing a folded chair into a thug-looking guy's chest. Sal couldn't figure out how his lean ginger boyfriend got the upper hand on that beefcake, or at least he couldn't until he noted the fiery rage in his eyes. Cat gasped.

Chapter Twenty-Four

"RY," SAL SAID into the now quiet room.

"This bastard killed my daughter." A demonic growl came from Ryder's chest. He didn't recognize his voice. Nor his life, at this point.

"He was following orders—" another thug started but snapped his mouth shut when Ryder raised the gun that must have come from the empty holster on the man's belt.

Luke stepped up. "Ryder, you do not want to do this."

"I think I do, Luke. I think I want to stop him from killing any more little girls." His hands shook along with his voice, loosening his grip on the gun.

"So do I." Luke put a steadying hand on Ryder's shoulder. "But his friend over there is right. He was acting under orders."

"That fucking makes it okay?"

"No, it means that killing him won't solve the problem." Luke's quiet tone both pissed Ryder off and calmed him down. Ryder didn't know what to feel. "Now, set the gun down and stand up slowly," Luke instructed.

Ryder glanced between Luke and Sal. The expression of anguish and fear on Sal's face mirrored what he had seen all those years ago when Ryder had told him about Felicia being pregnant with Gabriella. *Killing this bastard won't bring Gabby back, but it will keep me away from Sal, probably forever.* Ryder placed the pistol on the floor and allowed Luke to help him stand while a uniformed agent removed the chair from the thug's chest.

Luke flipped open a badge. "Everyone else, put your weapons down and your hands up."

"Well," Cat drawled next to Sal, "I guess FBI trumps local undercover consultant." She, too, drew out a gun and badge.

"What the fuck is my life?" Sal muttered next to her.

Luke exchanged nods with Ryder, as though giving Ryder permission to go to Sal, with the understanding that he not leave the building.

As soon as Sal saw what Ryder intended, he met him in the middle and pulled him in for a hug. "Thank you for staying with me," Sal whispered against his hair.

"Thank you for grounding me." Ryder pressed their lips together, ignoring the others in the room. And for the first time since he lost his daughter, he felt lucky.

Epilogue

"GODDAMN IT!" JASON threw the stick in his hand harder than necessary. His breath came in short spurts. Petey whined next to him. "Not going to chase it?" The pit bull stared up with knowing, sympathetic eyes. Jason shifted his weight to his good side and dragged his bad one the ten yards to the house. Yes, he should have been in his chair, but he had spent more time sitting in the last month since the arrests than he had in the half year prior. Ted had been arrested for drug trafficking, which he claimed to have done to support his gambling habit. He had been released on bail, though the judge was worried enough to insist on an ankle monitor and house arrest until the trial. Jason had avoided his calls. What was there to say? Ted had lied about everything since he'd started "helping" Jason. He had sworn up and down he got the pot from a medicinal grower in DC. Jason felt stupid for believing him. Which made him angry at himself and Ted.

As far as he and Sal went, as much as Jason had wanted to be angry with his brother for forcing him to stay home that night, he was glad to not have been in the middle of that. Of course, Sal didn't need to hear those exact words. Jason had to have some pride.

But mostly, Jason hurt. A lot. Without access to cannabis, his pain management prospects were once again limited to the crap the doctors prescribed—addictive or ineffective. When he reached the kitchen, he swallowed three ibuprofens, in hopes of taking the edge off. *I should know better than that.* Jason gave Petey a treat and led the dog into the living room. As soon as he sat down, a heavy knock sounded at the door. From the couch, Jason eyed the upright lock securing the door. Unfortunately, whoever waited outside was concealed by the closed blinds and drapes.

Another, more insistent knock. Petey let out a bark. "Okay, okay. I'm coming." Jason hoisted himself to his feet and crossed the room an inch at a time. His eyebrows jumped to his hairline when he opened the door to find Luke, the FBI agent, sans uniform, standing on the porch. "Hi, um, Sal and Ryder are gone into town."

Luke smiled. The sunrays accentuated the jade-green color of his eyes and started a tiny fire in Jason's gut. "I'd actually like to talk to you, if you have a minute."

Jason licked his lips. Luke had saved him from being in the middle of the bust. *So, why am I so nervous?* "Sure, come in. Can I get you something to drink?"

"No, thanks, I'm fine."

Jason silently cheered at his response as Luke took a seat. He couldn't have not offered, but God was he glad to avoid the trek back to the kitchen.

"How are you feeling?" Luke asked after a moment of quiet.

Can he see my limp? Is he mocking me? Judging from Luke's sympathetic expression, Jason doubted it. "I'm getting by."

"I'm sure you are." Luke crossed and uncrossed his legs. "Have you been able to find a suitable replacement for the cannabis?"

Jason narrowed his gaze. He reminded himself that Luke had helped him when he didn't need to before. It was unlikely that he was setting up a trap now. "No. The doctor-prescribed solutions don't work better today than they did a year ago."

Luke dug through his messenger bag, extracted a brown paper sack, and handed it to Jason.

Holding the bag closed tightly in his fist, Jason kept eye contact with the other man. "Is this...?"

"Yes."

Jason's jaw dropped, along with his inherent trust. "You're a fed. An undercover FBI agent. How could this be anything except a setup?"

"Why would I set you up, Jay? After I put my reputation on the line to keep you safe?" Luke asked, never letting his gaze drop. "I could get in trouble if I was caught. But I don't think you have any reason to turn me in."

Jason's head spun. The slight weight of the bag set his thoughts in motion. "But...why?"

Luke blew out a breath. "Because you don't deserve to suffer over a technicality. Because the fact that you could get in trouble for taking away your pain here, but not a couple hundred miles north is ridiculous. Mostly because I can."

Jason knew he should be skeptical, but damn if Luke's eyes weren't drawing him in, making him want to trust him. "How?"

"I'd rather not say. But I can promise you it's safe and I'll be able to get it at least once a month."

What's wrong with me? Well, I fractured my hip years ago and am in constant pain without this semi-illegal drug. So, I'm desperate. "Okay. Thank you." Jason paused, but continued before he could think himself out of it. "I would like more information, though. Maybe once we get to know each other better?"

Goddamn, that smile was back, and even more brilliant than before. "I'd like that, as long as you know nothing that does or does not happen between us will be contingent upon me helping you."

Jason hoped what he was saying was true. Because he didn't know what to do with the influx of emotions being transmitted through their gazes. But he thought maybe he wanted to find out.

About the Author

Liz Borino has been telling stories of varying truthfulness since she was a child. As an adult, she keeps the fiction to the page. She writes stories of human connection and intimacy, in all their forms. Her books feature flawed men who often risk everything for their love.

When Liz isn't writing, she's waking up early to edit, travel, and explore historic prisons and insane asylums—not (usually) all in one day. Liz lives in Philadelphia with her two cats and her significant other.

Email: liz.borino@gmail.com

Coming Soon from Liz Borino

Angel's Intuition

Excerpt

JULY 2013, LANGLEY, VIRGINIA

CIA Agent Aaron Collins pushed his shoulders together as he strode through the hallway to his supervisor Mick Keller's office and rapped on the door. As if he'd been waiting for him, Keller swung it open. "Come in, Collins, come in. Have a seat. Can I get you a drink?"

"No, thank you, sir," Aaron replied, shifting in the hard, wooden chair. His boss wrung his hands as he circled his large desk. "Is everything all right?" *Clearly not*, he answered himself. Bosses tended not to call emergency meetings on Friday afternoons to discuss the company's upcoming party.

Keller sat behind his desk and adjusted his glasses. "I need you to brief Foster on the POW situation in Afghanistan. The two of you are switching cases."

Aaron blinked. "My team and I have been working with the military on that mission for months. We're three weeks from deployment."

"Yes, Foster will assume your leadership role."

"Foster? He's a paper pusher!"

"Collins." Keller's voice held a warning.

Yeah, God forbid the agency admits the truth about the competence of their employees. "Sir, he really is not qualified."

"He will be once you brief him. We need you here, Collins," Keller told him.

Aaron tilted his head to the side. "Why do you need a field agent here?"

"You're one of our best."

"And...you're afraid to send me because you have reason to doubt safety?"

"It is a rather volatile situation," Keller hedged.

Of course, it's volatile! The fucking enemies have our men! "What aren't you telling me?"

Keller shook his head. "It wasn't my decision."

"Well, whose decision was it? Have you thought of calling them an idiot?"

"Not all of us have your finesse."

"I'll be there, or you need to give me a reason that I can't, beyond the stuffed shirt above you said so," Aaron said.

Keller removed his glasses and massaged his eyes. "No, that's all the reason either one of us require. Your job is here for the next three months."

"I have the most information about this mission." Even as Aaron spoke, he knew the battle was over.

"None of us know very much." He sighed. "I'm sorry."

So am I. "Can I still get updates?"

"You know we can't." Keller paused, then added, "He'll be all right, Collins."

They weren't talking about Foster's competence anymore. Now Keller referred to Aaron's husband, Jordan, an Army captain also assigned to this mission. "Of course, he will. I only wish I could help."

Also Available from NineStar Press

Connect with NineStar Press

Website: NineStarPress.com

Facebook: NineStarPress

Facebook Reader Group: NineStarNiche

Twitter: @ninestarpress

Tumblr: NineStarPress

www.ingramcontent.com/pod-product-compliance
Lightning Source LLC
Chambersburg PA
CBHW060534190726

48283CB00003B/724